Perfect Little Princess

Perfect Little Princess

Avril Sabine

Cracked Acorn Productions
Australia

Perfect Little Princess

Published by

Cracked Acorn Productions

PO Box 1365

Gympie, Queensland 4570

Australia

978-1-925131-55-0 (Kindle)

978-1-925617-36-8 (EPUB)

978-1-925131-78-9 (Print)

Genre: Young Adult Contemporary

Copyright 2015 © Avril Sabine

Cover design by Caitlyn Petersen

For everyone who has found a way to make their
imperfect life perfect for them.

Maddy hates living with her overbearing father and is determined to live with her mum. She's sick of not being able to be herself. But no one is listening to her wishes and when she learns why, she begins to fear that not only will she be stuck living with him until she finishes school, but her family has other secrets they're keeping from her.

*

This story was written by an Australian author using Australian spelling.

Chapter One

Maddy glanced over her shoulder and swore under her breath. Was he following her? She hadn't thought he'd seen her, but maybe he had. If she could get to her class she might be able to avoid him. He was the last person she would have expected to see at her school. He shouldn't even be in Brisbane. Her luck was absolute crap and this proved it.

She slipped through the crowd and into her next classroom, barely resisting the urge to look over her shoulder. She dumped her books on her desk as she slid onto the hard plastic seat, leaning back to stare at the ceiling as if the answer to her problem was there. White paint and a couple of fans, lazily turning, gave her no clue about what to do. He hadn't said anything about starting a new school after the holidays. Why hadn't he mentioned it? She would have been more prepared.

A stack of books dropped onto the desk beside her and startled Maddy from her thoughts. She looked over to meet the grin of her best friend, Sasha. Maddy's answering grin was forced. "Hey."

"I'm so over school. I can't wait until the next holidays. Why do they have to be ages away?" Sasha slid into the seat beside her.

"It's only the first day back."

Sasha sighed. "I know. They should shoot the person who decided the length of school holidays. It's the middle of spring, who wants to be stuck in a classroom at this time of year? I'd rather be on a beach."

"At least the next ones are longer. And include Christmas. That should make you happy."

"It's only the start of October. That's months away." Sasha's words were almost a moan.

Maddy's grin came more easily at her friend's expression of disgust. Sasha was always good at distracting her. Looking her friend over she took in the changes she'd barely had time to focus on earlier. This was the first chance they'd had for more than a quick hello this morning. "I like your new hair cut."

Sasha's expression immediately brightened. "Thanks." She ran her fingers through her long brown hair that now had auburn highlights and a fringe that ended sharply below her hazel eyes, thin enough to be able to see through. Before the holidays Sasha's hair had all been one length, like Maddy's light brown hair.

"It suits you. I wish my father would let me do something with my hair instead of expecting me to plait it neatly back like some little girl from the last century." She shook her head slowly. "No, make that from two centuries ago." Her gaze was drawn to the door as another group of students entered the classroom. Her heart felt like it skipped a beat. Yep, it was official. Her luck was absolute crap. She slouched at her desk and tilted her head down, wishing she'd ignored her father and not plaited her hair back from her face. The way her day was going she'd end up grounded anyway. Maybe it wasn't too late to undo the plait and hide behind her long hair.

"Are you okay? You don't look so good." Sasha leaned forward to peer into her face.

"Gee, your compliments are gonna go straight to my head." Maddy couldn't resist another glance towards the crowd near the doorway. Why? She wasn't sure exactly what she wanted answered. Why her? Why him? Why the hell was he at her school? Maybe all those questions.

"Very funny." Sasha glanced over her shoulder. "Do you know him?"

"Know who?" Maddy dropped her gaze to the desk, focusing her light brown eyes on the initials drawn heavily on the edge. Lightly running her fingers over the indent, she frantically tried to think of something she could tell Sasha. She couldn't discuss this right now. In fact, it was all she could do to remain in her seat. She wanted to run and hide.

"Aww come on, even you're not that oblivious. The boy who's surrounded by every brainless blond in the class. Both the natural and bottle ones."

She looked at him. 'The boy' Sasha had called him. She knew him as Logan. He had a ready grin and was laughing at something that had been said to him. Even his dark brown eyes were filled with humour. His hair, a shade lighter than his eyes, was streaked at the ends from hours outside, dark where his cap covered it. His head turned in her direction, as if he felt her gaze rest on him. She quickly returned her attention to the desk. She couldn't meet his gaze. What could she say to him? This was a disaster. But what else was new when it came to her life? "He looks new to the school."

"That wasn't what I asked. I could figure that out for myself. Do you know him?"

The teacher stepped into the classroom and strode towards his desk as he spoke. "Everyone take their seat. Holidays are over. Time to put your nose to the grindstone."

She was relieved. Talking wasn't tolerated in Mr Gallo's class. She would have a reprieve from the questioning. It wouldn't be much of a reprieve. Sasha wasn't one to drop a subject until she'd learned everything possible about it. And it looked like Sasha wouldn't be the only one looking for answers. Twice she'd caught Logan glance at her and both times she'd pretended not to see him. But she could only pretend for so long. Eventually he'd approach her and she didn't know what to do about that. When the bell rang for the next class, she was the first one through the door. She couldn't talk to him in front of everyone. No way. That would be an absolute disaster. World war kind of disaster.

Lunchtime found her headed towards the library, eating a sandwich on the way. The library should be quiet on such a sunny day and Maddy hoped to avoid both Sasha and Logan. They'd have questions she couldn't answer. Not until she could think of how to deal with the situation. Situation! What a bland word to describe something that made her feel queasy, frantic and wanting to find the nearest hole to crawl into.

It was nearly time for the bell to signal the end of lunch before Sasha turned up in the library. She stood over Maddy, hands on her hips and glared at her. "You want to tell me what's going on?"

Maddy glanced around the library. There was no one close enough to hear. That was as long as Sasha kept her voice down. And if she didn't answer Sasha quickly it looked like voice raising might be a very real possibility. "I think I might have a bit of a problem."

"Then why didn't you tell me instead of hiding here?"

Maddy sighed. "Will you accept cowardice as an answer?" She stared up at Sasha, mentally begging her friend to understand.

With a sigh, Sasha pulled a chair out from beside Maddy and dropped onto it. "You told me you had a boring holiday and nothing interesting had happened when I rang you last night."

"Mitchell was hanging around. You know he tells my father everything I say and do." Life had got worse when her father had married Marla, Mitchell's mother, a few years ago. Not that she'd expected things to have improved. Not with how little Marla seemed to think of her.

"Your stepbrother has the friendliest grin I've ever seen. It's a perfect example of false advertising."

Maddy laughed softly. "Isn't it just?" She sighed. "The new boy-" she waited for Sasha to nod, "is called Logan. I met him while I was at Mum's this holiday."

"And?"

A million answers tumbled through her mind, but only one really mattered. Maddy glanced around again. The coast was still clear. She leaned near Sasha before she whispered, "His kisses are amazing."

Sasha's eyes widened and her mouth dropped open. Then she narrowed her gaze. "You're stringing me along, aren't you?"

Maddy shook her head. "I swear I'm not. It was the last day there. I don't even know exactly how it happened. We were all hanging out at the beach. Everyone was complaining about the holidays ending. Most of them live on the coast and were making plans to get together this weekend. One of the other guys lives in Cairns with his mum and was visiting his dad for the holidays."

"Can we get to the good bit? The bell will ring before you tell me."

"Well, one minute Logan and I were saying

goodbye and wishing the holidays weren't ending and the next thing we were kissing. And I don't mean a friendly kiss on the cheek."

"Out of ten?"

Maddy grinned. "Eleven."

"You're shitting me."

"Nope."

"I hate you, you know."

Maddy laughed. "Sure."

"I wish I'd seen him first."

Maddy's smile disappeared. "He'll probably never want to see me again. I completely ignored him. Yesterday I was kissing him like… well, like…. ahh," she waved her hand to fill in for the words she couldn't speak. "Today I treat him like he doesn't exist. What am I going to do?" Her voice rose as panic threatened to explode.

"You want me to talk to him? I can tell him your father's hero is Hitler and he wants to be just like him."

Maddy smiled sadly. "If it wasn't for Mitchell…" again she finished her sentence with a wave of her hand. Who was she kidding? Her father probably had a million spies at her school. She knew he was friendly with the principal and who knew how many teachers.

"Don't worry about it. I'll tell him to pretend he doesn't know you. I'm sure he'll understand once I explain everything." Sasha rested her hand on Maddy's shoulder.

Maddy groaned when the bell rang. She rose to her feet. "He'll probably hate me forever."

"If he does, can I have him?" Sasha linked her arm through Maddy's.

"No way. My revenge would be harsh if you two hooked up."

"Hmm. I don't know. I think he'd be worth it."

Maddy elbowed her friend lightly and Sasha giggled. "Yeah, right, Sash."

"Nah, you're right. I wouldn't swap your friendship for a thousand hot guys. Well… maybe a thousand, but not just one."

Maddy grinned. "A thousand, huh? What would you do with that many?"

"I'd figure something out. Probably have them all waiting on me hand and foot and thinking I'm a goddess."

They stepped out of the library and into the crowded hallway. "I think you've been reading your mum's romance books again. She'll kill you if she finds out."

"They're not that bad. I don't know what her

problem is. Anyone would think I was in primary school the way she goes on about them." Sasha stopped in mid-step and pulled Maddy to a halt. "Don't look now…"

Maddy couldn't resist. Glancing in the direction Sasha had looked away from, she met Logan's gaze through the crowd. She wanted to run to him and beg him to forget the way she'd acted earlier. One step and then she halted, a voice bringing her to her senses. She turned to see her stepbrother walk towards her, laughing at something one of his mates had said. Maddy turned back towards Logan and mouthed the word 'sorry' before she looked at Sasha. At a quick nod from her friend, she headed towards Mitchell and away from Logan.

Mitchell glanced at her as they passed each other. No greeting. No acknowledgement. Only that single glance. Maddy forced herself to keep walking and not turn to look over her shoulder. Hopefully Sasha would take Logan aside and explain the situation. She didn't dare check in case Mitchell glanced back too. He'd pounce on the slightest thing she did that was out of the ordinary. She really didn't want to start the term grounded. Visits to her mum were all that made life bearable.

Chapter Two

The rest of the day dragged and Maddy's gaze constantly returned to her watch. Time seemed suspended and the second hand moved extremely slow. She wished Sasha was in one of her afternoon classes so she could find out what Logan had said, but at least she didn't have any classes with Mitchell today. She didn't think she could have hidden her impatience from him.

Once again Maddy was the first one out of the classroom. Within minutes she was out the front of the school, hiding in the shadows of a cluster of trees so she could keep an eye out for Mitchell. She nearly jumped when she heard someone move behind her. She turned around.

"Logan."

"I've heard some original excuses, but yours would have to take gold."

"Logan–"

"What's the real story? When I asked who you were, one guy told me the porcelain doll and another the ice princess. Not what I would have called you yesterday."

Maddy tried to ignore the stab of hurt his words caused as she continued to glance around, her gaze frequently returning to Logan. "Didn't Sasha tell you about my father?"

"He doesn't go to this school. How would he know what you do here? Or who you talk to?"

"Mitchell would tell him."

"Who?"

"My stepbrother. He's in year eleven too."

"Yeah, right. Like all the guy has to do with his time is spy on you. Either you're paranoid or very creative. So forget it. You're obviously not the person I thought I'd met during the holidays." Logan turned to walk away.

"Logan–" she broke off when she saw Mitchell headed for the front gate.

Logan faced her. "What?"

She'd run out of time. She had to reach Mitchell's side before he stepped through the gates or she'd have to put up with a major interrogation. "I'm sorry. You're right though because I have to be someone else here. My father has different rules to Mum. Just please pretend you don't know me. I don't want to risk my time with my mum." She turned and dashed towards the gate, on Mitchell's heels as he stepped through. "Hey."

Mitchell glanced towards her without comment.

"Good day at school?"

Mitchell remained silent as he strode along the footpath.

Maddy tried to keep her words light while the entire time her heart felt like it was breaking. "Did you get a stack of homework too? You'd think they'd give us a break being the first day back."

Mitchell glanced at her again, a scowl on his face. "Shut up, Madeline."

"Sure thing, big brother." Maddy smiled sweetly as Mitchell glared at her. He turned away, his broad shoulders casting a shadow on her. He had close-cropped sandy blond hair and blue eyes. He also played whatever team sport was in season and was a perfect student. The perfect son. The son her father had wanted and she'd failed at being. Mitchell was his son now and they got along perfectly. In a way Maddy had never been able to. They talked, joked, laughed and shared stories. All the things she wished her father would do with her rather than be cold and overbearing.

Maybe it would have been a little better if she could have talked to Marla like Mitchell talked to her father, but that would never happen. Half the time Marla acted like she didn't exist. Considering Marla didn't have much time for her own son, it didn't really surprise Maddy.

Things hadn't always been like this. She'd once got along with her father and had worshipped the ground he'd walked on. Had thought he could do anything. Things had slowly changed as she'd grown older and started to question his orders when she'd tried to become her own person with her own beliefs.

Maddy pushed those thoughts from her mind. It always depressed her and she was depressed enough as it was. She looked around, trying to find a distraction. She saw Sasha hop on the bus, looking over her shoulder the entire time so she stumbled up the stairs. She grinned and waved as soon as she noticed Maddy watched her. Maddy returned the wave and wished she could return the grin. It was impossible. She was more likely to burst into tears than anything else. She watched Sasha disappear inside the bus and desperately wished she could join her.

"I don't know how you can stand that girl. If her father wasn't Dad's boss…"

Maddy looked away from Mitchell. She could easily imagine the rest of his threat. He'd make sure her father hated Sasha and didn't let her spend any time with her at all. It was so unfair how her father believed everything Mitchell said. But she guessed when he smiled that perfect smile of his, that made everyone think he was their best friend, the devil would probably believe him.

She thought of all the job opportunities for a smile like that. Car salesman. Insurance salesman. Con artist. She almost grinned. Yep. Con artist. And then hopefully the police would catch him and he'd end up in jail. She was partway through thinking about the courtroom saga this would cause when her father pulled up in front of them, having waited for enough traffic to clear before he arrived.

Getting in the back of the car, she returned her father's polite greeting before staring out the window. She remained silent while Mitchell talked sports with her father. Her father. No one would believe it. It was like she was the stepchild. As soon as they arrived home she retreated to her room, the silence pressing in around her. The room was immaculate, not an item out of place. Her timber bed had a white bedspread, which seemed stark against the cream coloured walls and carpet. White vertical blinds hung at her window and apart from a desk with only a laptop on it, the rest of her gear was shut away behind the doors of her built-in-wardrobe. She automatically pulled out her homework and sat at the desk, the books a blur in front of her.

He hadn't believed her. But why should he? No one had a father like hers. A father who belonged in a world long since gone. What had Sasha said to Logan? She desperately wanted to know. And what had he said back to Sasha? The same he'd said to her? If only she had the internet in her room, or even a private phone line no one else could listen in on. She needed to talk to Sasha. She wanted to hear a friendly voice, or see some friendly words.

Maddy wiped the back of her hand across her cheek, surprised it came away damp. She wanted to live with her mum. She hated it here. And just like the end of every holiday, her mum had ignored her pleading, even when she'd pointed out that now she was sixteen she should have a say in where she lived. Her mum had tried to tell her that her father was only being protective. That everything he did was to keep her safe. When her mum had asked if he hit her or raised his voice at her, she'd had to answer no. He was far too controlled to ever raise his voice.

She swallowed past the ache in her throat that made her want to scream or cry. Or quite possibly both. She hated that her mum was right and her father would never hurt her. But, if he protected her any more than he already did, he'd probably smother her to death. Maybe that was his plan. Then he'd only have his perfect son.

Chapter Three

The next day Maddy learned that Sasha had done as promised, but Logan had laughed at her. He hadn't believed a single word she'd spoken. Maddy didn't blame him. She supposed it was a fairly unbelievable story. Sasha also told her she'd found out Logan had moved schools because he'd been caught playing a practical joke on a teacher at his previous school. A teacher that no one liked. She wasn't able to find out all the details, but he'd managed to change schools instead of being expelled.

Over the next couple of days Maddy didn't know whether to be relieved or annoyed that Logan ignored her. Although a few times she caught him watching her in Mr Gallo's class and she hastily looked away. When he started to hang out with Mitchell on Wednesday Maddy felt anger rush through her. She had to force herself to keep away from him instead of going over to demand why he was hanging out with a loser like her stepbrother. Her hands clenched into fists and she glared at Logan as he laughed with Mitchell. She wasn't close enough to hear what was said. Then he looked up and saw her. Maddy's heart felt like it leapt into her throat as their gazes met and she was torn between wanting to yell at him and kiss him. She did neither.

Turning on her heel, she strode away. If he wanted to be friends with Mitchell, fine. It wasn't like she was allowed to have anything to do with boys when she was at her father's house. And she wasn't about to defy him again. Last time he'd stopped her from spending one of the holidays with her mum. No way could she go through another school holiday at her father's house. Not that he and Marla were home much, but she'd had to put up with Mitchell. She'd rather spend a week with a dentist. Or have a month of exams. Or… the bell rang and she sighed heavily. Anything was preferable to being at her father's.

She glanced back and saw Logan still watched her. Her feet slowed until she stopped and stared back at him. What was he thinking? Was he still angry with her for asking him to pretend he didn't know her? Did he remember the kiss they'd shared? The kiss she'd tried so hard to forget. Why was he watching her? Someone bumped into her and she turned to glare at them. When she looked back, Logan was walking away at Mitchell's side. Maddy stared after him. Why did he have to start hanging out with her stepbrother? She'd thought he had better sense than that. Mitchell was a backstabbing hypocrite who loved to get her into trouble.

"Hey, girl." Sasha dropped an arm around Maddy's shoulders. She groaned when she saw the direction Maddy looked in. "You are so not going to pine after him. That is pathetic. You do realise that, don't you?"

"How long has he been hanging out with Mitchell?"

"I don't know. Can't be long. I didn't see him with him yesterday. But I did see him at the oval this morning, kicking a ball around with all the other idiots. Don't they know mornings are something you suffer through? Not enjoy."

Maddy laughed on cue, a brittle noise that sounded fake even to her ears. "Don't ever change. You always distract me even when I'm so mad I want to do something completely stupid."

"What were you going to do?"

"Talk to him. Well, maybe not talk. It would have probably been somewhere along the lines of yell. And then, I might just have kissed him." She smiled wryly.

"My father would have grounded me for a year once Mitchell carried that tale home. Actually, probably for life."

"Forget about him. We better get to class before we end up with detention."

"It's probably better than going home."

"Yeah, but how long would your father ground you for ruining his schedule?"

Maddy sighed and headed towards her next class, Sasha at her side. "Life really sucks. Mine in particular."

* * *

Friday afternoon found Maddy repeating her words of earlier in the week. She dropped her head in her hands as she leaned her elbows on the desk in her room. "Life completely and utterly sucks."

"I wouldn't say it was that bad."

Maddy jumped from her seat and stared at Logan. He stood in her doorway. "What are you doing? Go away before someone finds you here."

Logan stepped into her room. "Rob and I are staying the night with Mitch. That is after we've gone to Deirdre's party."

Maddy glared at him. The party she'd wanted to go to. "Good for you. Now get out of my room."

"I really don't know what your problem is. You rarely smile, you dress like a nun and you wear your hair like a grandmother. And not even a grandmother from this century."

"Mind your own business."

"You weren't saying that last weekend. Actually, last weekend you were plastered all over me." Logan came further into her room.

"Shh. Do you want to get me grounded for life?"

"I think you exaggerate. Your dad's okay. We've spent the last half hour talking to him." Another step closer.

Maddy took several steps away. "Yeah, he's great if you're a boy. But apparently because he once was a boy he knows all about how they think and it's not very pretty. Especially about girls. So I get to stay in my castle and my hair isn't long enough to throw out the window for a prince to come up and visit me and there's a dragon constantly on guard."

Logan grinned. "Why don't you ask the dragon if you can come out and play for the night? Mitch said you never go to parties because you think they're childish."

"Good for him."

"Well?"

"Well what?"

"Do you think parties are childish? What about the ones we went to on the holidays? Were they childish? I could have sworn you had fun. Or was it all an act?" Logan was only a couple of steps from her now. "Even the last day."

Maddy froze. If she retreated any more her back would be against the wall. She stepped to the side and backed up towards the door. "If you won't leave, I will."

"Maddy-"

"What's going on here?"

Maddy closed her eyes, afraid to turn and look at her stepbrother. She was so busted. She could probably kiss goodbye spending any time at her mum's this year. She opened her eyes and looked at Logan. 'Please?' She mouthed the word, not wanting Mitchell to hear her.

Logan looked at Mitchell with a grin. "I think you're wrong. She doesn't avoid the parties because she thinks they're childish. She's more of a prude than the Victorians were."

"Huh?"

Maddy turned to see Rob was also in her doorway. Rob was not the brightest of people, but even she felt like echoing him. What did the southern Aussie state have to do with prudes?

"The Victorian era. England when Queen Victoria ruled. Eighteen thirty something to nineteen hundred and one," Logan said.

"Oh." Rob nodded his head. "Now I get you. I thought you meant the Australian state."

Great, Maddy mentally shook her head. Now she was thinking like Rob. Her crappy week was complete.

"Anyway, you were right about your sister." Logan glanced at Maddy before he turned back to Mitchell.

"Stepsister," Mitchell said at the same time as Maddy.

Logan shrugged. "Whatever." He strode towards the door. "Let's get ready. I haven't been to a good party in over a week."

Rob laughed. "Man, that must feel like forever."

Logan grinned as he ushered the two boys away from the door. "Yep. Years."

Maddy stared after them. Relief and anger filled her. What game was he playing? She closed her bedroom door and leaned against it. She hadn't actually believed he'd help her. With how angry he was she'd expected him to leave her to Mitchell's mercy. And mercy was not a word in Mitchell's dictionary. She didn't think there were many nice words in his dictionary. At least not when it came to her.

She pushed away from her door and walked unsteadily to her bed. Dropping heavily onto it, she leaned back. Her eyes closed and she took a deep breath. As she slowly let her breath out, she opened her eyes. Logan stood over her. She hadn't even heard the door.

Maddy's mouth dropped open and she tried to form words. They wouldn't come. Panic raced through her and she stumbled to her feet, ready to run. To be anywhere other than in the same room as Logan and risk her father or Mitchell seeing them and jumping to the wrong conclusion.

"You owe me."

"What? Why?" Her words were nearly a squeak.

"For spinning a heap of crap for your brother. Although I don't know why he'd care."

"Stepbrother." The word was automatic.

"Whatever." Logan shrugged. "You still owe me."

"It wouldn't have been a problem if you hadn't come into my room." Maddy was finally able to think clearly again.

"Then you shouldn't have ignored me at school. One day you're all over me, the next you act like I don't exist. Then you get your friend to spin some crap that only an idiot would believe."

"Please get out of my room. And it wasn't crap."

"Then why does everyone reckon you think you're too good to hang out with the rest of us?"

"You should always find out the original source of a rumour." Maddy smiled bitterly as she pushed past Logan. "Since you won't leave, I will." She locked herself in the bathroom and didn't come out until Mitchell banged on the door to demand she get out so he could get ready. He accused her of deliberately trying to make him late.

She ignored her stepbrother as she headed back to her room, pausing in the doorway. It was empty. This time when she shut the door, she locked it. She risked being grounded if her father found her door locked, but she was willing to risk one weekend at her mum's house. That was bearable. What she feared was she'd never get to stay there again. Panic filled her at that thought. There was no way she could survive in her father and Marla's house permanently. Something would snap and it'd probably be her mind.

As soon as the three boys left for the party, Maddy opened her door again. She leaned against the door frame and sighed, almost weak with relief. Logan didn't know what he was talking about. Life did suck. Hers in particular.

Chapter Four

It was nearly three in the morning when something woke Maddy. She lay in bed as she tried to figure out what it was. She heard it again. Her name was called softly through the door. Rushing to the timber obstruction, she leaned against it, her hand pressed flat on the cool surface. "What are you doing?"

"There's a padlock at the top of your door. Why's there a padlock? And who locked it?"

"Go away, Logan. Please." She closed her eyes and forced the pleading words away.

"When you tell me what's going on."

"You haven't believed a word I've said so far, so why should I bother wasting my breath on you?" Hurt and resignation tinged her words and she listened to the temporary silence on the other side of the door.

"Who locked you in there?"

"My father." When her father had first installed the lock a couple of years ago and told her he'd be locking her door of an evening while Mitchell's friend was sleeping over, she'd hoped he'd been kidding. But her father never joked. At the time she'd hoped Marla might say something, but as usual she hadn't noticed. Or if she had, she didn't care. "Go away and let me get back to sleep."

"Why did he lock you in?"

"Because you and Rob are here. Please go away before someone sees you." She listened. There was silence on the other side of the door. Was he still there? Surely she would have heard his footsteps if he'd walked away. Although she hadn't heard them when he'd came into her room earlier. "Logan?"

"Yeah?"

"Why are you still at my door? And what are you doing at my door in the first place?"

"You really couldn't come to the party, could you?"

"No."

"Why?"

"Because my father wouldn't let me."

"No. I want to know why he wouldn't let you. You and Mitch are pretty much the same age. So why can he go and not you?"

Maddy sighed. "Please, Logan. I really want to go

to my mum's house next weekend. I get to go every second weekend and all the school holidays as long as I'm not grounded."

"How could he blame you? You didn't ask me to come to your door."

"He'd say I must have encouraged you. Please, Logan." Her voice broke on the please and she swallowed past the lump that clogged her throat. Why wouldn't he listen? No one else had noticed the padlock, or if they had, cared.

There was a moment's silence before Logan spoke again. "Which day do you go to your mum's?"

"I catch the train Friday after school and she picks me up from the train station."

"Okay. Night, Maddy."

"Logan?" She waited for him to answer and thought he'd gone when he spoke again.

"Yeah?"

"Stay away from me at school, please."

"Night, Maddy."

She growled in frustration as she heard his footsteps move away from the door. What did that mean? Was he going to stay away from her at school? Or would he try and talk to her? She walked slowly to her bed and dropped face first onto it. Yep. Definitely official. More than official. Her life really did suck. Her eyes ached with unshed tears and it took her ages to return to sleep. Not that sleep was an improvement since she dreamt of her father calmly telling her she'd never leave her room again and locking her door, which had become metal with a small barred window in it. And no matter how much she called for someone to let her out, no one listened and she remained at the door, clutching the bars. Alone.

* * *

All the next week Maddy anxiously watched out for Logan and made sure she headed in the opposite direction each time she saw him. Once she came around a corner and nearly ran into him. She clutched her schoolbooks to her chest as Logan grabbed one of her shoulders to stop them from colliding, his books under his other arm.

Maddy pulled away from him and looked at the ground. It took every bit of willpower not to glance around to see who was nearby. "Sorry," she mumbled.

"I'm not."

The words were spoken so softly Maddy wondered if she'd heard correct. She glanced up in time to catch Logan's quick grin before he strode past her. She forced her feet to take her forward. Standing around like an idiot would only draw more attention to the incident. And that was the last thing she needed. Her next class was a blur as she tried to figure out what Logan had meant by his words.

Luckily lunch was next and she sat in a secluded area, under a large shady tree, with Sasha and told her what had happened. She'd already told Sasha about her weekend in the hope Sasha could give her some clue as to what Logan was thinking since she had no idea.

"Well?" she demanded when Sasha continued to stare at her.

"I don't know." Sasha grinned. "But I think he likes you." The last was said in a singsong voice.

Maddy groaned. "He can't. He'll ruin everything."

"Maybe not. He hasn't tried to speak to you yet and it's Thursday. You'd think he would have by now if he was going to."

"I don't know."

"I do. And I bet he plans to stay at his grandad's place so he can see you while you're at your mum's."

"You really need to stop reading your mum's romance books. I think they've warped your sense of reality."

Sasha grinned. "You're jealous because your father

would lock you up and throw away the key if he caught you with one. All I get is no phone for the day." She frowned. "Although that's almost as bad as torture."

Maddy's attention was caught by the group of boys that came into view. In the middle of them was Logan. She was so caught up watching him mock wrestle Rob that it took her a few moments to realise Mitchell was with the group. Sasha lightly shoved her and she turned to glare at her friend. "What?"

"I bet you didn't hear a word I said."

"Of course I did. You said losing your phone would be the same as torture."

"And after that?"

"Ahh…" Maddy looked towards Logan, who laughed. She smiled slightly as she watched him. When he laughed it was like he did it with his entire body, like it radiated from him. Even his eyes seemed filled with laughter.

"I knew it. Not a word." Sasha waved her hand in front of Maddy's face. "Who's in a fantasy world now? Want a tissue to wipe the drool off your chin?"

"Funny!"

"I thought so. Now stop staring at him before your brother notices."

"Stepbrother."

"Wicked stepbrother. Brother," Sasha shrugged. "Who cares when there isn't a word bad enough to suit him?"

Maddy dragged her attention away from Logan and dropped her arm around Sasha's shoulders. "Have I told you lately that no one in the world has a better best friend than me?"

"Does that mean I get an extra good Chrissie pressie?"

Maddy laughed. "You never know your luck." The bell rang and she glanced towards Logan as she got to her feet and held out her hand to help Sasha up.

"You're hopeless. He doesn't even know you're over here staring at him. What's the point?"

"Because I wouldn't dare do it if he could see. Then someone else might notice too."

"Why don't you ask your mum if you can live with her?"

"I did. Again. You'd think now I'm sixteen I'd have some say over where I live."

Sasha grabbed Maddy's arm and forced her to turn and look at her. "What did she say this time?"

"No."

"Really? Was that it? Didn't she say why?"

Maddy shook her head. "She just kept saying no. And that we'd been over this a million times and my father was entitled to some of my time too. When I'd asked too many times she got stern, kind of like my father, and said, 'I've already told you no', and walked away. I've never seen her imitate him like that before. It was actually scary. She didn't even act like that the time she had a fight with him and I asked about something I overheard."

"The time we thought your father might have been married before?"

Maddy nodded. "Yeah. That time." She frowned. "I can't remember exactly what she said-"

"I can. She said she wasn't the kind of woman to jump when a man ordered, like his first one. But you know, she might have meant a girlfriend, not wife."

"Yeah, possibly. But then why wouldn't she tell me that? Why refuse to answer me?"

Sasha shrugged. "Who knows? But then I've never been able to completely understand your mum. I mean, the woman chose to marry your father. I've never wondered why Marla married him. She's colder than he is. Your father might be a brilliant plastic surgeon and everyone raves over how talented he is, but his people skills suck."

"Yeah, I've always wondered that too. I don't know what she was thinking. And now I'm the one who has to live with him. Why should I have to pay for her mistake?"

"I wish you could live with me."

"Me too. But I guess I'm stuck where I am."

"Not this weekend you aren't."

Maddy grinned. "Nope. Not this weekend." Her grin evaporated. "Unless I get grounded." She grabbed Sasha's hand and dragged her out of the shelter of the tree they sat under. "Come on. Detention for being late for class wouldn't be good right now."

Chapter Five

Maddy closed the boot of her father's car, having placed her bag for the weekend in there. She opened the car door and was about to get in when she froze. "My assignment. It's still on my desk."

"I'm going to be late," Mitchell growled.

"It won't take me long." Maddy took the keys her father handed her, his lips tightly pressed together.

"It better not." Sinclair had dark blond hair and pale blue eyes that could cut deeper than any knife he'd ever wielded. And currently those eyes were an unfriendly blue with a hint of annoyance.

"It won't." Maddy ran to the front door and let herself in, glad it was her father taking them to school. Marla would have told her there was no time and in future she shouldn't be so disorganised. Her assignment was on her desk where she'd left it and she was nearly at the front door when the phone started to ring. She hesitated. Curiosity won and she picked it up. "Hello?"

"Maddy?"

"Mum?"

"Is your father about, love?"

"Ah, not really. He's in the car waiting for me. He'll probably start hitting the horn soon."

"I won't keep you then. Look, I'm sorry to call at the last minute, but I have to go away this weekend. Work related. Maybe your father will let you come the next weekend instead."

"Yeah, right."

"I'm sorry."

The car horn sounded once and Maddy began to wish she hadn't stopped to answer the phone. She wanted to argue and plead, but knew she didn't have the time. And she still wouldn't be able to go because then she'd be grounded for taking so long. "I've got to go. Dad's getting impatient."

"Do you want me to call him at work later or are you fine with telling him?"

"I can tell him. It'll probably put him in a good mood. At least someone around here will be happy this weekend." Bitterness filled her words and her body, making her hand tighten on the phone she was tempted to throw at the wall.

"I'm sorry, Maddy. I know you must be disappointed–"

She couldn't do this conversation. Not right now. "Bye, Mum." She hung up the phone and ran for the door. Locking the door behind her, she hurried over to the car to slide into the back seat.

Sinclair took the keys from Maddy's outstretched hand. "What took you so long? I have a full schedule today. It's unprofessional to be late from anything other than an emergency."

"Sorry." Maddy buckled up.

Mitchell turned in his seat to glare at her. "If I get detention I'll miss practice this arve. You'd like that, wouldn't you? I bet you did it deliberately to try and make me miss it."

"I couldn't care less what you think."

"Keep that up Maddy and you won't be going to your mother's this weekend."

Maddy opened her mouth to tell him she wasn't going anyway, but Mitchell spoke first.

"I don't know why you let her go, Dad. Every time she comes back she's more argumentative and treats me like I'm her enemy."

Maddy clenched her teeth. Every time he called her father 'dad' it made her want to yell at him. And hit him. He wasn't Mitchell's father. No, his father had walked out when he was three-months-old because he was as annoying back then as he was now.

"The psychologist I took her to said a transitional phase is normal," Sinclair said.

She hadn't wanted to go because she'd been worried the psychologist would side with her father and agree with him that she wasn't coping with being shuffled between two parents. But her father hadn't given her a choice. She'd been both surprised and relieved when the psychologist hadn't agreed.

"It might be normal in someone who lives between two parents, but it's annoying. Stopping the visits would mean we wouldn't have to put up with it. Madeline might not think her senior years are important, but I do. I don't need these kinds of distractions, Dad."

Maddy hated it when they talked about her as if she wasn't there. They pulled up in front of the school gates and she lost her chance to say something. Mitchell was out of the door with a goodbye. Maddy did the same. She hurried to catch up to her stepbrother. There was something she needed to make clear.

She fell into step beside him. "You know, if it wasn't for the fact I'd be grounded and miss staying with my mum, I'd be a lot harder to put up with. You might think about that next time you try and make Dad keep me from going."

"Shut up."

"I hope you understand exactly what I mean, Mitchell."

He stopped and faced her. "Are you threatening me?"

Maddy smiled mirthlessly, shrugging. "Take it how you want. But if you make every minute of my life hell by preventing me from visiting Mum, I'm going to want to make sure you feel every bit of pain I'm feeling."

Mitchell leaned in close. "Don't ever threaten me, Madeline."

"Then don't try and wreck my life and I won't have to."

"Hey, Mitch." Logan joined them with a friendly grin. "Will you be at the practice game this arve?"

Mitchell took a step away from Maddy and gave her one last glare before he turned to Logan. "Yeah. But I can't hang around afterwards. Dad picks me up straight after the game."

Maddy watched as they moved away, her attention on Logan. She jumped when someone clapped her on the back. Her startled look turned to a smile when she saw it was Sasha.

"Not long now and you'll be at your mum's and can quit pretending for a bit."

Maddy shook her head, fighting back the anger that filled her. "No, I won't. She rang this morning and said I couldn't come."

"What? No! What did your father say?"

"I haven't told him yet."

"Why can't you visit her?"

"She won't be there. She's away for the weekend. Something to do with work."

Sasha smiled, a look of calculation entering her eyes. "You know, that doesn't mean you have to have a terrible weekend."

"I don't like your expression, Sash. The last thing I need is to get in trouble."

Sasha airily waved her concerns away. "You won't. You could still go. Catch a taxi from the train station."

"I don't have the money to do that."

"I'll lend it to you."

Maddy shook her head. "I'd never be able to pay you back."

"It can be an early Christmas present."

"I don't know."

"You'd have the house all to yourself for the weekend."

"Well…"

"I've got nearly a hundred dollars on me."

"What on earth for?"

Sasha ignored the exclamation. "You'd have an entire weekend without your father, Marla or Mitchell. You could do what you want. Be yourself."

A reprieve from her father every second weekend was the only way she could get through each week. If she had to last a month without a break, she'd be ready to kill someone. Probably Mitchell. So it wouldn't really be wrong, it'd be saving a life. Maddy smiled reluctantly. Sasha made it sound so easy. "I just know I'm going to get caught."

Sasha threw her arms around Maddy with a squeal. "You're going to do it?"

Maddy nodded as she ignored the alarm bells sounding in her mind.

"You have to ring me the moment you get to your mum's house. And I want to hear every little detail on Monday. I wish I was coming with you."

"So do I." Maddy shook her head slowly. "You are such a bad influence. I can't believe I'm going to do this."

Sasha linked her arm through Maddy's as the school bell rang. "It will be marvellous. Wonderful. Amazing. Be-lud-ee purrrr-fect."

"You have a bad habit of exaggerating."

Sasha laughed. "Just you wait and see."

Maddy recalled her earlier question. "So why do you have so much money with you today?"

"There's the most perfect pair of shoes, I just have to have. But don't worry, I'll use Dad's credit card. That's what it's meant for. Emergencies. I can't wait for you to see the shoes."

As they headed for class, Maddy smiled slightly as she listened to Sasha describe the shoes in minute detail her hands helping with the explanation.

Chapter Six

By the time the bell rang for lunch, Maddy had changed her mind a dozen times. She strode to where her and Sasha sat, barely having the chance to sit beside Sasha before her friend was pressing something into her hands. She looked at the neatly folded square of plain paper. "What's this for?"

"Open it and see. It won't bite. At least I don't think it will."

"Come on, Sash. What's going on? You look like you're about to burst."

"Hurry up and open it. I don't know what's in it. I was asked to give it to you."

Maddy frowned at the piece of paper. It looked like an ordinary piece of white A4. She could see the shadow of writing and tilted it as if to see through the page.

"Do you know how hard it was not to open it?

Now hurry up before I take it back and open it for you."

Maddy unfolded the paper and looked at the phone number printed across the page with the words 'Grandad's house' scrawled underneath it. She grinned when Sasha squealed, bouncing on the bench seat they sat on. She shook her head, trying to tamp down her own excitement. "It's not that exciting."

"I told you he's going to be there this weekend."

"Possibly."

"He will be. You better tell me every little detail. I can't wait until Monday. I can't believe I said that. I so hate Mondays normally. That was so weird to say. I feel like I should be doing penance or something for saying it. Now remember, I want to hear every little detail. Make sure you remember all of it."

"Aye, aye captain."

Sasha continued to grin. "That'll be enough out of you or you'll have to walk the plank." She groaned. "How are we going to get through the afternoon classes? You have to ring him the moment you get in. And arrange to see him straight away. You've only got the weekend so don't waste a single second of it. But after you ring him, call me. I want to know what you arrange."

"I do know how to do this, Sasha."

"Well, I have to make sure. After all, you've spent nearly a fortnight in that oppressive environment your father calls a home. It's enough to crush your spirit and make you forget how to have fun."

"It's not that bad."

"Really?"

"Well… possibly."

Sasha squealed again. "I'm so excited for you."

"I kind of noticed," Maddy said dryly.

Sasha instantly sobered. "I'm drawing too much attention, aren't I?"

"A little."

"Okay. I'll try and contain myself. But I want to grab hold of your hands and dance you around the schoolyard."

"Anyone'd think it was you going away for the weekend."

"I wish."

"Maybe one day. I'd love to have you visit me at Mum's. But my father said I wasn't to invite you. Ever. He might change his mind one day. You never know."

Sasha nodded. "Maybe." But it was plain she didn't believe.

Maddy soon found Sasha was right and the afternoon classes dragged slowly by. When her father picked her up, she kept expecting something to go wrong. Nothing did and when they arrived at the train station, she kissed her father briefly on the cheek, grabbed her bag from him and boarded the train. All around her people hurried, a low hum of sound filling the air. A mix of footsteps, words, machinery and phones ringing. Her stomach felt like a troop of acrobats had taken up residence and she thought she might be sick. But no one stopped her. They didn't even glance at her. She sank into a seat and looked out the window. No one ran along the platform to demand she be thrown off. No one yelled out she was lying. The people out there didn't care what she did. Only she and Sasha knew her mum wouldn't be at the other end to meet her. And neither of them would be stupid enough to say a word to anyone.

She sank back in her seat and closed her eyes. A sigh of relief escaped as she felt the train start forward. Next destination- freedom. She smiled as her entire body relaxed. A weekend without Marla's constant disapproval, her father watching her every move or Mitchell ready to pounce on anything she did wrong. Wrong as dictated by her father. She needed this break so she could get through the next couple of weeks without killing someone. And Mitchell was right at the top of her list of prime candidates.

"Is this seat taken?"

Maddy's eyes flew open and she stared up at Logan. She opened her mouth to speak, but it was like she'd forgotten how. Instead she closed her mouth and shook her head. Until this moment she hadn't really believed he'd be headed for the coast this weekend. And she certainly hadn't thought he might be on the train with her.

Logan dropped onto the seat and let his bag slide to the floor at his feet. "What do you normally do on the train?"

"Homework."

"Seriously?"

"Yes."

"Will the real Maddy please stand up?"

Recognising the misquoted song, she smiled. "I don't think she exists."

"I thought I'd met her on the school holidays."

"Yeah well, she got packed away with the rest of the holiday fun."

"Think she'll be unpacked this weekend?"

"Possibly."

"That's good." Logan leaned close and dropped his voice. "Because I like the way she kisses."

She had to look away and think of something else or she knew her cheeks would be tomato red. It was going to be a long trip if he kept making comments like that. Although in the right clothes and with a better hairstyle she never seemed to be bothered by those kinds of remarks. Maybe she was right and the real Maddy didn't exist. She spent so much time being who she was expected to be that she wasn't sure if she knew who she really was anymore.

"What are you thinking of that's making you frown like that?"

She shook her head. "Nothing important." At least it didn't seem important to most of the people she knew. As far as her father was concerned, he had exact ideas on what she should be like, even if being that person felt like wearing a coat three sizes too small. But she wasn't going to share that thought. Logan knew far too many of her secrets already. "What do you normally do on long train rides?"

Logan grinned. "Depends on who I'm with."

Maddy decided that was another comment to leave alone. She had a good idea from the gleam in his eyes what he was talking about and it involved them sitting a lot closer than they were. It was time for another conversation change. "Why are you headed to the coast?"

"Would you believe me if I said I couldn't wait to see my grandfather?"

Maddy shrugged. "Not really."

"I came because I don't like to talk to someone through a locked door."

"Oh." Why did he have to keep steering the conversation to uncomfortable topics?

"So what was with that?"

Maddy looked away from him and out the window. A pity there wasn't something more interesting to catch her attention. Something she could have drawn Logan's attention to so it wasn't focused on her. "I've already told you."

"Not really. Well, not so I'd be able to make sense of it. What century is your father living in? He does know we're no longer in the Dark Ages, doesn't he?"

"Probably not. I'm surprised he's never thought of getting me a chastity belt."

"Nah, he'll want to do better than that. I bet he's got a nunnery all picked out for you. On your eighteenth birthday, instead of a party, you'll be given directions to it."

"That wouldn't surprise me." She started to relax again now the conversation had lightened.

Unlike other weekends, the train ride passed quickly and the hours seemed like minutes before they pulled into their station. Maddy followed Logan off the train and looked around. It felt odd not having her mum there, waving madly and rushing over to meet her. She felt kind of lost and stopped, wondering what to do next.

"Is anyone meeting you here? Didn't you say your mum does?" Logan turned and took a step towards her when he saw she'd stopped.

Maddy shrugged. "I've got to catch a taxi tonight."

"I've got a mate picking me up. He won't mind giving you a lift."

"Well…" She would prefer not to have to spend Sasha's money, but she didn't really know Logan that well. Being an eleven for kissing was probably not the type of recommendation you looked for when accepting a ride from someone. And she knew nothing about his friend.

"You don't have to. I thought you might want a lift." Logan grinned. "And while we're dropping you off you could check with your mum to see if we can pick you up in the morning and hit the beach."

"She won't mind. It's completely different from when I'm at my father's place."

"No padlocks on the bedroom door here?"

"No. When will your friend get here?" She changed the subject before he could ask her about the padlock again. She didn't want to explain. Not when she barely understood half of what her father did. And her mum's continual excuse that he was being protective wasn't enough of an explanation for her.

"He's actually my step cousin, but we were friends before we were cousins. I dialled his number and hung up while we were getting off the train. That was his warning to come and get me."

"Oh." She glanced around and tried to think of something else to say. They'd been able to talk so easily before. Until he'd mentioned the padlock. Now she worried he might ask about it again if there was a lull in the conversation. She saw nothing to inspire words. The couple of cars that had been waiting to pick up other passengers were gone. Streetlights shone on the car park they stood in and the traffic driving past was light.

"Do you want a lift?"

Chapter Seven

Maddy glanced around. The place was nearly deserted. She guessed she could go over to the petrol station and wait for a taxi, but she'd still be on her own. This weekend suddenly didn't seem like such a good idea. Nor did all the horror movies she'd watched. "Ahh, I suppose."

Logan grinned. "Guess I'll get to check out your other home. Do I get to see what this bedroom is like too?"

Maddy's nervousness evaporated as quickly as it had come and she returned his grin. "No."

"Aww, why not? Do you have embarrassing posters in there? Pink frilly sheets? Or is it another ice princess setting?"

She ignored the last comment, but her grin faded. "Of course not. Pink is not my colour."

"Then why can't I see it?"

A white sedan pulled into the car park and interrupted their conversation. The car was left running while the driver swung open his door and rose enough to lean over it. "That's fast work. Even for you, Logan." He had a crooked grin, bleach blond hair, no shirt and board shorts.

Logan draped an arm around Maddy's shoulders. "Mind if Maddy hitches a lift?"

"Nah." He straightened as they came close to the car and held out his hand. "I'm Davey Hillman."

Maddy took his hand. "Maddy Dowling."

"The Maddy from the school holidays?"

She glanced at Logan. "Ahh, possibly?"

"What are we hanging around the car park for?" Logan guided Maddy to the front passenger door and opened it. "You want the front?"

"Are you worried about what I might repeat, Logan?" Davey slid behind the wheel. He chuckled at the rude gesture Logan made before he closed the front door. "You know I do owe you for my dad marrying your aunt."

Logan hopped into the back seat. "You've been saying that for years. I think you're all talk."

"Really?" Davey glanced at Logan before he leaned towards Maddy who was avidly following the conversation. "Do you want to know what he said?"

Maddy nodded.

"Where does your mum live, Maddy?" Logan asked.

"Quiet in the back," Davey ordered over his shoulder. He turned to Maddy. "You don't sound very interested in knowing. Are you sure I should tell you?"

Maddy couldn't resist glancing at Logan. "Yes, please."

"She's a lot nicer than you, Logan. I reckon I should tell her."

"That's the last time I tell my aunt you looked out for me while I'm here," Logan muttered.

Davey laughed. "He said he wished he'd thought to get your phone number before you did your disappearing act."

"Is that all?" Maddy was disappointed. She'd thought it was going to be more interesting. Although, she had to admit she'd had the same thought.

"Yep." Davey continued to grin.

Maddy turned to look at Logan who grinned too. She shook her head. "And to think I agreed to get in the car with you pair. I'll probably want to murder one of you before you drop me off."

Davey put the car in gear and pulled out onto the road. "So, did he get your phone number?"

"I don't have a number he can ring me on."

"You don't have a mobile phone?" Davey sounded shocked.

"No."

"Hey, where am I taking you?" Davey asked.

Maddy gave him directions.

Davey turned a corner. "Man. How can you survive without a mobile phone? It'd just about kill me if I lost mine."

Maddy shrugged. "I've never had one."

"Never?"

Maddy shook her head. "No."

"You poor deprived child." Davey glanced in the rear view mirror. "I guess you expect me to play chauffeur tomorrow."

"Well, my aunt did say you were to look after me."

"Yeah, Mum seems to think you're so sweet and innocent. Her dear little nephew. Lucky she wasn't here the second night of the last school holidays when you were throwing up 'cause you can't handle drinking."

"It wasn't the alcohol. It was food poisoning from your cooking."

"Yeah, right. You just shouldn't drink. Not when you can't handle it, you poor little boy."

"I seem to remember playing nursemaid to you a few nights after that. It wouldn't happen to have been that bottle of Jack would it?"

Davey shook his head. "Nah. It was that new take-away place. I really did have food poisoning."

"That's my excuse. Find your own," Logan protested.

Maddy pointed out the front window. "My place is there. The lowset house with the big tree that hangs out over the road."

"It's all dark." Davey turned off the engine. He leaned across her to peer out the window. "Are you sure someone's expecting you?"

"Yeah. I've got a key. Mum said she'd be home late. I guess she's not back yet." Maddy rummaged in her bag for the key. Like a couple of days late. An awful feeling began in the pit of her stomach when she had trouble finding the key. It remained even after her fingers touched the cold metal. A glance at the house showed only darkness. How had she let Sasha talk her into this? Actually, Sasha hadn't needed to put in much effort to convince her. Why had she thought she could pull this off?

She forced her lips into a smile for Davey. "Thanks for the lift."

"No problem. You be right until your mum gets home? We can hang about for a bit if you want."

Maddy shook her head, the smile becoming easier. She didn't think they'd be willing to stick around all weekend. "No. Thanks though."

"I'll walk you to your door." Logan got out of the car.

Maddy stood on the grassed footpath and tried to see his expression in the shadows created by the tree. "You don't need to."

"Come on." Logan strode towards her front door.

With a sigh, Maddy followed him. It was a bit hard to argue with someone who didn't argue back. She fumbled with the key as she tried to unlock the door. When it swung open, she turned to Logan. "You can go now."

"You don't need me to look under your bed for monsters?"

Maddy grinned. "You just want to check out my bedroom. I already told you there's no embarrassing posters."

"Ahh, but are you telling the truth?"

"I guess you'll have to keep wondering." Maddy took a step back and reached her hand inside to turn on the lounge room light. She stared at Logan who blinked in the sudden brightness. "Night, Logan."

"I'll see you at eight." He leaned forward and brushed his lips across hers.

He was halfway back to the car before Maddy gathered her scattered thoughts. "Not that early. I want to sleep in tomorrow," she yelled after him.

"Quarter past eight," he yelled over his shoulder.

"Ten."

"Nope. See you." He hopped in the car and shut the door.

Maddy waved as they drove off, shaking her head. "Fifteen minutes doesn't make it a sleep in." She locked the front door behind her. "He's crazy."

Around her was only silence. She stared at the familiar room. The faded brown couches with their indistinct pattern, the battered coffee table covered in newspapers and magazines and the polished floorboards that had years of marks and scratches on their surface. Even with the couple of timber bookcases along one wall, that nearly groaned with books, the room felt empty. Quiet and empty, like it contained nothing and no one.

She forced herself to head to her bedroom and ditch her bag. She had the place to herself. It was meant to be exciting. She wasn't meant to jump at every little sound. Her stomach grumbled and she pressed her hand against it. Food. That's what she should get. Then bed. Especially if Logan was turning up at eight the next morning. Well, quarter past. But that wasn't enough extra time to call it sleeping in.

She peered in the fridge and pulled out bread and chocolate spread. Not a very nutritious dinner, but there wasn't anyone around to notice or complain. She took a large bite and sighed as the flavour filled her mouth. This was much better. She wandered to the lounge room and dropped into an armchair. No one to complain about what she ate, where she sat and how she sat. She swung her legs over one of the arms and leaned back against the other.

Her mum never complained about how she sat on the chairs, but she hadn't spent the last two weeks at her mum's place. She took another bite and groaned when the phone rang. For a moment she nearly ignored it. Then she started to wonder if it was Sasha ringing to check on her. She'd forgotten she'd told Sasha she'd ring.

Still trying to swallow her mouthful, Maddy picked up the phone. "Mmmm?"

"Mrs Dowling, I've got good news for you. Your mother's temperature has finally dropped. I know we were worried she'd be sick all weekend, but it looks like we were wrong. Why don't you have a sleep-in before you come back to the nursing home tomorrow morning?"

"Ahh-"

"Now don't you argue. I know you've been concerned about her the last few days, but she's on the mend now. It wasn't long after you left tonight that she came good. You make sure you take care of yourself. There's no need for you to be making yourself sick. Then how would you be able to visit your mum? She really looks forward to your daily visits. I know it doesn't always seem that way, but it really brightens her day."

She struggled to make sense of the conversation, thinking she should tell the woman she had the wrong person. "Ohh... uhmm..."

The woman continued talking, not giving Maddy a chance to say anything other than half formed sounds. "You go and put your feet up and take some time out for yourself. After lunch will be soon enough to visit tomorrow. Sleep in, you hear?"

"Ahh-"

"Good. I'll see you tomorrow."

Chapter Eight

Maddy continued to stand there, holding the phone even when she heard the woman hang up. Her mind raced as she tried to make sense of the conversation. Mrs Dowling? Surely it wouldn't have been a wrong number. How odd would that be? To call another Mrs Dowling. But if the call had been meant for her mum, why were they talking about her mother? "My grandmother," she whispered as she finally managed to hang up the phone.

She staggered to the armchair and dropped onto it, her sandwich forgotten. What was going on? Did she still have a living grandmother? As far as she knew all her grandparents were dead. A frown formed. Had anyone told her that, or had she assumed it? She'd definitely been told her paternal grandparents were dead. They'd been gone before she was born. First one and then a few years later the other. And her maternal grandfather had died when her mum was a little girl. She didn't remember anyone saying anything about her maternal grandmother. Why had she never realised no one had mentioned how she'd died? Did that mean she was still alive? And why hadn't anyone told her?

Still feeling dazed, Maddy rang Sasha. She kept the conversation short, using an early morning with Logan as an excuse for needing to head to bed. But instead of going to sleep, she continued to sit in the lounge room, her mind filled with unanswered questions.

The sound of the front door being unlocked brought Maddy to her feet. She stared at her mum, who froze in the doorway. Nearly a minute passed before Joscelin came in and closed the door behind her.

"I thought I'd left the light off."

Maddy nodded. She wanted to demand answers. Why had they lied to her? But no words came. She stared at her mum and wondered what was going on.

"Why are you here, Maddy?"

Anger welled up. She'd always suspected her mum of lying each time she'd said she wished she could see her more often. If her mum had really felt that way, she would have fought harder for a larger share of her time. "I thought you were meant to be away for work."

Joscelin smiled wryly. "Fair enough. I hope you didn't organise a party or something because I'm desperate for sleep."

She'd expected an apology. Not humour. "No party. But I do have a phone message for you."

Joscelin's smile vanished. "Who from?"

"Your mum's temperature dropped and they said not to come in to the nursing home until after midday. To sleep in. They thought I was you. Whoever it was talked non-stop and I didn't get a chance to correct her before she started telling me all kinds of interesting things." Anger kept her voice sharp.

Joscelin took a step forward, hand outstretched. Looking away, she dropped her hand. "It's not what you think."

"Really? I think I have a grandmother, I've never met, shoved in some nursing home. Are you telling me that's not true?"

"Please Maddy, you've got to keep quiet about this."

"Why?"

"You shouldn't even be here this weekend. I trusted you to tell your father you couldn't come."

"Guess I'm about as trustworthy as my mum. I wonder if it's genetic."

"Now Maddy-"

"No! Why did you lie to me about her?"

"I never lied. I didn't tell you. There's a difference."

Maddy shook her head, an image coming clearly to mind. "I remember Dad saying something about me not having any grandparents when I was younger. Sasha was going to stay with her grandma for the holidays and I wished I could escape too. It was when her dad made all those changes at the private hospital he runs. I remember her having an argument about him not wanting her around so he was ditching her."

"Maddy-"

"I want to see her."

"No."

"Then I'll ask Dad if I can."

"He doesn't want you to have anything to do with her. His parents are probably lucky they died when they did or he would have got around to rejecting them too if they'd started to do and say odd things when they got old. Image has always been important to him. Although old age probably wouldn't have dared altered them too much since he got his ideas from them about image. And life reinforced their teachings." Bitterness tainted Joscelin's words.

"You can't stop me from seeing her. I won't tell him. Have I ever told him about what you let me do here? Please, Mum." Why did they do this to her? Why lie and smother her and never trust her?

"I'd love you to see her, Maddy. But I can't risk it. For all I know he has people at the nursing home who tell him what goes on. I'd never be able to afford to pay for her to stay there."

"What do you mean?"

Joscelin walked unsteadily across the room and dropped onto the couch. She kicked her slip-on shoes off and rubbed her forehead. "Why do you think I stopped fighting to have you full time? He was paying for Mum to stay in a nursing home. When you were about three she started forgetting where she was and what she was doing. She didn't live near us. I had to fly down and see what I could do for her. The doctor she was seeing suggested a nursing home. I was devastated. I wanted to bring her home." Joscelin fell silent as she stared into the distance.

"What happened? Did you bring her home? Why can't I remember meeting her?"

"Because you didn't. We always meant to fly down and see her, but your father's work kept interrupting." Joscelin's lips twisted into a mocking smile. "I guess nothing has changed there."

"How did she end up on the coast? I mean, haven't we always lived in Brisbane?"

Joscelin nodded. "Yeah. Your father said he'd pay for a nursing home. I wanted to bring her to Brisbane, but he wouldn't agree. He didn't want me taking you to visit her. Said you were too young to understand what was going on and it'd confuse and upset you. I guess he didn't believe me when I said I wouldn't take you to see her. When we divorced, he stopped paying for the nursing home. I tried to look after Mum, but she was a full time job. It was impossible to work and look after her. When I woke up one morning and she was gone, the front door wide open, I knew she needed to be in a nursing home. And at the time, the public system had such a long waiting list."

"Why is Dad paying for the nursing home?"

Joscelin dropped her head into her hands. "Because I stopped fighting him for you."

"What?" Surely she hadn't heard right. Her mum had not only chosen someone else over her, but her father had blackmailed her mum so he could have custody of her?

Joscelin looked up at Maddy who continued to stand. "I knew you could take care of yourself and you'd be safe with him. Probably safer than living with me, but Mum," her hands moved in agitation. "She needed help. She needed to be safe. Your father loves you, Maddy. He'd never let anything happen to you. He might be a little overzealous in how he goes about it, but he'll always keep you safe."

Yeah, to the point he wouldn't allow life to happen to her. She ignored that part of her mum's words. It was a never ending argument between them. Her hands curled into fists. She wanted to demand that she deserved someone to look after her too. "I want to meet her. There's got to be some way of getting in to see her."

"I don't know. I can't think about this right now. I haven't slept properly in days. Can we talk about it in the morning?"

Maddy stared at her mum, wanting to hold onto her anger and not feel any sympathy. Her brown eyes seemed washed out and the only colour was from the darkness underneath them. Her dark brown hair was pulled roughly back from her face and hung in wisps from where she'd run her fingers through it numerous times, as she was doing that very moment. Her hair was a couple of shades darker than Maddy's with a few stray strands of grey.

Maddy breathed out heavily. "Okay. As long as we do talk in the morning."

"I want to be out of here before eight. You'll have to get up at seven if you want to talk."

Maddy wanted to argue. So much for sleeping in. But she supposed seven was better than the six her father expected them to rise. Regardless of if it was the weekend. He didn't tolerate laziness, which is what he considered sleeping in to be. Even Marla never slept in. "Fine. I'm going out at eight-fifteen anyway." She didn't explain where or with who, her mum could ask if she wanted more information. She was sick of being the only one who was expected to live an open book life. Why should she? Their lives were riddled with secrets.

Joscelin staggered to her feet. "Goodnight, Maddy."

She watched her mum leave the room, reeling from everything she'd learned. Why couldn't she have had a normal family?

Chapter Nine

When Logan arrived the next morning, Maddy was still thinking about everything her mum had told her during breakfast. She opened the front door when he knocked and stared at him. He wore board shorts, a sleeveless shirt and the faded cap he'd worn when she'd first met him. She scowled at his smile and was tempted to shut the door and climb back into bed.

"Did your mum get in okay last night?"

Maddy nodded.

"Where is she today?"

"Out."

"What's wrong?"

"It's not morning yet. I wanted to sleep in. But I couldn't. I had breakfast with Mum at seven and when I would have crawled back into bed after she'd left I had to get ready to go to the beach with you instead." Her glare was ruined by a yawn.

"Are you sure your mum exists? You didn't imagine her, did you?"

"Of course I didn't imagine her."

Logan peered over her shoulder. "You haven't murdered her and stored her in the chest freezer, have you? Maybe I should have a look?"

"And I guess that'd include checking under my bed too."

"Just to make sure you're not hiding any dead bodies." Logan nodded seriously.

Maddy smiled, her annoyance at the early morning evaporating. "Nice try, but no luck. Now are we going to the beach or what?"

"Yep. Grab your gear and let's go."

Maddy picked up the medium sized backpack she'd left by the front door and slung it over one shoulder. When she reached the footpath, she saw Davey waited in his car for them. She smiled in greeting. "Hey."

Davey grinned. "I thought it had been the lack of light."

"Huh?" Maddy slid into the front seat, Logan waved her towards, before he got in the back.

"But no, you're still pretty. Actually, you're even prettier today. So what's a pretty girl like you doing hanging out with my cousin? Don't you know there are heaps better guys than him?" Davey glanced over his shoulder before he pulled out onto the street.

"Are you adding yourself to that list?" Maddy asked.

"Of course." Davey grinned.

Maddy stared up at him. She'd been wondering last night, but now she was in her sundress, with her bikini underneath and her favourite cap, she felt more like herself and able to ask personal questions. "How old are you?"

"Eighteen. So I'm not too old for you at all. Two years is a good gap."

"I've not long turned sixteen. At the start of the last school holidays."

"There you go, perfect gap."

Logan leaned forward, resting his hands on the front seats. "I wouldn't worry about him. I've heard girls complain he's a hopeless kisser."

"Yeah, but I've got a car and license. You've only got your learners and you have to bum a ride. Not very cool, cuz."

The smile that had been forming vanished as Maddy wished she had her learners. It was so unfair her father wouldn't let her get it yet. Especially since Marla had let Mitchell go for his.

"Material possessions are meaningless." Logan

made a flicking motion with his hand as if to shoo them away.

"But I notice you don't turn your nose up at a lift," Davey pointed out.

Maddy looked from one to the other. "Do you pair always hassle each other?"

"Hassle?" Logan's voice was full of innocence. "Never!"

"Yeah, never. We're the best of friends. Always saying such wonderful things about each other." Davey tried for an equally innocent tone.

"Yeah, right." Maddy made sure her disbelief could be clearly heard.

Davey parked the car. "Swim anyone?" He swung the door open, the warmth of the day rolling into the car, bringing with it the tang of salt.

Logan tore off his shirt as he clambered out of the car. "I'm dying for one."

"Yeah, me too." Maddy walked beside Logan as he headed along the path through the trees, the sounds of the ocean ahead of them. Reaching the beach, she dropped her backpack on the sand and slipped off her dress, tossing it on top of her backpack. Her sandals were soon kicked off and she sank her toes into the sand. "I miss the beach when I'm stuck in Brisbane."

Davey ran towards the waves. "Last one in the water gets to wash my car."

"Not fair!" Logan raced after him. "You cheated."

Maddy watched them with a grin. There was no way she was going to join that race. She wasn't about to let either of them think she was willing to risk having to wash the car.

* * *

After a morning at the beach, they headed to a takeaway shop and ordered burgers. They sat at a table out the front, sheltered by a bright umbrella. Maddy took a bite of her burger and leaned back in the plastic chair, relaxed and a little tired after so long at the beach.

"I've got things to do this arve, but if you're not busy this evening, do you want to go to the movies?" Logan asked.

Davey swallowed his mouthful. "He might be busy, but I'm not."

Maddy smiled. She knew Davey only said that to tease Logan, he wasn't serious. He'd probably give her a lift somewhere if she asked, but he wasn't interested in hooking up with her. Not like Logan was. "That's okay. I should probably get my homework done since someone distracted me from doing it while I was on the train."

"You'd choose homework over me? I'm heartbroken." Davey put on a suitable expression to match his words, pressing his hand theatrically against his heart.

"Yeah, right." Maddy rolled her eyes. She turned to Logan. "What do you have to do next?"

"Visit my grandad."

Maddy frowned. "Ahh, aren't you staying with him?"

Logan grinned and shook his head. "Nope. I'm staying at his house."

"With me," Davey added.

Maddy felt more confused. "Make sense, why don't you?"

"Come to the movies with me tonight?"

Maddy stared at Logan a moment then nodded. "Only if you start making sense."

"Grandad has really bad osteoporosis and is living in a nursing home since he needs regular supervision. He tells everyone he's got glass bones." Logan smiled fleetingly, his fondness for his grandfather evident in his expression. "He didn't want to sell his house when he moved to the nursing home. Him and Grandma bought it when they got married and it's right on the beach. She's only been gone a couple of years. He said it'd be like losing her all over again."

"So I live there and take care of it. But since I'm at uni during the day, there was no one to watch out for him," Davey said.

Maddy latched onto the words that had triggered an idea. "Which nursing home?" She grinned when Logan told her. "Can I come too?"

"What are you up to, Maddy?" Logan looked at her suspiciously.

She sighed. Did she really want to spill her secrets? How else would she get him to agree to take her? And she really wanted to meet her grandmother. Desperately. She wanted to see the person her mum had chosen over her. Reaching a decision, she outlined her night and even told him she wasn't meant to be here this weekend. Her hands were clasped tightly together in her lap as she waited for one of the boys to speak, unable to meet their gazes.

Davey shook his head. "Your father sounds like a complete bastard. No offence."

Maddy shrugged. "He can be sometimes." She wanted to tell Logan to hurry up and answer her. How long was he going to wait before he said if she could join him on his visit to the nursing home?

"Pretty amazing that they're both at the same nursing home," Davey said.

Maddy shrugged again. "Mum said it was the best one in the area." She looked at Logan, wanting to shake him.

"That wasn't fair of your mum to let him have you so she could keep your grandma in a nursing home," Logan said.

Maddy made a conscious effort not to shrug again. As much as she complained about her father, and sometimes her mum, she always felt the urge to defend her parents. It annoyed her sometimes. Made her feel weak. At least she never felt like defending Marla and Mitchell. "I don't know. Since I've never met her, I wouldn't have a clue. But I guess it would have been scary for Mum to wake up and find Grandma missing. I know if I was looking after someone and they disappeared I'd probably have a heart attack. And besides, it's not too bad at my father's." If you didn't want to have a life.

"What crap. He padlocks your bedroom door of a night." Logan glared at her.

"Only when Mitchell has friends stay over." She wished he'd drop the subject.

"A padlock? Seriously?" Davey looked from one to the other.

Logan nodded while Maddy shook her head.

"He does. It was at the top of her door and well and truly locked. It must have been the biggest one he could find," Logan said.

"I wasn't disagreeing. But it's not like you think. He's only trying to protect me." *Or so he says.* She didn't think Mitchell's friends were that untrustworthy, but what did she know? Absolutely nothing if you asked her father. "Besides, it isn't that big." *A big one would have looked tacky and you couldn't have that.*

"How would that protect you if there was a fire? Are you expected to stay in your room and burn alive because you're locked in and can't get out?" Logan demanded.

"I could get out the window. Anyway, it's none of your business." She gave up on Logan taking her to the nursing home and turned to Davey. "Can I get a lift to the nursing home too?"

When Davey nodded and started to speak, Logan interrupted him. "How are you going to get in there? They don't let people wander around. You need to have a reason for being there."

"I don't see why you're so angry." Maddy rose to her feet. "Forget it. I'll find my own way." She slung on her backpack and stalked away from the table, ignoring both boys when they called out to her.

Chapter Ten

Running footsteps hit the concrete path behind Maddy, but she refused to turn and see who it was. When the footsteps reached her side, she kept her head straight while she glanced sideways to see who walked with her. It was Logan. She walked a little faster, but he kept up. She dropped back to a normal walking pace after a few minutes. He continued to walk quietly beside her.

After nearly five minutes of silence Maddy glanced over at him. "What?"

Logan smiled ruefully. "Sorry."

Maddy stopped and stared at him. Logan pulled her out of the middle of the footpath, to the shade at the front of a clothing shop, so people wouldn't bump into her.

She frowned. "What are you sorry for?"

"You're right, it's none of my business. But it bothers me."

"Why does it bother you?"

Logan remained quiet for a long drawn out moment. "Because it's unfair. Mitch gets to go where he wants and with whoever he wants. I nearly punched him Friday morning when he bragged to Rob about one of the times he got you grounded. He hates you. I don't know why, but he does. And your stupid father hangs off every word he says. It's so.... antiquated."

"Yeah, my father was born in the wrong era. Most of the fights he had with Mum were about what was appropriate behaviour. That and wanting to get her under his knife. He thinks there's no excuse for ugly people in the world with all the advances in plastic surgery." Marla believed the same if the amount of plastic surgery she'd had was any indication.

"How about lack of money? Not everyone can afford it. And I don't think they should have it just because they can. I mean, who wants a world filled with all the same people because that's what everyone thinks means beauty? How boring would that be?" Logan frowned and bent close to peer into her face. "He hasn't altered you has he?"

Maddy shook her head, unable to speak with

Logan so close. She remembered what it had felt like to kiss him. Her gaze dropped to his lips. They were centimetres away.

"Maddy?"

She blinked, drawing away from him a bit. "What?"

A smile slowly formed on Logan's lips. "I asked you why he hadn't, but you seemed distracted by something."

Maddy couldn't stop the colour that filled her face. "Mum made it part of the custodial agreement that he couldn't until I was eighteen. She hopes I'll say no then."

"What's wrong with the way you look?"

"He wants to take a fraction off my nose. Make my cheekbones a little more prominent and my bottom lip a bit fuller so my lips match in size. Apparently everything is a fraction off perfect. I think he wants to make me into one of those porcelain dolls with the heart shaped face that some of the kids think I already am. He's always trying to turn me into his perfect little princess." She couldn't keep the bitterness from her voice.

Logan reached out and traced her cheekbone with his fingers. "Don't let him change you. There's nothing wrong with you the way you are."

"I know," she whispered. "I hadn't planned to let him anywhere near me with a surgical knife. I actually had nightmares about it when I was younger."

"How did we get so completely off track? I was going to apologise and ask if you want to come to the nursing home with me."

Maddy grinned. "Yes. Definitely."

Logan draped his arm around her shoulders and turned with her so they could walk back to Davey. "I don't know how you can meet your grandma, but maybe my grandad can help. His body might be giving up on him as he says, but his mind is sharper than a tack."

"What's he like?"

"Old."

Maddy elbowed him lightly in the ribs. "Be serious."

"You'll have to meet him. He's unique. So, are we still on for the movies tonight?"

"If you really are feeling apologetic you should let me choose which movie we watch."

Logan groaned. "Not a chick flick. There's no way I could sit through one of those."

Maddy's eyes widened innocently. "You mean to say you were actually planning to watch the movie?"

Logan laughed and leaned in close so his lips brushed her cheek before resting near her ear. "Maybe the start of it."

* * *

Maddy stood beside Logan as he signed them in at the nursing home. She tried to relax, but it was hard. She kept thinking someone was going to demand why she was there. And what if she ran into her mum? Would Joscelin say something? Maybe she shouldn't do this. What if her father found out and stopped paying for her grandmother to stay here? Just because she didn't know the woman that didn't mean she wanted something to happen to her.

The woman behind the counter looked down at the book and smiled. "Have a nice visit with your grandad, Logan. And Maddy with no last name." Her smile became a grin for Logan. "I bet you've forgotten it."

Maddy read what Logan had written. 'Logan Ridley and Maddy.' She looked up at him, worried what would happen when he put her last name down. She opened her mouth, but closed it when he draped an arm around her shoulders, pulling her against him.

"Of course I know it." He grinned.

"You're as bad as your grandad. I bet he doesn't remember half the names of all the girls he's kissed over the years. Most of them he probably forgot within minutes of meeting them. The stories that man tells." The woman's grin remained in place.

Logan laughed. "Now that'd be an exaggeration. I bet it was only a quarter of them. But once he met Grandma, he only had one name to remember."

The woman giggled, turning to Maddy. "You watch these Ridleys. They're charmers. Both the younger and the older one."

Maddy smiled weakly, hoping the issue of her last name was over. The woman looked to be barely twenty. She bet if anyone could distract her, it would be Logan at his most charming. She'd seen him in action a few times during the school holidays. Within minutes, she was proved right when Logan waved over his shoulder as they wandered off to see his grandad, no last name written down for her.

Logan led her through the grounds of the nursing home, his fingers entwined with hers. The pathways were concrete, suitable for wheelchairs and walking frames. Shady trees and covered walkways sheltered them from the sun and the further into the grounds they walked, the slower Maddy's steps grew.

"Are you okay?"

Maddy nodded. What could she say? She was the one who'd demanded he bring her. She'd look like an idiot if she turned and ran as quickly as she could to the nearest exit.

Logan led her to a garden seat placed strategically under a shady tree with a flower garden at its base. "What's wrong?"

Maddy shook her head and stared at her lap, one hand resting on her leg, the other still held by Logan. What could she say without looking stupid?

"Grandad won't bite." When he received no reply, Logan reached out and brushed his fingers along her jaw line, tilting her head up. "I'm lost here, Maddy. What's wrong?"

Maddy turned her head away. "What if my father finds out I've been here? And then what if something happens to my grandma because I snuck in to see her and Mum can't afford to keep her here. Maybe I shouldn't see her." She was a self-centred idiot, as bad as her father.

Logan sat quietly for a moment. "Okay. You don't have to decide straight away. Or even today. But come and meet my grandad. He likes to meet my friends. And I won't say anything to him about your grandma unless you want me to."

"How old is he?"

"He's still in his sixties. Really young for how bad his osteo is."

"I thought it was a female thing."

Logan shook his head. "Not exactly. Although eighty percent of people with it are female. Grandad puts his down to living too well." Logan grinned. "By that he means too much drinking and smoking, the wrong foods and not enough exercise."

Maddy smiled fleetingly before her frown returned. "I really don't know what to do. I want to meet her. I thought I'd never meet any of my grandparents and now I'm worried I'll miss out. What if she died next week? Whatever she had this week could come back and I'll never get to meet her. But she could live another decade, if she had the proper care and wasn't left to wander out onto a highway and get hit by a car." Graphic images filled her mind and she shuddered.

"I reckon you should see her. Grandad will help us figure it out so your father never learns you saw her." Logan grinned. "He loves plotting and planning."

Maddy stared at Logan. It looked like his grandad wasn't the only one who enjoyed plotting and planning. The gleam in Logan's eyes told her he was looking forward to helping. She took a deep breath and let it out. Determination filled her. Her father dictated enough of her life. She needed parts of it that were her own. Besides, she wanted to meet the woman who'd caused her to live with her father, Marla and Mitchell. "Okay. Let's do it."

"Good." Logan dragged her to her feet. "We're nearly at Grandad's room. In his building, as well as a communal kitchenette and sitting area everyone also has their own bedroom, ensuite and patio. Plenty of privacy for our discussion."

Chapter Eleven

When they reached a building, Logan held the door open. He stepped to the side and let the elderly lady, who was about to exit, through. She smiled when she saw Logan and patted him on the cheek.

"Logan, sweetie. Your grandad will be so pleased to see you. You're such a good kid. My grandkids haven't visited for over a month and here you are, a fortnight later and back again."

"Hi, Mrs Lewitt. Did you do something different with your hair? It looks nice."

Mrs Lewitt patted her short curly, silver hair. "Oh you. You're as bad as your grandad." She noticed Maddy. "And who is this? Is this your girl, Logan?"

Logan laughed. "Slavery was abolished ages ago, Mrs Lewitt."

"Oh you. You know what I mean."

"Come in or get out. You're letting the hot air and flies in," a voice growled from inside.

"Oh mind your manners, Albert. That's the last time I visit you if all you're going to do is snap and snarl at everyone." She turned back to Logan. "You have a lovely visit with your grandad, you hear?" She patted him on the cheek before she slowly walked away.

Logan gestured towards the doorway and Maddy stepped inside. A cluster of armchairs sat in front of her, a man slouched in one of them. A few wisps of hair remained on his head and his bright blue eyes seemed startling in his lined and faded face.

"Hi, Mr B. How are you today?" Logan took Maddy's hand again.

"Hmph. As if you really care. The only reason anyone visits death's waiting room is because you're looking to inherit. If there's nothing left to get, no one bothers to come." Albert glared at them.

"Huh? Really? Guess I better have a chat to Grandad about that. He's ripping me off. I visit him way more than my parents and aunt so he should be leaving the house to me."

"Don't give me that innocent expression, Logan. I'm a wake up to you." Albert shook a finger at him.

Logan grinned. "And I'm a wake up to you." He

glanced around the room, which had a kitchenette at the other end. They were the only ones inside. He pulled a pack of unopened cigarettes out of his pocket and tossed them towards Albert. They immediately disappeared into Albert's pockets. "You didn't get them from me. After all, I'm not old enough to buy them."

"Don't know what you're talking about, boy."

Logan laughed. "That's the spirit, Mr B." He turned to Maddy. "Come on, I want you to meet my grandad."

"Hmph. But I'm not good enough to meet your girl."

"I thought you didn't want to be hassled." Logan's grin stayed firmly in place.

"Told you thinking isn't your strong point." Albert's glare hadn't lost its intensity.

"So you keep telling me. Maddy, this is Albert Brax whose favourite pastime is terrorising the staff."

"That's enough cheek out of you, boy." He rose slowly to his feet and held out his hand to Maddy. "You look like a smart girl. What are you doing with this one?"

Maddy sent a sideways glance to Logan before she replied with a straight face, "I guess we're all entitled to lapses in judgement." She took his hand, surprised the frail body had the strength for such a firm handshake.

"What is it? Annual pick on Logan day?" Logan's frown was ruined by the laughter in his eyes.

"You mean to say we're only allowed one day a year to pick on you, Logan? Where's the fun in that?" Maddy asked.

"If you come to your senses, you can come and visit with me for awhile." Albert lowered himself onto his seat with a groan.

"Aww, Mr B. don't tell me you actually like someone," Logan teased.

"Go visit your grandad instead of standing around speaking nonsense," Albert growled.

Logan laughed. "See you later."

"Hmph."

Logan knocked on his grandad's door and called through it, "Are you presentable, Grandad? Can we come in?"

"We? You have company with you? Come on in then," came the deep voice from the other side of the door.

Logan swung the door open and Maddy stepped into the room that had a bed in one corner, a couple of armchairs, a television at the far end of the room and two closed doors. She guessed one of them led to an ensuite and from the style of the other one, it was probably a built-in-wardrobe. Past the chairs was a sliding door that led onto a patio with a small outdoor setting.

Sitting in one of the armchairs was a man with salt and pepper coloured hair, only slightly thinned. He had rounded shoulders that had probably once been broad and the same dark brown eyes as his grandson.

"Well, and who do we have here?"

"Grandad, this is Maddy. Maddy, my grandad, Clifford Ridley."

"Hi, Mr Ridley." Maddy smiled weakly. This was the man who Logan wanted her to tell her family secrets to? No way. She'd expected some little old man who was too sickly to leave his room and would have a nurse at his side. This man reminded her a bit too much of her father. The kind of man who was used to being in charge.

"Just Cliff will do." He held a hand out to her and she took a step forward to take it. "Have a seat." He waved towards the other armchair and then looked over at Logan. "You can sit on the bed." He turned back to Maddy. "So what's a pretty little thing like you doing with my grandson? I'm surprised your parents would let you anywhere near him." He winked and grinned at her.

Maddy grinned back at him. He had a sense of humour, so maybe he wasn't too much like her father after all. "People keep telling me that. Maybe I should start listening if everyone is saying the same thing."

"I hope this isn't your way of trying to get out of going to the movies with me tonight." Logan plumped the pillows up against the wall and rested against them.

"Since it's my pick I might wait until after the movies to listen."

"We didn't finish discussing that," Logan protested.

Maddy smiled at him and turned her attention to Cliff. "You know, this place isn't what I thought it would be like. When I think of nursing homes, I always think hospital like. This is rather homey."

"And you think of nursing homes frequently?"

Maddy shook her head. "Not until recently." She looked at Logan. She could see the question on his face. She forced herself to nod. She couldn't back out. Who knew when she'd get the chance to meet her grandmother again?

"Maddy found out her grandma is in this nursing home."

"Found out? Sounds like there's a story in that." Cliff looked from one to the other.

Logan nodded. "Just a little one." He proceeded

to tell Cliff all he knew, with Maddy filling in the occasional detail. Cliff asked a few questions and then stared at them thoughtfully.

"Are you sure there isn't more to it? It seems a bit odd your father would want nothing to do with a person because they were losing their marbles in their old age," Cliff said.

"Who knows what other secrets they're keeping from me. But, it sounds like something my father would do. He's very image conscious. He expects certain behaviour from those around him and if he doesn't get it, you're in major trouble. He doesn't like scenes and he certainly doesn't like odd behaviour. I can't count the amount of times he's told me, 'You're embarrassing not only yourself, but everyone around you'. And I remember most of the arguments he and Mum had, when they were together, was about the way Mum looked. He didn't like that she wouldn't do something about how she was ageing. She saw them as character lines while he saw them as wrinkles wrecking her beauty. He said it made him look bad since his business is beauty."

"He doesn't sound like a very pleasant man," Cliff said.

Maddy shrugged. "I don't know. He's extremely respected in his field. He's one of the top plastic surgeons. And no one ever complains about his work. He also does charity cases. You know, like burn victims and stuff."

"I bet no one ever has anything nice to say about his bedside manner," Logan said.

"Probably not." Maddy shrugged again. It wasn't like she could really argue the comment, even though she wanted to.

Cliff rose from his chair. "Let's take a walk. I know a couple of women here called Sara, but I don't know if either of their surnames is Leason. We can have a wander and find out. I know one Sara who has Alzheimer's and was sick recently. Maybe that's your grandma."

Maddy stood up too. "But you can't let her know I'm her granddaughter. I don't want to risk it getting back to my father."

"Leave it to me. I'll take care of all the details." Cliff picked up a cane that rested against the wall near his door. "If it's the woman I'm thinking of, she tries to rope everyone into playing cards with her."

Logan joined Maddy and took her hand again. He waited until Cliff was out of the room. "I told you he'd figure something out."

"You did. Now we have to hope it works."

Cliff poked his head back through the doorway.

"Are you two coming?" He grinned. "Or am I interrupting something?"

Maddy nodded then quickly shook her head. "We're coming and no, you're not interrupting anything." She pulled away from Logan and stepped out of the room, a glare for him. When Cliff headed for the exit, she followed. She slowed her pace to match the older man's and listened as he greeted everyone he passed. She was amazed he seemed to know everyone by name and asked specific questions. Like if they were over a particular ailment, or how an outing had gone or if a family member, who he also knew the name of, was well. She was astounded he could keep all the facts straight.

After awhile, she asked, "Is there anyone here you don't know?"

Cliff grinned. "I'll let you know if I discover one."

Chapter Twelve

Finally Cliff stood in the doorway of Sara's room and smiled at her in greeting. "How are you today, Sara? It's good to have you back from the hospital."

The woman lay propped up against a pile of pillows in her bed. She was small enough that she looked lost in the single bed. Her straight, grey hair was shoulder length, brushed neatly back from her face, and her hand shook as she placed it against her cheek.

"Do I know you? How do you know my name?"

"We've met a couple of times. I guess you're a more memorable person than I am." Cliff smiled and ushered Maddy and Logan into the room. "This is my grandson and his girlfriend. You haven't met them before."

Now she was in the room, Maddy noticed her mum sat in a chair in the corner of the room. She tightened her hold on Logan's hand and watched as her mum started to speak.

Sara spoke up before anyone else could. "Sally! Where have you been? I've been waiting for you for ages. Tim stole my doll again. I want you to get it back."

Maddy glanced behind, but there was no one there. She looked at Sara again. "Me?" she asked hesitantly.

"Don't you know who you are anymore, Sally? I have trouble remembering people. I guess forgetting yourself isn't much different. Do you want to play cards? There should be a deck somewhere." Sara struggled to get out of bed. "Can we play Old Maid? That's my favourite. You like it too, don't you?"

Joscelin rushed to Sara's side. "Don't try and get out of bed, Mum. You'll end up falling and hurting yourself."

"Do I know you?" Sara peered up at Joscelin.

"Yes. Remember? We talked about it before. I showed you the photo album. I'm your daughter."

"Do I have any other children?"

"No, Mum." Joscelin's voice was soft and it broke on the last word.

Cliff stepped forward, his hand out. "I've seen you around a few times. Joscelin, isn't it?"

With a nod, she took his hand. "I'm sorry, I don't know who you are."

"Cliff. Your mother is a mean card player. She's roped me into a few games while I've been here. If you don't mind, I'm sure Maddy would be happy to play a game with your mother."

"Oh, but Maddy-" Joscelin began.

Cliff interrupted her. "Now don't worry about Maddy. I know you don't know her, but she's a good kid. I'm sure she won't mind at all."

Maddy had moved far enough into the room to notice the wink Cliff directed at her mum. She met the searching look her mum gave her, trying to pretend she didn't know her. If this was the only way she'd be able to get to meet her grandma, she'd take it. The woman lying in the bed was nothing like she could have imagined. Her mum was right. Sara did need someone to take care of her. There was no way she could look after herself. Maddy's heart plummeted as she realised she'd harboured the hope that her mum had been wrong and she could have moved in with her.

"Don't you want to play with me, Sally? Have I done something wrong?"

Maddy hurried to the side of the bed. "Of course

not Gr… ah… Sara. I'd love to play cards with you. Old Maid, wasn't it?"

Sara nodded enthusiastically while Joscelin opened the set of drawers beside the bed and removed a pack of cards. Maddy took them when her mum handed them across the bed. Their gazes met and held. Maddy could see the worry in her mum's eyes.

"Thank you, Joscelin." Maddy bit back a smile when her mum opened her mouth to correct her then closed it, her lips in a tight line. Instead she gave a curt nod.

"Here you go ladies." Cliff slid the wheeled table over to hang above the bed. He tapped the surface. "Plenty of space to play a game or two."

Maddy slipped the rubber band off the cards and slid it onto her wrist before she started to shuffle them. She forced her lips into a smile. "Anyone else joining the game?" She removed one of the cards from the deck and popped it unseen under the mattress. "Out of sight. Wouldn't want anyone to be tempted to cheat." She sat on the edge of the bed.

"I'll play." Logan moved to the other side of the bed and sat on the edge of it.

"I'm going to go have a chat to that lovely carer out there." Cliff waved towards the door. "She looked terribly lonely."

Logan laughed. "Sure, Grandad."

"If I don't see you later today, I'll see you when you visit tomorrow." Cliff turned from Logan to Joscelin. "Would you like to join me? Maybe we can have a coffee."

Joscelin glanced at Maddy, who now dealt the cards, then nodded. "I'll be back soon." She looked from Maddy, to Logan and then rested her gaze on Sara who didn't even notice her words. Joscelin sighed and headed for the door.

Maddy looked down at the fan of cards in her hand and removed all the pairs. "Who goes first?"

"Me. Oh please, Sally. Can I?"

Maddy nodded. It was hard to believe those childish words came from the woman in the bed in front of her. What must it be like to remember nothing but your childhood? What things had she done that she'd never remember? What things had she once thought special that no longer existed for her? She was going to keep a diary from now on. Just in case. Well, she'd try and keep a diary, but if all the other times she'd attempted to keep one was any indication, her intention would last two days. It wouldn't help that she'd only be able to keep it at her mum's house. After they'd played Old Maid, with

Sara winning, they played several hands of Go Fish. Maddy was fascinated by everything Sara had to say.

She felt anger build for what her father had stolen from her. She'd never had a chance to know the woman her grandma had once been. It wasn't fair. How could he have such stupid ideas on what was and wasn't acceptable? Why did he have to make everything so difficult?

"Sally?"

When Logan rested his hand momentarily on her shoulder, Maddy realised Sara must have been trying to get her attention for a bit. "Sorry. I was distracted."

Sara nodded. "Have you got a five?"

Maddy looked at her cards. She spotted the red card and handed it over. A smile lit up Sara's face as she excitedly put the cards in the pile at her elbow on the table. Maddy glanced down at her cards before she turned to Logan. "Queen?"

He shook his head, then grinned. "No need to go calling me names."

Maddy smiled, glad Logan was with her. She didn't know if she could have faced this moment alone. It was good she didn't have to. She watched as Logan turned to Sara and asked for an eight. Maddy's gaze dropped to her hand. Yep, she had one of those. And she better start to pay attention or she'd lose. Again.

After Sara won, they played another couple of hands of Go Fish and a round of Snap before they returned to Go Fish. At one point Joscelin poked her head back in and smiled as she saw them laughing. Maddy met her mum's gaze and nodded slightly before she returned to the game.

As they played, Sally continued to speak of things she thought had happened only recently. Her biggest complaint was about her brother Tim who loved to hide her doll.

Sally took a card from the centre pile. "My doll was so dirty when I found her shoved under the house. It's not fair he keeps hiding her. I don't hide his stuff. Well, maybe I let those bugs out of the jar, but I just wanted to have a look at them."

"What were they?" Maddy asked.

"Mostly ladybugs. But there were a couple of shiny Christmas beetles too. Do you think they're called Christmas beetles because they look pretty enough to decorate the tree?"

Maddy shrugged. "Possibly."

"Could be to do with them being around at Christmas time," Logan said.

Sara smiled at him. "I haven't met you before, have I?" She looked slyly between Maddy and Logan.

"Have you known my sister long? Does Daddy know about you?"

"Ahh…" Maddy didn't know how to answer that question.

Sara's smile became a grin. "Or what about William? Does he know? I thought you were sweet on him. I bet he won't be happy to meet Logan."

Maddy looked at Logan. Her eyes begged him to help her answer. She didn't want to confuse Sara. Or would this day be forgotten by morning? She didn't know. But if it wasn't, she didn't want to make a tangled mess of what really had happened in the past and what she told Sara was happening. She frowned. She was beginning to make as much sense as Sara.

Logan smiled easily. "Nah, William and I are mates. I'm keeping Sally company while he's not about. Just looking out for her."

"It's because of that Malcolm who keeps hanging around, isn't it? I saw you kiss him the other day," Sara said.

"I never." Maddy tried to look indignant. Surely that would be Sally's response to an interfering younger sister. Not having one, she wasn't completely certain.

Sara giggled. "Yes you did. Out the back under the mango tree. I bet you thought no one would see. It's really dark under it, but I was in the tree and saw you. And you didn't even tell him off for kissing you."

"Hmm, I wonder what William will think of that," Logan teased.

"You wouldn't tell him, would you?" Maddy began to enjoy the role-play.

"Well, I'd have to think about it. I'm sure I could be convinced to keep quiet."

Maddy smiled. "Really?"

Sara giggled again. "I bet he wants a kiss too. Daddy says that's all boys want. He told me to stay far away from them."

"At least until you're older." Maddy's smile faded as she realised what she'd said. Sara was older. Way older than her. And yet now she was like a child. How fair was that?

"Whose turn is it? I've lost track."

Maddy met Logan's gaze, grateful he'd interrupted her thoughts. They'd been rapidly spiralling to extremely depressing depths. "I've lost track too."

"It's mine," Sara exclaimed. "Do you have a six?" She grabbed the card Maddy reluctantly held out. "Another pair." She placed them on the table.

Maddy frowned. "Are you sure you're not cheating?" She glanced behind her. No mirror. How would Sara have known the last three cards to ask?

Maybe she didn't hold her hand up high enough when they talked.

Sara had a suitably innocent expression on her face. "I never cheat."

Maddy's eyes narrowed. "Why do I find that statement hard to believe?"

"You only say that because you're not winning. Are you going to have your turn or are we skipping you?" Sara asked.

Play continued until Logan's mobile phone rang. After a quick look, he slid it into his pocket. "We have to go, Sara. My cousin will be here to pick us up soon."

Sara pouted. "But we haven't finished our game."

"What about we play tomorrow?" Maddy began to gather the cards.

"You won't forget, will you? Sometimes you say you'll do something and you forget all about me, Sally."

Maddy slid the rubber band over the cards. "I promise."

Sara held out her hand. "Pinkie promise?"

Maddy linked her little finger with Sara's. "Pinkie promise."

Sara grinned. "Good." She held out her arms.

Maddy wrapped her arms around Sara and lightly

held her, worried she might break the small, frail body. She reluctantly pulled away and Sara grabbed hold of her hand as she did. The skin was paper dry and the fingers were bent and swollen with arthritis. "I'll be back tomorrow." She let Sara tug her close again.

Sara pressed a kiss against her cheek. "Love you, Sally. You're the only one who plays games with me."

"I love you too." Maddy pulled away and forced a smile to her lips when all she wanted to do was cry. She didn't want her grandma to call her by another person's name. She wanted her to say 'love you, Maddy.' How many years had she missed out on moments when her grandma might have known who she was and said those words? Had she been this bad the moment she'd been diagnosed or had there been times when she hadn't been confused? She'd have to ask her mum.

Logan wrapped an arm around Maddy's waist. "See you tomorrow, Sara. And you won't win every game then. Are you sure you don't cheat?"

Sara giggled, shaking her head. "No. Not me."

Chapter Thirteen

Maddy let Logan lead her from the room. She caught sight of her mum sitting in the communal area, a book lying open on her lap. Maddy turned away. She saw one of the staff watched her.

"Hey, Anne," Logan said easily.

"How are you, Logan?" The woman turned her attention from Maddy.

"Good." He grinned. "Great actually." He glanced at Maddy. "I've spent the day surrounded by lovely ladies so how could I be anything else?"

Anne laughed. "You are fast becoming as bad as your grandad. Maybe you spend too much time with him."

Logan's grin stayed firmly in place. "Nah, I need to spend more time with him. He's got so much more to teach me."

"When the day comes that he's taught you

everything he knows, we'll have to slap a warning sign on you." Anne's gaze strayed to Maddy. "That was a lovely thing you did for Sara."

Logan chuckled. "As if she had much of a choice. Grandad kind of bulldozed her into it."

Anne nodded. "Yes, he does have a tendency to do that. He's so charming that even while you're saying no, you're already doing whatever he suggested."

"I actually ended up enjoying myself," Maddy said.

Anne lowered her voice and leaned close. "You know she cheats, don't you?"

"I knew it," Maddy exclaimed.

"Yes. She's very good at it and you've got to be quick to catch her. She's such a character though. And a real sweetheart. It's hard to say no to her. Like kicking a puppy," Anne said.

"Tell me about it. She somehow talked me into coming back tomorrow."

Anne patted her on the shoulder. "If you've got other plans for your day she'll probably forget."

Maddy hesitated. She really wanted to come back, but would it look odd if she argued about it? "Well, she did make me promise. Are you certain she'll forget?"

Anne shrugged. "It could go either way. Tomorrow she might be firmly in the present and today will be part of the far past or forgotten altogether. Or she might still be in the past and waiting for her sister to come and play cards with her. Or she might be even further back in the past. Anything is possible."

"Oh." Maddy hesitated again. "I'll come back. I hate to break a promise. Even one that was dragged from me."

"We're coming to see Grandad anyway," Logan said.

"Do you know who her sister ended up with?" Maddy asked. "I mean, if she thinks I'm Sally, it'd be handy to know. Especially since she accused me of kissing one boy while another one was my boyfriend."

Anne gestured towards Joscelin. "You'd have to ask her daughter. But from what we've gathered Sally had a lot of boyfriends and Sara loved to spy on her sister. She used what she learned to get her sister to spend more time with her. Sally was the only one who ever had time for her."

Maddy felt sorry for Sara. And Sally. "Kind of makes me glad I don't have a little sister."

Anne returned the grin. "Trust me, they're a pain at times." A bell chimed. "That's one of my charges. I'll see you two tomorrow."

Maddy waited until Anne had left the area before she glanced at Joscelin. She wanted to ask her about Sara and Sally, but guessed here was not the place. Instead, she turned to Logan. "Do you think you and Davey could drop me home for a while?" She made sure her words were loud enough to be heard by her mum.

"Sure." Logan smiled. "As long as you're not going to ring me later and claim you need to wash your hair so you can't go to the movies after all."

Maddy laughed. "It probably does need washing after being at the beach all morning." She walked beside Logan towards the exit, his arm still around her. She heard footsteps follow them, but didn't check to see if it was her mum.

"So cruel," Logan said.

"I guess if I wash it the moment you drop me home I'll still be ready to see a movie with you." She paused. "Possibly."

"Not only cruel, but heartless as well." Logan waved to one of the residents they passed and received a smile in answer.

"Nah, not me. But if I had the incentive of movie choice, I'd be ready a lot quicker."

"I knew there had to be a reason behind your cruelty. Very sly. Do you cheat at cards too?"

Maddy looked up at Logan, stumbling slightly. The thought of being like her grandma stunned her. Until now she'd only had her parents to compare herself to. There'd been no other family members even talked about. Her father had always said when she'd asked about his parents that they were in the past and one should never dwell on it. The past tended to hold you back. Her mum hadn't been able to talk about her parents and Maddy had thought it was because she mourned their deaths. Now she didn't know what to think.

"What?" Logan stopped at the edge of the road to wait for Davey.

Maddy shook her head.

"Then why were you staring at me?"

"Do you think I'm like my grandma?"

"I bet she would have easily been able to lead a double life too."

"I do not," Maddy exclaimed.

Logan laughed. "What do you call it? Right now, your father wouldn't recognise you as his perfect little princess who wouldn't even glance at a boy let alone be this close to one."

"I'd be grounded for life if I did. Sometimes I hate living a double life, but I don't have a choice. You saw Sara. Could you risk her life because you didn't like where you lived? It's not like I'm in any danger there." Her father would never let anything happen to her. Not one single thing.

Logan sighed. "It's not right."

"Neither is the fact that my grandma can't recall her life."

Davey pulled up, ending the conversation. When Maddy got in the front seat, she saw her mum pull onto the road ahead of them. Great, just what she needed. She'd hoped to get home before her mum and have a few minutes to put her thoughts in order before she had to answer the questions she knew her mum would ask.

Maddy sat quietly in the car and listened to Logan and Davey tease each other. She was glad they didn't need her to help carry the conversation. She had too many things to think about. There were a million questions she wanted to ask her mum. Things she should already know. Stories about her family she wished she'd been told when she was little. Were her great aunt and great uncle still alive? Had they married? And which boy had her aunt ended up with? Or was it none of the ones Sara had mentioned. And what about Sara? What had she done with her life? Other than have a child and lose all memory of it.

Maddy sighed. Why couldn't she have been born into a normal family?

"You okay, Maddy?" Davey asked.

"Families are a pain," she muttered.

"You think you've got problems." Davey jerked his thumb towards the back seat. "I'm related to him now."

Maddy smiled like Davey expected her to. "Do you want a sympathy card?"

"That'd be nice," Davey said.

"Then I should get one too." Logan leaned forward to join in the conversation.

Maddy turned in her seat to look at him. "Why would you need a sympathy card? You're so lucky to have a cousin like Davey."

Logan clutched his heart. "Ouch. I think I'm bleeding."

"Next you'll be wanting me to kiss it better."

Logan looked hopeful. "Will you?"

Maddy stared thoughtfully at him. "Nah. You don't look wounded enough."

Davey laughed as he pulled up in front of Maddy's house. "You know Maddy, if you were only going with him to the movies because no one else'd take you, I could take you."

"Well…" Maddy looked towards Logan.

"Now I am seriously wounded."

Maddy laughed at Logan's sad expression. "I guess I should go with him. I wouldn't want to emotionally scar him for life. He seems too fragile to survive. I mean, look at him."

Davey nodded. "Yep. Definitely a delicate little daisy."

"I'll show you who's delicate." Logan unbuckled and made a threatening move towards Davey.

Maddy opened the car door. "I'll leave you to argue this out together."

Logan was out of the car before Maddy. "I'll walk you to the door. In case you want me to check under your bed for monsters."

Maddy swung her backpack to her shoulder. "Nice try, Logan." She glanced back at Davey. "I'll see you later."

Davey nodded. "Yep. Guess I'll be playing chauffeur. Again." He grinned.

Maddy smiled. "Thanks." She walked to the house with Logan. "What time will you be back?"

Logan glanced at his watch. "Hour and a half." He rested his hands on her hips, taking a step closer. "Unless you want me to stick around. Your mum didn't look too happy with you earlier."

"I'll be fine. She's usually realistic about things."

"Then I'll see you later. Do you think she'll let you stay out late? There's a party we can head to after the movie."

Maddy nodded.

Logan smiled as he continued to stare down at her.

She wondered if he planned to kiss her. If he was, he was taking his time about it. Becoming impatient, she rose slightly on her toes so she could press her lips against him. Thoughts about the conversation she needed to have with her mum evaporated from her mind and her hands entwined at his neck. When she finally pulled away from the kiss, she was the one smiling.

"Impatient, aren't you?"

Maddy grinned. "Sometimes."

"Good." Logan grinned before he slowly let her go and headed back to Davey's car.

Maddy watched him walk away, waving as the car drove off. As soon as they were out of sight, her grin faded and she sighed. Now she had to face her mum. It wasn't like she was worried about what her mum would say. Not in the same way she worried about what her father had to say. No, she was worried her mum wouldn't tell her stuff. Worried she'd continue to be kept in the dark about her family history. How many other secrets were there hidden in her family that she didn't know about? Maybe Tim had gone from stealing dolls to stealing jewels. Or maybe international secrets and was a spy. Tim Bond, stealer of secrets and little girl's dolls. And what about Sally? Maybe she'd married a dozen different men and made a fortune out of divorcing each of them. Or she could have run away with a sailor and never been heard of again because their ship sank and they were living on a deserted island. Maddy smiled, pushing her wild thoughts aside. Hopefully she'd soon know.

Chapter Fourteen

Maddy found her mum in the kitchen, eating a salad sandwich. Her stomach grumbled when she saw the food.

Joscelin gestured towards the fridge. "I made you one too. I wasn't sure how long you'd be so I put it in the fridge."

Maddy saw the plate with the sandwich on it the moment she opened the door, gladwrap keeping it from drying out. She took it to the table and sat across from her mum. "Thanks."

Silence descended as they ate. Joscelin finished first and sat back to watch her. Feeling uncomfortable, Maddy placed the last few bites back on the plate and returned the stare.

"How do you know Logan? I thought you were out with Melissa today. You normally hang out with her and Carrie, don't you?"

"I met him through Melissa." Well, it was close to the truth. She'd been at the beach with Melissa who'd noticed Logan and suggested they talk to him.

"Rather convenient that his grandfather is at that nursing home."

"I guess life thought it owed me a break with all the crap I have to put up with."

"I don't have any choice, Maddy. It's not like he beats you or anything. Your father would never let anything happen to you. He'd protect you with his life."

"And that's the problem. Not even life is allowed to happen to me."

"Do you want me to demand more of your time? Is that it? In a couple of years you'll be old enough to live on your own. And then what? Should I sacrifice my mother's last few years of her life for your selfishness?"

Maddy's lips thinned. The conversation wasn't going the way she'd planned. "Of course not. But you could have told me. I would have understood. You didn't ask me how I felt about it. You let me think you couldn't be bothered to fight for me. That you didn't care how I felt."

"Part of the deal was that I couldn't tell you."

Maddy snorted. "Just like part of the deal is that I can't attend parties while I'm at your place?"

Joscelin shrugged. "That's a normal part of growing up."

"I would have thought knowing my grandma was a normal part of growing up too."

Joscelin dropped her head into her hands, covering her face for a moment before clasping her hands together on the table. "I risk enough letting you go out as much as I do when you're here. Every time the phone rings I think it's him checking up on you. Every time you return to him I worry you'll let something slip. And then what? I'll be left either trying to take care of my mother on my own or get no more contact with you."

"I'm not an idiot. I'd never say anything to him that'd risk my coming here. I value my freedom too much."

"But you could accidentally-"

"No. Never." Maddy shook her head. "I watch every little word I say. Which isn't hard since he prefers that I don't speak."

"What do you mean?" Joscelin's voice was sharp.

She bit back a sigh. After all the time she'd been trying to make her mum fight for her, it was ironic that this was the first time Joscelin had sounded concerned about her living with her father. She thought of Sara and the frail body she'd held that afternoon. "Nothing. It's just not fair that he'd rather talk to Mitchell than me."

"I'm sorry."

Silence fell for a moment until Maddy broke it. "Why is he like that? I mean he loves hearing about all the things Mitchell gets up to. Sports, parties, girlfriends. All of it. But I only have to glance at a boy and he freaks."

"He has his reasons. I didn't realise when I agreed to marry him how badly those reasons had effected him."

"What reasons?"

Joscelin shook her head. "They're his secrets to tell. Maybe you should ask him."

"You've got to be kidding. You can't have forgotten what he's like. I'd be grounded for questioning his orders."

"He isn't that bad."

She started to argue her mum's statement, but the thought of Sara brought a halt to her words.

"If you don't want to ask him then you'll have to get used to not knowing. It's too big a secret for me to tell you."

"What about your family? What happened to Tim and Sally?"

Joscelin sighed. "Tim became a soldier and died young. By then his father, my grandfather, was dead and my grandmother was devastated. Tim was her favourite. When she died, Sally took in Mum, who was sixteen, and looked after her. When Sally married Robert a year later, my mum was angry and terrified she'd lose her sister and end up alone. She worked on breaking them up. She also broke up Sally's second marriage. I've forgotten who he was. When Sally found another boyfriend, she moved to England with him where they eventually married. Mum always regretted driving Sally away. She used to talk about how fear of something happening could cause a person to make that fear come true. She had a lonely childhood and losing everyone except her sister made her cling to the only person she had left. It took losing her sister for her to come to her senses."

She thought of Tim, Sally and Sara for a moment before wondering about Sally's husband. "Was Sally's last husband a sailor?"

Joscelin looked at her strangely. "You ask the oddest questions sometimes."

"Was he?"

Joscelin shook her head. "No."

"Is Sally still in England? Did she have any kids?" Maddy prompted when Joscelin fell quiet.

Joscelin nodded. "Yes. I've got two cousins, both women, and I get Christmas cards from them every year."

"Do they have kids?"

"Yeah. The oldest, Marie, has a boy and two girls and the youngest, Carol, has three boys. I think one of her boys was born the same year as you."

Maddy stared at her mum. "I always thought we had no family."

"I'm sorry."

"Have you met any of them?"

Joscelin shook her head. "They keep inviting us over, but we couldn't go."

"Us? They invited me too?"

"Maddy, there's no point in thinking about it. Your father would never let you go."

"I won't be living with him forever."

"I guess not."

"Can I write to them? Can I have their email addresses?"

"I'll email Marie later and let her know you want to get to know your cousins."

"Cousins." Maddy savoured the word.

"Well, the kids would be your third cousins."

Maddy grinned. "I've got cousins. Do I have any other family?"

"Look Maddy, make sure you don't tell any of this to your father. He wouldn't let you come here. He had words with Aunt Sally one year. She rang up and wanted us all to come out for a white Christmas. She's a very blunt lady and your father didn't take it too well."

"He never takes it well when people disagree with him."

"Well the point is, you need to keep this to yourself. Okay? It was part of the agreement. He felt they'd be a negative influence on you."

"I'm not an idiot." She was getting sick of having to remind her mum that.

"Good. Now what plans have you got for tonight?"

Maddy glanced at the kitchen clock. "No!" She leapt to her feet. "I have to get ready. Logan will be here in half an hour. I haven't even washed my hair and it's a mess." She reached the doorway before she turned back. "Oh. A movie. Then a party. I'm not sure when I'll be home." She hurried from the kitchen before her mum could reply. If her mum didn't want her to stay out late for the party she could follow her and argue the issue. But she didn't think her mum would have a problem, as she'd looked more than a little guilty over everything she'd kept secret. Maddy wondered if it was guilt from choosing her mother over her daughter that had her being so lenient all the time. Or if there were any other secrets putting that expression on her mum's face, but there was no more time to sit around and chat. She'd barely have enough time to get ready.

Logan knocked on the front door as Maddy ran a brush through her hair. It had taken longer to blow dry than she'd expected. She heard the murmur of voices from the lounge room and pulled on a pair of jeans and a top that ended above her belly button. She checked in the mirror. Happy with the look, she hurried to the lounge room.

Logan sprawled in an armchair, his jean clad legs stretched out before him as he talked to Joscelin. He stopped and grinned when he spotted Maddy. Coming to his feet, he strode towards her. "You look good."

"Thanks." She turned to her mum. "I'll see you in the morning."

"If you're awake before I head out." Joscelin rose to her feet. "Be sensible and call me if you need me."

Maddy nodded and crossed the room. She kissed her mum on the cheek. "I'm always sensible." She grinned and grabbed Logan's hand as she headed for the door.

They were nearly at the car when Logan said, "Always sensible?"

"Of course."

Logan laughed. "I seem to remember the second last day of the holidays–"

Maddy turned and kissed him before he could mention what she'd done. Eventually drawing away from him, she said, "You didn't even say hello to me."

"I'll have to remember that."

"What? To say hello?"

"To bring up uncomfortable subjects when I want you to kiss me."

"That wasn't why I kissed you. It was because you're slow about saying hello."

"Sure." Logan's tone said he didn't believe her.

She ignored him and turned to open the car door. "Hey, Davey."

"What? No kiss for me?"

Maddy laughed and leaned close to peck his cheek. "Happy?"

"I'm never going to wash that spot again." He lightly touched where she'd kissed.

"Idiot."

Davey grinned. "So I hear you're coming to our party later."

"Ahh, possibly?" She looked over her shoulder to Logan, who was in the back seat.

"Yep."

"Your party?" Maddy asked.

Logan smiled. "Have you thought about what movie you want to see?"

"I'm not easily distracted."

"Neither am I. So, what movie?"

Maddy shrugged. If he wanted to avoid the topic she wanted to discuss he could pay for it. She managed to keep a grin off her face. "I'll have to see what my choices are. I'm leaning towards a sad story with a lot of romance. What do you think?"

Logan groaned. "I knew I should have brought my i-pod."

Maddy pouted as theatrically as her grandma had earlier. "Don't you want to enjoy the movie with me?"

Chapter Fifteen

Davey laughed. "Guess I should be grateful I'm not taking you to the movies after all."

Logan's expression became one of extreme suffering. "Of course I want to enjoy the movie with you, Maddy. In fact, if you wanted to watch a horror I'd be willing to hold your hand and make sure you weren't too scared."

"A horror! Never. They're the worst movies. My favourites are dramas and romance." Maddy struggled to keep a grin from breaking free as she saw the uncertainty that briefly crossed Logan's face. Horrors would have to be her second favourite genre, right after action. But he'd find that out soon enough.

Davey pulled up as close as possible to the cinema, but it was still half a block away. "Off you go children. Don't do anything I wouldn't do." He grinned wickedly. "You won't need me to pick you up will you?"

Logan shook his head. "Nah. We'll catch a taxi."

They stood on the footpath and waved as Davey drove away. Logan slid his arm around her waist and they ambled towards the cinema. Along the way they smiled in greeting to a couple of kids they knew.

Once inside, Maddy nearly laughed at the relief on Logan's face when she picked an action movie. They bought popcorn, lollies and soft drinks before finding seats at the back of the theatre. By the end of the movie, Maddy decided she'd have to see it again. She could barely recall any of it. Logan had been too much of a distraction. She smiled.

"What?" Logan asked as they waited for a taxi.

Maddy's smile widened into a grin and she shook her head.

"It must have been something."

Maddy shrugged. "Possibly."

"Or are you stringing me along like earlier?"

"When did I string you along?" Her eyes widened innocently.

Logan grinned. "Hate horror and your fave movies are romance? Ring a bell?"

Maddy laughed. "I couldn't resist. You looked so

worried. Would you have gone along if I'd picked a romance?"

"Yep. But I probably would have seen even less of it than I saw of this one."

Maddy laughed again. "That's what I was smiling about."

Logan frowned. "Huh?"

"When you asked before. I was thinking I'd have to see this movie again since I didn't get to see much of it."

Grinning, Logan leaned close and lowered his voice. "I didn't hear you complain at the time."

"I'm not now." A taxi pulled up and Maddy hurried over to it.

A moment later, Logan climbed in the back seat beside her and gave his address to the driver. Several minutes after the taxi moved off, he turned to Maddy. "Will you ignore me Monday?"

"Nothing has changed, Logan." Her smile faded and she looked away from him.

"But if–"

"No. Don't even think it."

"You don't know what I was going to suggest," Logan protested.

"If it involves you being closer to me than twenty metres, you can forget it."

"I'm closer than that during Mr Gallo's class," Logan said dryly.

"Don't ruin the weekend," Maddy pleaded. She waited for him to agree, but he fell silent, looking out the window.

A few minutes later, Logan turned to her with a wry smile, threading his fingers through hers.

Before Maddy had a chance to ask him what he was thinking, the taxi pulled up at the front of a house that must have had every light turned on. Music and noise poured out the open windows and people looked to be everywhere. They were in the yard, their silhouettes at nearly every window and a couple were even in the street.

Logan paid the driver and thanked him before they got out. He took Maddy's hand and led her to the open front door. The noise increased the closer they came until they were completely surrounded by it the moment they stepped inside.

Maddy trailed behind Logan, her hand clasped firmly in his as they manoeuvred through the press of bodies. She recognised a couple of faces from the crowd that hung out at the beach and smiled in greeting. All of them were older than her and she guessed they were probably Davey's friends. Logan let go of her hand when he reached a closed door and pulled out a key and unlocked it.

He turned on the light and stepped back so Maddy could enter the room. Once the door was closed, the hum of the air conditioner helped drown out some of the noise. Maddy glanced around the bedroom and guessed it was Logan's.

"I didn't know you had your own room here."

Logan shrugged. "I stay here a bit. I have done since I was little."

"Why?"

"Both my parents work and when I was younger they didn't want to put me in a school holiday program so I spent all my holidays with my grandparents. I still come out here regularly. My choice since I no longer have to be babysat. I've got a lot of friends here. And I like hanging out with Grandad. And Grandma when she was alive."

"Did you choose everything in the room?" Maddy looked at the random pattern on the bedspread that was a mixture of earth tones with splashes of black. The curtains were a cappuccino colour with a darker fleck through them and the desk, bookcase, chest of drawers and double bed were all made of light coloured timber. The floor was covered in a thick pile carpet that was a warm cream colour, the bed had a handful of shirts strewn over the end and the built-in-wardrobe was only partially closed.

"Pretty much." Logan bundled up the shirts and tossed them on the already cluttered floor of his wardrobe before he shut the door. "Maddy–"

Not liking his tone, she interrupted. "I hope you're not going to try and continue our earlier conversation."

"I want to be able to talk to you when you return to your father's house."

"I wish you could too." Maddy sighed. "Don't be difficult, Logan. If he saw me even looking at you he'd ground me for a year."

"I think you're exaggerating."

"What about the padlock? You can't have forgotten that."

Logan ran his fingers through his hair and started to pace. "So I'm meant to pretend I don't know you? What about if I want to go to something you'd normally take a girlfriend to? Do you expect me to take someone else? Would you like that?"

"I'm going home." Maddy turned to the door.

Logan hurried over to her and stepped between her and the door. "Maddy–"

"No. I don't need this crap. Fine. Go get a girlfriend who doesn't have to hide that she knows you. Now get out of the way." She tried to push him away.

"I'm sorry."

Maddy sighed. "Stop doing that."

"Doing what?"

"Sounding so sincere when you say you're sorry. How am I meant to stay mad at you when you do that?"

"Hopefully you won't." He reached out and drew her close.

Maddy sighed again and rested her head against his chest, his heartbeat echoing in her ear. "Are we going to argue over this every other day?"

"When do you come to your mum's house again?"

"In another fortnight. Why?"

"That's a long time. Does that mean I can't see you, speak to you or have any contact with you at all during the next two weeks?"

What could she say other than yes? She wished things were different, but they weren't. Two days out of every fourteen didn't seem like much. He'd be mad to put up with that.

"Maddy?"

"No contact at all." She pulled away enough that she could see him. "I wish it was different."

"I reckon he's insane."

Maddy smiled slightly. "Nah, just obsessive about my safety. Sunday night when I get home he'll drill me about what I've done this weekend. Mum and I talk about what to say on the way to the train station. Just in case he ever rings and checks with her. He never has, but it's something he might do. We plan it out right down to our meals."

"Don't go back."

"Logan-"

He closed his eyes momentarily. "Forget I said that."

Maddy pulled away from him and put her hands on her hips. "If you keep this up, I'm going to feel worse than I already do about staying with my father. I won't even want to see you here if you do that."

Logan turned away from her, his head bowed. He turned back abruptly. "Do you want to check out the party?" He smiled slightly.

Maddy stared at him. "Are you bi-polar or something?"

Logan grinned. "You're right. I'll drop the subject. Let's have some fun instead. If I can't be with you until the end of the month, I want to make the most of every second."

"Okay." Maddy smiled, relief washing over her. "Sounds good to me."

The next few hours sped by. Logan introduced her to lots of people she guessed she'd never remember and Davey interrupted them when they were dancing, stealing her away for a dance. Logan laughingly took her back again. She had a couple of drinks and even though she was tempted to have more so the alcohol could temporarily help her forget her problems, she stuck with soft drinks. She didn't want to feel miserable the next day. She wanted to enjoy every minute of Sunday since she'd be spending it with Logan. A few minutes after she thought that, she realised it was already Sunday.

Chapter Sixteen

When Maddy was ready to go home one of Davey's mates, who hadn't been drinking, gave her a lift. Logan came with them as well as another girl who lived along the way and was ready to leave.

Maddy snuggled against Logan in the back seat of the car, tired but unable to stop smiling. Music surrounded them from the stereo and the girl in the front sang along to it, her words more than a little slurred.

Logan bent to her ear. "Did you have a good night?"

"Yeah."

"Want to go to the beach in the morning?"

Maddy groaned. "It is morning."

Logan laughed softly. "How about eight?"

"What's with you and eight in the morning? Are you obsessed with it or something?"

"No, just with spending as much time as possible with you."

Maddy stared up at him and wished there was more than the odd flicker of light from streetlamps to show the expression on his face. "What if I say I want to sleep in?"

The car pulled up and the driver walked the girl to her front door. They were left alone in the dark.

"Then I'll turn up and wake you. Do you think the same trick that worked for Sleeping Beauty would work for you?"

Maddy grinned. "It could be worth a try."

"Maybe I should practice first, just to make sure I've got it right."

Maddy didn't disagree and within seconds his lips were on hers. Minutes later, there was a rap on the window. The driver grinned at them before he got back in the car.

"Don't go fogging up my windows. I need to be able to see out of them."

"You're lucky I don't have anything to throw at you," Logan grumbled.

The driver laughed and headed for Maddy's house, once they gave him directions. Still smiling she snuggled against Logan. She wondered if she should ask what the driver's name was again, but she didn't bother. She yawned. What she really wanted was to crawl into bed and sleep for ten hours. She guessed that wasn't about to happen. Not the ten hours part anyway.

As usual, Logan walked her to the front door. He also kissed her goodnight and reluctantly pulled away from her.

"I better go before Paul hits the horn."

Maddy nodded. That was the driver's name. She'd known it had been a common one. "Tell Paul thanks for the lift. I meant to say it, but I guess I'm more tired than I thought."

"Everyone local takes turns. That way we've always got a way to get everyone home safely at the end of the night. The ones that live further away organise their own driver."

"That's a good idea."

"Grandad's rule if we want to have parties there." Logan grinned. "Not a bad trade off."

The car horn broke the silence of the night. Maddy grinned. "Whoops."

Logan laughed. "I'll see you at eight." He ran back to the car.

She watched the car disappear before she closed the door and locked it. Leaning against the door, she couldn't stop smiling. She was tired, but happy. A lamp was left on in the lounge room so she could find her way to her bedroom, the house was quiet and Maddy guessed her mum was in bed asleep. She didn't blame her since it was nearly three. Maddy pushed away from the door and slowly made her way to her room.

Dropping onto her bed, she kicked off her shoes and peeled away her jeans. There was no way she could manage a shower. She'd probably fall asleep in there and drown. Could you drown in a shower? Or only in a tub? She didn't know, or care. She wasn't going to take the risk.

Down to knickers and her shirt, she shoved back the blankets and rolled onto her stomach. She frowned as her eyes closed. She was sure there was something she needed to do. The front door was locked. She was certain she'd done that. The lamp could stay on in the lounge room. No way was she dragging herself out there to turn it off. But there was something. She yawned. If only she could remember. All thoughts evaporated as she fell asleep to dream of dancing with Logan.

* * *

Maddy woke, remembering what she'd forgotten to

do. Set the alarm clock. She yelped when she saw Logan stood over her. Checking her sheet covered her, she was relieved to find it did.

Logan grinned. "Aww, there goes my plan to wake you properly."

"What are you doing in here?" She sat up, clutching her sheet to her chest.

"Your mum let me in on her way out. Said she would have woken you if she'd realised you had plans for the day. I told her that was okay, you said for me to wake you."

"I did not." Maddy glared at him.

Logan nodded. "Yep. You did. Told me it'd be worth a try to wake you like Sleeping Beauty."

Maddy shook her head. "I was joking. Now get out so I can have a shower and try and wake up. How can you look so disgustingly cheerful after five hours sleep?"

"Three. The party was still going when I got back."

Maddy threw her pillow at him. "Out."

Logan caught the pillow and retreated.

"Give me my pillow back."

He glanced over his shoulder, grinning at her. "Come and get it."

"Logan!" She growled when Logan ignored her and kept walking. As soon as he was gone, she stumbled out of bed and closed the door. Grabbing her swimmers and a sundress, she pulled her robe on over her knickers and shirt so she could use the bathroom. When she opened her door, there was no sign of Logan.

She quickly showered, changed into her clothes and brushed her teeth. Feeling more human, she went in search of Logan. He was in the kitchen and had made her jam on toast. She smiled as she watched him clean up his mess.

"You're almost forgiven for waking me." She sat at the table.

Logan put the toast in front of her. "I didn't want to waste all day waiting for you to get ready."

Maddy took a bite and closed her eyes. How could it be after eight already? It felt like she'd barely gone to sleep. She yawned then took another bite.

"Are you planning on going back to sleep there?"

Maddy opened her eyes slightly. "Why do you sound hopeful?"

Logan grinned. "Because I get to wake you."

Maddy shook her head and ate her breakfast. As soon as she'd finished, she dusted the crumbs off her fingers, ditched her plate in the sink and filled a glass from the tap for a drink. Upending it in the draining rack she turned away from the sink. Before she could leave the kitchen Logan reached out and snagged her around the waist.

"Are you properly awake or do you still need help waking up?"

Maddy smiled. "Still slightly tired." She met his lips and her eyes closed. When he pulled away, she opened her eyes. "I don't feel any more awake."

Logan laughed before he kissed her again. "As much as I'd like to stand here all day and do this, Davey will be back to pick us up soon."

Maddy frowned. "How did he know I wasn't ready?"

"I told him when your mum said you were still asleep."

"Oh."

"Although he did bet me you wouldn't be ready." A horn sounded outside. "Come on, that'll be him. What else do you need?"

"My bag from yesterday. It's got my hat and sunscreen in it. Oh, and I need another towel." Maddy hurried from the room and grabbed her gear, including a change of underwear, and reached the front door as Davey hit the horn a second time.

Logan rose from the armchair he sat in, her pillow laying on the couch across from him. He linked his fingers with hers as they headed out the door. Maddy tilted her head back as they walked to the car. It looked like it was going to be a perfect day. The blue sky was cloudless and the day was warm, but not yet hot.

"Morning," Davey said as she opened the front door.

Maddy wrinkled her nose. "Liar. It won't be morning for at least another couple of hours."

Davey laughed. "Guess you can't handle these late nights."

"I'm not used to them. Lights out at eight-thirty at our house. Then everyone rises at six, regardless of what day it is. I hate early mornings."

Davey shuddered as he pulled out onto the road. "That's almost child abuse. Weekends are for sleeping in." He glanced at Logan in the rear view mirror. "You hear that, cousin?"

Logan shrugged. "You're all a bunch of wimps. Do you run for cover the moment it looks like it might rain, too?"

"I'll show you who's a wimp when we reach the beach," Davey warned. "I'm going to dunk you until you beg for mercy."

"I can swim faster than you."

"I can run faster. I'll catch you before you reach the water."

Chapter Seventeen

Maddy smiled as she listened to them jokingly argue the entire way to the beach, applying her sunscreen so she didn't have to do it when they arrived. Davey had barely parked the car before Logan unbuckled, dropped a kiss on Maddy's cheek and dashed for the beach.

"Getting slow old man," Logan called over his shoulder.

Davey threw the car keys to Maddy and pounded across the sand after Logan. "You're going to be begging for mercy."

Maddy pulled on her cap, shouldered her backpack, locked the car and slowly followed them. She put the keys in one of the pockets of her backpack and left it high enough on the beach so the waves wouldn't reach it while they were swimming. She dropped her dress on top of it and raced for the water, the sand already warm under her feet.

The morning passed far too quickly and after lunch, at the same take-away shop, Davey dropped them at the nursing home. They didn't stay as long as the previous day since they both had to catch the train. Davey waited for them out the front of the nursing home and Maddy's feet dragged as she headed for his car.

"You look like you lost your best friend. Didn't you have a good visit with your grandma?" Davey asked as she closed the car door.

Maddy nodded. "I wish she knew who I was. I don't want to be Sally. I'm her granddaughter, not her sister."

"At least she'll interact with you. I've seen some of them refuse to have anything to do with their family because they don't remember them." Logan closed the back door.

Maddy sighed. "Ignore me. I'm being a whiner."

Logan reached forward and put his hand on her shoulder. "That's okay. I guess you need a break from being perfect all the time."

Maddy faced him with a glare. "Quit grinning at me. I'm annoyed with you. I hate being called perfect."

"I guess I'm missing an 'in joke' here," Davey said.

"Yeah. I believe the actual term is a perfect little princess," Logan said.

Maddy turned to Davey. "The kids at school say it. And my father expects it of me."

Davey frowned. "They obviously don't know you."

Logan laughed. "And that is an understatement."

Maddy couldn't help smiling. Then she sighed. "I wish the weekend wouldn't go so fast." She groaned as they pulled up in front of her house. "I can't believe it's over already."

"Not quite." Logan hopped out of the car.

"See you, Davey." Maddy smiled at him before she slid out of the car.

"You take care, Maddy," Davey called out.

Maddy nodded before she closed the door. She fell into step beside Logan. "What do you mean by not quite."

"We've still got the train ride back to Brissie."

"That will pass far too quickly. And I really should do my homework on the way. I haven't done any yet."

"Do it when you get back to your prison."

"You forget I've got an interrogation to deal with when I return to jail."

Logan smiled. "Don't think about it. You'll ruin the weekend." He leaned forward to kiss her.

Maddy sighed when they parted. "I'll see you at the train station."

"Yep. Smile, Maddy. It's not the end of the world. Twelve days will pass quickly."

Maddy forced a smile to her lips and watched as Logan sauntered to the car. She waved as they drove off, standing alone on the doorstep. Why did the days you wanted to last forever always go by so quickly? She knew the next twelve days would drag. They always did when she waited for something. And they dragged even slower the more she wanted the days to pass.

Reluctantly Maddy went inside, showered and changed into one of her 'perfect little princess' dresses. As soon as she was ready, she sat at the kitchen table and had a snack while she discussed with her mum what to say during the interrogation. The conversation continued in the car and finished not long before they arrived at the train station.

They sat in the car, both silent for a moment. Maddy could see Logan waited for her near the entrance to the train station. He remained where he was and she was glad for the chance to say goodbye to her mum without an audience.

"Watch what you say to your father."

"I always do, Mum."

"She was talking about you this morning, your grandmother. Even though she thought of you as her sister, she remembered you were coming."

Maddy smiled slightly. "That's good, I guess. She tried to con me into visiting tomorrow. I wish I could have said yes."

"I do too." Joscelin gave her a one armed hug. "I wish you could stay."

"Me too."

"It was a hard choice to make. If it wasn't for my mum I would have fought to keep you. But I know you're capable of looking out for yourself. She isn't."

Maddy nodded, even though she wasn't completely sure she was as capable as her mum thought. "Will you get in touch with your cousins about me emailing their kids? Let them know I've only got infrequent internet use. Maybe tell them I'll email during the next school holidays."

"I will. And take care, Maddy." Joscelin looked over to where Logan stood. "I won't wait around to watch you onto the train. It looks like you have company."

"Yeah." Maddy couldn't resist a smile.

"Does he know…" Joscelin's voice trailed off.

"Yeah. He's not real happy about it, but he's not going to say anything either."

"That's good. I'm glad you've now got two friends you can talk to in Brisbane. You know it wouldn't hurt you to make a few more friends at school. Being unable to hang out with them on the weekend shouldn't prevent you from making friends."

There was no point in correcting her mum. It was more than being unable to hang out together on the weekend and there was still only one person she could talk to. If her father ever caught her talking to a boy he'd ground her for life. She leaned forward and kissed her mum on the cheek. "See ya."

"Love you, Maddy."

"Love ya." She slid out of the car, carrying her bag.

Logan met her half way. "I was beginning to think you'd changed your mind about returning."

"I wish."

He glanced over her shoulder. "Did your mum say anything about me waiting for you?"

Maddy laughed. "She's nothing like my father."

"So what did she say?"

"That she wouldn't stick around so we could spend some time together."

"Okay. I'd say she's the complete opposite of your father then."

Maddy nodded. "Yep. Pretty much."

They sat together on a bench seat on the platform while they waited for the train. Conversation was sporadic and Maddy wondered if Logan was thinking about the coming weeks of no contact too. When the train arrived, they found a seat together and sat quietly, hands clasped. Maddy rested her head on Logan's shoulder and was startled to find she'd fallen asleep. She blinked sleepily, meeting Logan's gaze.

He smiled. "I didn't want to wake you, but we're nearly there."

Maddy looked out the window, trying to figure out where they were.

"About ten minutes until we arrive."

"Oh." Her fingers tightened on Logan's.

"I'll see you at school."

"You won't be able to talk to me."

"I know. But at least I'll know you're okay."

"Yeah." She didn't know what to say. She decided to kiss him instead. Didn't they say actions spoke louder than words?

Logan smiled when she pulled away from him. "I'll be counting the days." He rose to his feet. "I'll wait until you're gone before I get off."

Maddy nodded. "Okay." She certainly didn't want her father to see Logan on the train with her.

His smile faded before he turned and headed towards the back of the train.

She clasped her hands in her lap and tried to think of something else. Anything other than watching Logan walk away. Her throat started to feel tight and her eyes watery. She blinked hard. There was no way she could explain tears. She had to hold on. If her father thought something was up he'd interrogate her even longer and she was too tired to last all night.

The train pulled to a stop and Maddy took a shaky breath, rising to her feet. There was no point postponing the inevitable. Better to get it over and done with.

It wasn't hard for her to spot her father. There seemed to be a space around him as if people didn't dare come too close. "Hello, Dad."

He took her bag. "How was your weekend?"

"Good."

"What did you do?"

Maddy managed not to sigh. No matter how politely it was done, it always felt like an interrogation. It continued through the drive home and started up again after dinner. When Maddy was finally able to escape to bed, she released the sigh she'd held back for ages. It was going to be a long wait. Back to enduring more crappy days.

Chapter Eighteen

On Thursday, while Maddy sat in Mr Gallo's class, she was once again thinking about how long it was until she could go to her mum's house. It wasn't helped by how many times Logan had looked in her direction. When he glanced back at her for about the twentieth time she mouthed the words 'stop it.'

He faced the front of the class and Maddy closed her eyes for a moment. How was she meant to concentrate with him only a couple of seats away?

"Are you paying attention, Ms Dowling?" Mr Gallo demanded.

Maddy's eyes opened and she froze. What could she say? He always asked a question about what he'd said to make you prove the claim you were listening. If she said no, he was likely to give her detention. She kept her gaze on Mr Gallo even though she wanted to look towards Sasha or Logan in the hope they'd have the answer.

"Well?" Mr Gallo started to stride towards her.

Logan snorted. "Maddy always listens. It's us mere mortals that have trouble paying attention all the time."

Mr Gallo turned his attention on Logan. "Is that meant to be funny, Mr Ridley?"

"Of course not, Mr Gallo. Just a statement of fact. It's hard to compete with perfect people."

Maddy held her breath as she waited to see how Mr Gallo would answer. Everyone knew he was annoyed when he addressed students formally.

"How about you tell me what we were discussing moments before you decided to do your comedian attempt?"

"Sorry. I wasn't paying attention." Logan smiled wryly. No one dared to laugh at his comment as they would have in another teacher's classroom.

"Then maybe detention during lunch will help you learn to pay attention." Mr Gallo turned on his heel and strode back to the front of the classroom. He faced everyone, his gaze not missing a single student as it travelled around the room. "Anyone else find they need a lesson in concentration?"

The class remained silent. A few shifted

uncomfortably. Maddy could almost hear the sigh of relief that came from the class when Mr Gallo returned to teaching. She glanced at Logan, but his attention was focused on the front of the class now. What was he thinking? He was going to get them both in trouble. Maybe she could change classes. She quickly dropped that idea. There was no way she could explain that to her father. She forced herself to pay attention. She didn't need detention too.

The moment the bell rang, she bolted for the door. It was that or risk giving in and talking to Logan. That would be completely crazy.

Sasha fell into step beside her. "What's the rush? Is there a fire somewhere?" She grinned.

"Very funny. I'm going to kill him."

"I think it's cute."

Maddy rolled her eyes. "You would. Someone will notice if he keeps staring at me instead of paying attention to his work. And then my father will make me go back to an all girls' school. Your dad making negative comments about the school not being good enough wouldn't work a second time."

"Maybe we can arrange-"

"Don't go there, Sash."

"Yeah but-"

"I'm not listening."

Sasha poked her tongue out. "You're no fun."

"I know."

Sasha draped an arm around her shoulders. "I didn't mean that. Cheer up, will you? People will think I'm depressing to be around."

"Sorry."

Sasha stopped. "This is my next class, but don't think this conversation is over. It's lunch next. And no hiding."

Maddy smiled. Her friend knew her too well. "Okay."

The next class went quicker than Maddy expected and she was soon sitting in a corner of the library talking to Sasha. Or more accurately, arguing with Sasha.

"But I'm sure I can organise something," Sasha said.

"I'm not going to risk it. Come on, Sash. One week is nearly over. I don't want to have to put up with all this waiting only to be caught doing something at the last minute and miss out on going to Mum's."

"But we could have a study session at my place. I could invite-"

"Please. Stop. You know your mum is a major gossip. It'd get back that we had a boy there. It's okay. I'll survive until the following weekend."

Sasha sighed heavily. "I want to help."

"I know. And I'm lucky to have you as a friend. But there's nothing either of us can do."

"It's so unfair."

"Yeah, I know."

"There's got to be some reason why your father goes overboard with protecting you."

Maddy shrugged. "It doesn't matter if there is. No one will tell me anything."

"I can't believe they hid the fact your grandma is alive from you for all these years."

"Yeah, I know."

Sasha smiled suddenly. "We could google him."

"How will that help?"

"There's all sorts of stuff online. Come on. Let's see when we can book some time to use the internet."

Even with Sasha wheedling, they still couldn't get a slot before Monday lunch. They wandered off with Sasha complaining about how unfair everything was. Maddy certainly wasn't going to disagree. That was a fact she was very familiar with.

* * *

The rest of the school week was uneventful and Maddy reluctantly said goodbye to Sasha Friday afternoon. Her gaze caught Logan's across the school grounds and she hurriedly looked away.

"I could kiss him goodbye for you." Sasha grinned.

"Don't even think about it."

Sasha laughed. "Have a good weekend."

Maddy shook her head. "If you're trying to be funny, it's not working. You're being mean."

Sasha hugged her. "You better run. I spotted Mitchell headed for the gate."

With a quick hug back, Maddy ran to catch up to her stepbrother. She was too depressed by the thought of a weekend stuck at her father's house that she didn't bother to hassle him. Instead they stood quietly together. Maddy glanced around and saw Logan stood by the school gates. She stared at him. What did he think he was doing watching her like that? She frowned. He grinned and turned away. She thought of some uncomplimentary names for him while she waited for her father to turn up. He better not get her grounded.

* * *

Saturday afternoon Maddy was seated at her desk working on an assignment. A sound behind her made her turn around. She leapt to her feet when she saw Logan standing in the doorway.

"Out," she hissed.

"Maddy, I just had to-"

"No. Out. Please." She moved towards him, making shooing motions with her hands.

Logan grabbed her hands. "Will you listen for a minute?"

Maddy drew away from him. "No. Come on, Logan. Don't do this."

"A couple of minutes and then I'm gone. Okay?"

Maddy nodded, then her eyes widened as she looked past him. "Dad."

"What's going on here?"

Logan turned to face Sinclair. "Maddy's in Mr Gallo's class with me. I was checking if I'd taken down the homework pages correctly. It didn't seem like the same amount he usually gives." Logan grinned. "Good thing I checked too." He glanced at Maddy. "Thanks. I would have ended up with detention for not paying attention."

Maddy smiled weakly. "That's okay. It wasn't any trouble." She glanced at her desk. "If you don't mind, I'm in the middle of an assignment."

"No problem." Logan wandered out of the room.

She barely managed not to watch him go, keeping her gaze on the carpet.

"A moment before you return to your assignment, Madeline."

"Yes, Dad?" She stood with her hands clasped in front of her and her head down.

"You know how I feel about you having a boy in your room."

"He only wanted to ask a question about school."

"You should have told him to step into the hall. There was no reason why he couldn't talk to you from the hall, was there?"

"I didn't think of it. I was surprised he talked to me. Boys don't usually talk to me, even to ask me questions about schoolwork." She felt like patting herself on the back for that comment. Instead she reminded herself to keep her head down and her expression neutral.

"Then maybe if something like this occurs again you'll remember to follow the rules. You will not be going to your mother's house next weekend."

"What?" Maddy's head rose and she stared at her father in disbelief. "But I didn't invite him into my room."

"Nor did you send him out. Are you going to

argue this with me, Madeline? You can miss out on two weekends."

Maddy forced her gaze to the floor and held onto her temper. Her fingernails dug into her palms and she made herself relax them. She'd kill Logan when she saw him again. "No." Don't argue, don't argue, she repeated the words over and over in her head until the words were all one. It was bad enough she'd miss out on one weekend, two would be hell.

"In future, you might remember the rule of no boys in your room. I'm very disappointed in you, Madeline."

She remained standing as she listened to her father's footsteps leave the room. Tears pooled in her eyes and she fought back the urge to scream. How dare Logan cause her to be grounded? She'd kill him. Slowly and painfully. She fought the urge to angrily pace her room. Instead she seated herself at her desk again. Work was impossible, but she rested her fingers on her keyboard and tried to look busy in case her father returned. How was she going to get through another two weeks? It'd kill her. Anger swirled through her, hot and strong as her fingers tightened into fists, her knuckles white. Why hadn't Logan listened?

Chapter Nineteen

Monday morning she gave Sasha a note to take to Logan. She'd written, 'Thanks for getting me grounded'. Even after two nights, her anger hadn't decreased. And Mitchell mentioning it, as often as he could, didn't help. Nor had being made to ring her mum and tell her she'd been grounded while her father listened in.

Sasha met up with Maddy before her second class. "He wants to talk to you."

"Too bad."

"I thought he was going to be sick when he read your message. He actually went white. I've never seen anyone do that before."

"It's impossible."

"If I can organise it, will you meet with him?"

"Possibly."

"Come on, Maddy. I know you're pissed off at him,

but wouldn't you like to tell him in person instead of using me as your punching bag?"

"Sorry, Sash."

"That's okay. I'd be angry too."

"Okay. Organise it."

"Cool. I promise I'll organise a meeting no one will notice."

Maddy smiled slightly at Sasha's excitement. "I swear you're only happy when you're planning something you're not meant to be doing."

Sasha laughed. "Nah, I'm also happy when I'm buying shoes. See ya."

Maddy's smile momentarily widened as she watched her friend walk away. She didn't know what she'd do without Sasha. There was no way she'd ever have survived living with her father without her best friend.

Not wanting to end up with detention, she hurried to her next class, wondering what Sasha would organise. By the time the morning break arrived, she was impatient to learn the details, but Sasha refused to say anything as she led the way to their destination.

"Come on, Sash. Where are we going?" Maddy asked again.

"You'll see soon enough."

Maddy looked around and frowned as she figured

it out. "The storage rooms? But we can't get in there. I'm not about to stand around in a hallway and risk someone catching us together."

Sasha held up a key. "Am I amazing or what?"

Maddy grabbed the key. "Where'd you get this from?"

"I have my sources." Sasha grinned.

"Come on. Tell me."

"Staff are idiots sometimes when they decide which students can be trusted. One of the boys who does the scenery, for the end of year play, has a copy of the key so he can store the finished stuff. He also has trouble resisting a smile."

"You're terrible, Sash."

Sasha smiled broadly. "Absolutely. Now don't you lose that key or I'll probably never be able to get it from him again."

Maddy could only nod. She'd spotted Logan waiting for her.

"And hurry up and say what you've got to say to each other. This break isn't as long as lunch. And you can't meet up with him at lunchtime because we have plans. Not to mention lunch is when people most often use the storage rooms."

Maddy glanced at Sasha. "Plans?"

"Internet."

"Oh. I forgot."

"I thought you might since you've only been able to focus on murder." Sasha smiled when she glanced ahead. "Luck."

"Thanks." Maddy faced Logan when Sasha headed back the way they'd come. He stared at her. She took another step forward and then the thought of someone catching them together made her move quicker. She unlocked the storage room and they slipped quietly inside. Once the door was again locked, Maddy stared at him.

"I'm sorry." He reached for her.

Maddy took a step back. "You seem to say that a lot."

"I thought you'd be angry at me."

"I am." Maddy smiled mirthlessly. "I've planned your death in graphic detail. Do you want to hear my favourite method?"

"Ahh, not exactly."

"Didn't you say you liked horror movies?"

"Not if it's my life being made into one. Maddy–"

"How could you do that to me?" The words burst from her.

"I didn't think he'd ground you."

"I told you he would."

"But I had an excuse all sorted. How could he ground you over helping someone?"

Maddy sighed. "Because you were in my room." No one ever understood. Half the time she didn't.

"What can I do to make it up to you?"

"Nothing, Logan. While you get to do whatever you want for the weekend I'll be stuck in my room doing schoolwork or reading acceptable books. Do you know what that's like?"

"No."

"Good answer. If you'd said yes or you could understand I would have been really, really, really mad."

Logan reached for her again. "I'm so sorry." He drew her close. "Would it make you feel any better if I stayed home all weekend too?"

Maddy held herself stiffly, but didn't pull away. "You'd do that?"

Logan nodded.

Maddy stared at him, wishing the dusty windows let in more light. "I guess that would be fair."

"Why don't you escape out your window one night? I'll organise a lift for you."

Maddy shook her head. "A security camera is focused on my window. If I'm going out that window the house better be burning down around me."

"What's your father's problem?"

"I don't know." Maddy groaned as the bell went, a far off sound they could barely hear.

"I miss you." Logan's arms tightened around her as he kissed her.

When they broke apart, Maddy said, "Me too." Her anger had evaporated and she wished she could have held onto it. At least it had stopped her from the sad feeling that washed over her at the thought of being stuck at her father's house.

Logan checked the corridor before they left the storage room. It was clear. They each headed in a different direction. Maddy sighed when she was nearly at her class. She'd forgotten to ask him to stop staring at her.

Maddy automatically smiled when she reached the door of her next class and saw Sasha waited for her, impatiently shifting from one foot to the other. She surreptitiously handed the key over. The last thing she needed was for someone to wonder what she'd been up to. "Thanks."

Sasha nodded. "I'll see you in the library at lunchtime."

Maddy slipped into the classroom and settled into

her seat. Her mind returned to the kiss. And as often as she tried to keep her thoughts on schoolwork, her mind just as often returned to thinking about Logan. She was glad when it was lunchtime and she could escape the scrutiny of teachers.

Sasha was at the computer before her and already doing a search. Maddy pulled up a chair and sat beside her friend. "Found anything yet?"

"Tonnes. The problem will be in finding enough time to sort through it."

"I guess we better hurry since we've only got our lunch break."

"I probably should have put our names down for more days, but I didn't think about it."

"We'll do that when we finish up here." Maddy clicked on another page and glanced through it.

After a few minutes, they split the window and had two articles open at a time to read through, taking turns to use the mouse. By the end of lunch, they'd found nothing interesting and put their names down for more time on the internet. They were lucky to get a slot for the next day.

"You'd think he was a saint the way some of those articles go on about him," Maddy grumbled.

"People always say you shouldn't believe everything you read in the news."

Maddy grinned. "And that is the absolute truth."

* * *

Maddy was barely through the front gate Tuesday morning before Sasha grabbed her and dragged her to a quieter spot. She handed Maddy a piece of folded paper.

"What's up?" Maddy opened the page and stared at the newspaper heading. 'Neglected Child Ends In Shallow Grave.'

"I continued our search at home last night. Hurry up and read it, Maddy. There was an article about a charity organisation he did some free work for a couple of years ago and they referred to his dark past and had a link to this article."

Maddy noticed it was from a Sydney newspaper and was from eighteen years ago. Her father's name jumped out at her.

Prominent plastic surgeon Sinclair Dowling and his wife Hannah mourn the loss of their oldest daughter, twelve-year-old Elspeth, who went missing a week ago. She was found yesterday in a shallow grave. Police are continuing investigations. The family refused to comment and their younger daughter Eleanor has been removed from school.

Friends and neighbours had much to say. One horrified neighbour said, "We all expected something like this. The girl was out till all hours and hung with the wrong crowd. Of course things were going to end badly. Her parents are as much to blame as the one who killed her."

Maddy's legs felt like jelly and the words in front of her wavered until they were black squiggles. She stumbled to the half a metre high garden wall and sat on the warm concrete. Leaning forward, she swallowed hard. Her stomach rolled unnaturally and she wondered if she was going to be sick. A sister. No, two sisters. One of them dead. What had happened to the younger one that she'd ended in a shallow grave? Maddy tried to look at the page again but her fingers trembled so hard she dropped it.

"What's going on?"

Maddy stared up at Mitchell, Logan beside him. She shook her head and reached for the page. Mitchell beat her to it. "That's mine." She struggled to her feet, glaring at Logan when he held out a hand to help her. "I don't need your help."

"Who gave you this?" Mitchell waved the page in front of her.

Chapter Twenty

Maddy had no idea what to tell Mitchell. Her head still reeled from what she'd read.

"We don't know," Sasha said. "It was in Maddy's locker."

"It's all lies." Mitchell crushed the page into a ball.

Maddy grabbed it off him. "There's a URL at the top of it. I'm not an idiot. I was going to check it out."

Logan held out his phone. "Here. Check it now."

Maddy shook her head. "I don't know how to use it."

"I bet I could figure out how." Sasha took a step towards Logan.

Logan's fingers moved across the touch screen and he glanced over to read the URL on the page Maddy had tried to smooth flat. Within minutes the article was on his screen. "It looks real."

Mitchell swore. "I didn't even know he'd been

married before Joscelin. I bet Mum doesn't either. Who else knows about this?" He glared at the girls.

"I wouldn't have a clue." Maddy held Mitchell's gaze, not daring to look towards Sasha. There was no way she'd dob her friend in.

"Do you think they'll tell the whole school?" Sasha asked.

"If anyone opens their mouth about this I'll beat them so badly they'll wish I'd killed them," Mitchell growled.

Logan closed the internet and slid his phone back into his pocket. "Have you been to your locker yet, Mitch? If they didn't leave one for you, then it's only Maddy they're hassling."

Mitchell pointed at Maddy. "Don't move from here." He strode away, Logan at his side.

"Oh. My. God." Sasha placed her hand on her heart. "I swear I was clinically dead when Mitchell read that article."

"What are we going to do?" Maddy hissed. "He's going to kill us if he finds out who's behind the article."

"Then we have to make sure he never finds out." Sasha grinned. "You know, this could be a good thing. Did you see his face? I thought he'd explode.

I never knew he was so conscious of what people thought about him."

"Oh no, get that look off your face."

Sasha's look became all innocence. "What look?"

"No. Whatever you're planning, no way."

"Spoilsport." Sasha poked out her tongue. "Uh oh, here comes trouble."

Maddy turned to see Mitchell striding towards them, Logan still at his side. She folded the page and put it in her pocket, the creases making it impossible for it to lie flat. "I guess he found out it's someone after me. Like we didn't already know he wouldn't find anything."

"Stay calm. We can pull this off." Sasha's lips barely moved.

"I hope."

"What did you do?" Mitchell demanded as he stopped in front of them.

"What do you mean?" Maddy frowned. Surely he hadn't figured it out already.

"To piss off whoever left that article for you."

Maddy shrugged. "I wouldn't have a clue. Sasha's the only person I talk to."

"That might be the problem," Logan said.

Mitchell turned towards Logan. "How could that be the problem?"

Logan held up his hand, palm towards Mitchell. "Don't kill the messenger. I've heard people complain your sister is a snob, that's all."

"Stepsister," Maddy and Mitchell automatically said together.

Mitchell glared at Maddy. "This is all your fault."

"No it's not. It's yours. I can't talk to anyone without you carrying tales to Dad. So of course they think I'm a snob." She glared back at him.

"He asks me. What am I meant to do? Lie to him?" Mitchell demanded. "It's better to tell him first. Before he finds out."

"Maybe there's a way we can fix this. If she wasn't seen as acting like she was better than the rest of us, whoever sent the article might back off and leave her alone," Logan suggested.

The bell rang and Mitchell swore again. He pointed his finger at Maddy. "Don't say a word about this to anyone and if you get any more articles you bring them straight to me."

"Whatever." She hated it when he bossed her around. They were the same age. Well, he was a few months older, but he still had no right to act like he was way older.

"I'm not messing around here, Madeline. I won't have this story getting around school. The girl was a slut. I don't want anyone knowing trash like that was in our family," Mitchell said.

"Fine. But she was only a kid. How bad could she have been?"

"Read the article again. You obviously didn't read it properly the first time." Mitchell turned abruptly and strode off.

Logan reached out and rested his hand on her shoulder for a split second before he followed Mitchell. Maddy sagged against Sasha, sighing.

"How much of it did you read?" Sasha slipped an arm around her shoulders.

"The first paragraph."

"Then make sure you're alone when you read the rest of it. She wasn't a sweet little kid. Come on. We better get to class before we end up with detention."

Maddy let Sasha lead her to her next class. Her mind still struggled to keep up with the sudden turn her world had taken. First a grandma she didn't know about, as well as numerous cousins, and now sisters. She recalled her mum had avoided the question she'd asked about any other family she might have. Was that deliberate? Did her mum know about her sisters? Why did her parents have so many secrets? What was wrong with them that they couldn't tell her things she really should know? Unless her mum hadn't bothered because neither of her sisters were still alive. How could she find out? Would her mum tell her the truth if she asked? She had no idea and guessed it would be ages before she'd have the chance to ask.

* * *

When Sasha met her at the gate Thursday morning, Maddy had a feeling of dread pool in her stomach. She knew Sasha was up to something by the quick glimpse of mischief she'd seen in her eyes, but she couldn't say anything. Not with Mitchell beside her. Before she had a chance to take the piece of paper Sasha tried to hand her, Mitchell snatched it and read it.

"Where'd you get this?" Mitchell waved the piece of paper under Sasha's nose.

"I saw the corner sticking out from under the door of Maddy's locker and pulled it out. I didn't want to risk anyone else getting hold of it if it was the same as the last one."

Maddy tried to take the page, but Mitchell kept it away from her. She glared at him. "It's mine."

"Are you sure you don't know anything about this?" Mitchell demanded.

"I haven't seen the bloody thing. Now hand it

over." Maddy's eyes narrowed, her hand held out as she waited to see what plan Sasha had cooked up.

Mitchell shoved it at her. "I'll see you at lunch. Whoever it is will not get away with it." Mitchell strode away, his expression becoming friendly as he called out greetings to his friends.

"What have you done now?" Maddy hissed as she looked down at the paper. "Sasha!"

Sasha grinned unrepentantly. "Whoever sent that message is obviously a nasty piece of work."

Maddy shook her head and again read the message Sasha had created. 'Saturday ten a.m. to three p.m. at the Botanical Gardens. If you can't follow orders I can't keep quiet.' Lowering her hand, she met her friend's gaze. "What are you planning?"

"Escape. Wouldn't you like to get out for the day? I mean, you were meant to be going to your mum's this weekend. I just wanted to give you a day out. I know you hate spending your weekends stuck in your room."

Maddy sighed. It was too late to do anything about it now. She'd have to go along with it. Unless they confessed they were behind the note, they were committed. She had a feeling Mitchell would take it the wrong way and she'd be in even more trouble if she told him it was all a hoax. "Thanks. I think." A hint of sarcasm was in her words.

Sasha laughed. "You're welcome."

"Hey."

Maddy turned to face Logan. "Hi." Her word was a whisper and she looked around to see if Mitchell was about.

"It's okay. He sent me with a message." Logan smiled.

Maddy wasn't sure how much of a difference that'd make. There were possibly others who told her father what she did around here. "I never took you for an errand boy."

Logan's smile became a grin. "I guess it depends on the errand."

"I'll leave you two to chat." Sasha started to move away.

Chapter Twenty-One

Maddy grabbed Sasha by the arm, her gaze still on Logan. "No you don't."

"You try and do someone a favour and they resent you for it." Sasha shook Maddy's hand off.

Maddy ignored Sasha's comment. "What does he want, Logan?" She was conscious of the stares from the other students.

"He said you better come up with a plan before lunch since this is all your fault. And you better make sure you join him at lunch because he won't be happy if he has to track you down. What's happened? He didn't say."

Maddy handed the piece of paper to Logan and waited for him to read it. When he handed it back, she folded it and slid it into her pocket. She was puzzled by his grin. "What?"

"It's almost like someone is actually trying to help you."

"Why would you say that?" Maddy was worried Sasha's plan was too obvious.

"Because Mitch is going to have to find a way to get you out of the house when you're grounded. And you better include me too."

"And me," Sasha piped up.

Maddy sighed heavily. This was getting too complicated. "The only thing I can think about is that my father is big on education."

Logan pulled his phone out. "Let's see what's at the gardens then."

The bell rang and Maddy groaned. "Tell me what you find out at lunch."

Logan nodded before he returned to looking at the screen of his phone. Maddy watched as he slowly walked away, the other students making way for him when they saw he wasn't paying attention. Maddy looked at Sasha when she linked her arm through hers.

Sasha grinned. "He's so hot he makes me want to pant like a dog."

Maddy shook her head. "That's a disgusting visual."

Sasha laughed. "Maybe. But there's nothing disgusting about the way he looks."

Maddy couldn't argue with that comment. Instead she returned to what had been preying on her mind all night and morning. "I read the rest of that article last night. I think I understand why my father is so paranoid about what I'll get up to. Everyone thought Elspeth was a saint until they looked beneath the surface. No one had a clue what she was up to. She came and went as she pleased, she had friends way older than her and when they actually found her body, tests showed she was drunk."

"Yeah, but you're not her." Sasha started to walk towards their first class, tugging Maddy along with her. "He shouldn't be treating you like he expects you to be exactly the same. Besides the article said her mum had a drug problem, yours doesn't. It's a completely different situation."

"Were there any other articles?"

"Some. But they all said pretty much the same. Elspeth was the daughter from hell and the only people who would mourn her were her parents and sister who didn't even know the girl they were mourning."

"I can't believe everything written about her in that article, she was only twelve. She was in primary school."

Sasha shook her head. "No, actually she wasn't. She

was in an accelerated learning program and in grade ten at the time. It was in one of the other articles I read. So she was with kids way older than her all the time."

"Oh." Maddy thought about that for a moment. "What really bothers me is I don't know what happened to her sister. My half-sister. Is she still alive?"

"I tried to find that out, but didn't have any luck. The articles were all focused on how horrifying it was that such a respected member of the community let his daughter run wild. And that no one even knew she was missing for nearly two days. She'd lied about where she was going." They reached Sasha's classroom and she handed an envelope to Maddy. "See you at lunch."

Before Maddy had time to ask why she wouldn't see her at morning tea, Sasha was inside her classroom. Maddy opened the envelope as she headed to her first class. There was a piece of paper and a key. She smiled when she read the words 'morning tea' on the paper. She slipped it into her pocket, which was certainly getting a lot of use today. If she guessed right, the key was for the storage room and somehow Sasha had either given Logan a similar message or planned to give him one. Or maybe he had asked Sasha to organise the meeting.

Maddy could barely sit still during class. Morning tea took ages to arrive. When it did, she was at the storage room door not long after the bell rang and unlocking it. Logan was by her side as she stepped through the door. They locked it behind them and grinned at each other.

"I rather like your friend."

Maddy laughed. "Me too." With another laugh, she threw herself into his arms. "I only wish morning tea was a lot longer."

"Yeah. I'd meet you here at lunch, but your brother will wonder where we are if we do."

"The storage room is sometimes used during lunch so we can't meet here then anyway. Do you have any ideas about what we can tell my father to get me out of the house on Saturday?"

"Some." Logan paused, looking uncomfortable. "Do you know who's sending the messages?"

"Do you swear you won't tell Mitchell?"

"Of course not."

"He's your friend."

Logan shook his head. "I only hung out with him to get an invite to your house." He grinned. "I couldn't suddenly stop hanging out with him after I figured out being at your house wasn't any help." He paused. "Now I wouldn't have a clue what he is."

"Sasha."

Logan frowned. "Huh?"

"The first time was an accident. We were trying to find info online about my father. We wanted to see what secrets he had in his past. He never wants to talk about it. Anyway, we ran out of time to finish our search at school so Sasha continued when she went home and printed up the article she found."

"And Mitch got his hands on it. Nice save."

"Yeah. Then Sasha had the idea of using it to make Mitchell help me get away from the house on the weekend. I would have told her she was crazy if she'd explained to me what she'd planned to do. Which is probably why she didn't tell me. Now we have to go through with it or Mitchell will be suspicious and probably find some way of getting me into trouble over it."

"Can I pick our next destination?"

"Logan!"

"What?"

"You're as insane as Sasha. If we get caught my father will ground me for life. He'll probably lock me in my room and throw away the key."

Logan's arms tightened around her. "I'll rescue you if he does that."

Maddy rested her head on his chest with a sigh. "I'm worried about what'll happen to Grandma if I'm caught. What if he blames it on Mum and won't let me see her or pay for the nursing home fees? Mum said she'd tried to get financial assistance, but she didn't qualify. Something to do with the value of the house my father bought her as part of the divorce settlement, but there's a clause that says she can't sell it or mortgage it until I'm eighteen. Something to do with ensuring she has a stable living environment for me." She shrugged. "Probably another one of his excuses so he can control everyone around him."

The bell rang and Logan groaned. "I don't get to spend nearly enough time with you. Tomorrow same time?"

Maddy nodded and kissed him. She had to agree with Logan. They didn't get to spend anywhere near enough time with each other.

Chapter Twenty-Two

Saturday morning Maddy sat quietly at the table and ate her breakfast. Marla sat across from her talking to Sinclair about the charity function she needed to attend that day since she was one of the women who'd organised it. Maddy half listened, glad her mum wasn't into all the charity stuff Marla was into. That was all Marla seemed to do with her time these days. Most of it related to promoting her husband and the places he worked.

Marla rose from the table and dropped a kiss on Sinclair's head. She was perfectly dressed, in an understated outfit that was both suitable and classy according to Sinclair's view. "Have a lovely day, dear." A small smile briefly made an appearance and she left the room. No lengthy smiles or even grins to cause wrinkles on her perfect skin.

Maddy had overheard her mention to a friend that

all the excessive smiling her friend did would cause numerous unsightly wrinkles. Ever since that moment she'd been tempted to collect a selection of jokes she could say every morning in an effort to make Marla smile. She was interested in finding out how determined Marla was not to wrinkle her skin. Her attention was drawn back to the table when her father spoke.

"What are you planning to do today, Mitchell?" Sinclair sat across the table from him.

"We're looking at Aboriginal Culture in one of my classes and the teacher mentioned there was a bush tucker walk at the Botanical Gardens. I thought I might go there today and have a look. I was wondering if Madeline could come along too since we both have the same class. The teacher said it'd be beneficial to what we're studying. I know she's been grounded from going to her mum's, but well, I guess I was also feeling sorry for her. I mean, it was my friend that got her in trouble," Mitchell said.

"That's very nice of you Mitchell, but I wouldn't think of putting that amount of responsibility on you."

"Dad, you know I'll take good care of her. I was honoured when you first asked me to look out for her at school. I thought you trusted me."

It was only years of practice that allowed her to keep her surprise from showing on her face. How dare her father ask Mitchell to look out for her at school? They were the same age. She didn't need a babysitter spying on her.

Sinclair stared at Mitchell for a moment, then nodded. "I know you'll take good care of her. I've been very impressed with your level of responsibility. All right then. Make sure she's always in your sight and be home before dark." He drew out his wallet and handed over fifty dollars. "Have something nutritious for lunch. No junk food."

Mitchell pocketed the money. "Of course not, Dad. I'd never pollute my system with junk food." He turned to Maddy. "Make sure you bring a hat. It's going to be a hot day according to the weather report."

She was tempted to say what a liar he was and that she'd seen him eat junk food at school. She managed to control the impulse. "Don't I get a say in the decision? What if I don't want to be stuck out in the heat all day?" She didn't want to sound too eager and risk her father thinking something was up. "And who wants to go on some boring bush tucker walk? It sounds like something old people would do."

"Don't argue, Madeline. Your brother has made a

nice gesture. Now go and get ready." Sinclair stared at her until she dropped her gaze.

"Fine." Maddy pushed away from the table and headed for her bedroom. She kept her smile hidden until her door was closed. A thrill coursed through her and she had to hold back a squeal of excitement. She'd see Logan this weekend after all. And best of all, she had something to keep Mitchell in line with. Life was looking up. As long as Mitchell didn't find out it was her and Sasha pulling his strings.

They caught a train into the city and from there a bus to the gardens, arriving a little before ten. Sasha and Logan were waiting for them. Mitchell scanned the area for anyone he might recognise, jumping slightly when Logan clapped him on the back.

"Relax. It's a nice day. Enjoy it."

Mitchell glanced around again. "I want to know who sent that letter."

"I doubt they're going to have a sign on them confessing to it. Come on, why don't we go for a walk and have a look at the bush tucker trail?"

"Dad will ask us about it," Maddy said.

Still grumbling, Mitchell led the way to the information booth and then, armed with a map, headed for the trail. Maddy and Logan hung back a little, walking side by side, hands occasionally brushing. She glanced sideways at Logan for what was probably the hundredth time and he grinned at her.

Logan leaned close to her ear. "Don't you normally complain when I stare at you? How come you're allowed to do it?"

Maddy pushed him away from her and sped up a little. She controlled the smile that wanted to break free when he fell into step with her again. When Mitchell glanced back at her with a glare, she couldn't resist smiling. Not only was she out for the day, but it was annoying Mitchell. What more could she want? She glanced at Logan. Well, maybe to hold his hand as they walked along the shaded pathway.

The day passed rapidly. They wandered around the gardens, joined one of the tours, had lunch in the cafe and after three they made their way to the bus stop. The only person who wasn't in a good mood was Mitchell. He kicked a stone ahead of him, scowling at it.

"Lighten up, man." Logan clapped him on the back.

"We wasted our time. I bet whoever sent the message wasn't even there." Mitchell turned his glare on Maddy. "This is all your fault."

"Like I asked to have a sister like Elspeth."

"I didn't ask to have a sister like you either."

"Fine! Then I'll let everyone know the truth and we won't have to worry about someone holding it over us." Maddy's hands went to her hips and she returned Mitchell's glare.

"Hey, no need to get into a fight about it. And Mitch, surely it's not such a big deal if everyone knows. You never even knew the girl. She's no relation to you at all," Logan said.

"Stay out of it," Mitchell snapped.

Logan shrugged. "Just trying to help."

"Well don't. And if you dare tell anyone, you'll regret it."

Logan's easygoing attitude was immediately replaced by anger. "Don't threaten me. I didn't do anything. And neither did Maddy or Sasha so quit snapping at them like you have been all day. No one will probably even care about Elspeth."

"You wouldn't have a clue. You should have heard what they said when Mum married her father." Mitchell pointed a finger at Maddy. "I had to listen to their crap for months because of the way she treats people."

"As if I have a choice. I'd be stuck in my room for life if I was too friendly with anyone," Maddy snapped.

"All you have to do is stand up to him. Your problem is you have no backbone," Mitchell said. "You let him treat you the way he does. You're old enough you could tell him where to go and move in with your mum."

Maddy laughed bitterly. "Now who wouldn't have a clue? If you'd seen the fights I had with Dad when I first had to live with him you wouldn't say that. It didn't take me long to learn how to behave. You see, I had this stupid idea that all the comments Mum had made about how to act over the years were her ideas. I didn't know it was her way of stopping me from getting into trouble. And what about you? You spin him bullshit all the time so he lets you do what you want. Why don't you stand up to him?" Maddy's voice became a parody of Mitchell's. "As if I'd pollute my body with junk food."

"Bus is here," Sasha said when Mitchell started to speak.

Logan was the first to move, Mitchell the last. They sat halfway down the bus, Maddy and Sasha in one seat, the boys in another.

Sasha whispered in Maddy's ear, "Do you think that's why he hates you?"

"I don't know."

"He's never liked being teased. I've seen him pound

on one of his mates who laughed at him for something stupid." Sasha frowned. "I can't even remember what it was about now, just something you wouldn't normally bother about. Well, most normal people wouldn't. They'd laugh it off."

"We can't do this again."

"We'll have to do something. We can't stop suddenly. How would you explain that?"

Maddy sighed. How had things become so complicated? "Fine. But no more outings."

"You're being boring."

"No, I'm being practical. Look how mad Mitchell is. I hate to think about what he'll tell Dad when we get home."

Sasha grinned. "You better warn him not to try and get you into trouble in case he has to spring you for the day if you get another one of those letters."

"I won't be getting another one of those letters."

"Yeah, but he doesn't know that."

Maddy nodded thoughtfully. "It has possibilities."

"You can sit with him when we catch the train from the city. I'll keep Logan entertained so the two of you can talk."

"Don't be too entertaining," Maddy warned.

Sasha laughed and glanced over to where the boys sat quietly. "Can't I have a little fun?"

"Nope." Maddy smiled, knowing her friend was only teasing. At least Sasha's comments helped to take her mind off the interrogation she was sure to receive from her father that night. As well as helped her to stop thinking about all her other problems for a minute.

Chapter Twenty-Three

When Maddy and Mitchell stepped in the school gate Monday morning they were greeted by Logan holding a folded page. He handed it to Mitchell.

"I was here before Sasha so I thought I should check." Logan crossed his arms over his chest and waited for Mitchell to read the message.

Mitchell swore and shoved the page at Maddy. "I'm fed up with this." He strode away from them.

Logan took Maddy's arm and moved her even further from the crowd. "Aren't you going to read it?"

"Should I?"

Logan grinned. "Sasha and I spent hours figuring this one out."

With a sigh, Maddy looked at the page. 'I am the puppet master and I have your strings in my hand.' She laughed softly. "No wonder he was pissed off. Was that deliberate? Finding the comment that would bug him the most?"

Logan's innocent expression failed miserably. "Now would I do that?"

"Yes."

"Hey." Sasha joined them. "Think it was a nice touch that Logan got to the message first today?"

Maddy slowly shook her head. "What am I going to do with you pair?"

"I've got some suggestions for what you can do with me," Logan said.

"I can imagine," Maddy said dryly.

"Think we can manage a night excursion?" Logan asked.

"No. No more. Come on Logan. We'll get caught if we keep it up." Maddy folded the paper and slid it into her pocket, her gaze on Logan, pleading with him to listen. "Last time you didn't listen to me I ended up grounded."

"Tell me you hated Saturday," Logan said.

Maddy looked away. "That isn't fair."

"Life usually isn't. Meet me later?"

Maddy sighed. She was beginning to recognise that stubborn look. She'd tackle the problem later. "Same time, same place." She smiled. They mightn't get much time, but it wasn't safe to use the storage rooms outside of morning tea. Most people were too busy trying to eat to worry about anything else in that short a break.

"Absolutely." Logan turned to Sasha. "I'll see you at lunch?"

Sasha nodded and the two of them watched as Logan strode away. Sasha turned to Maddy. "Are we eating lunch with your brother? I didn't even think to check with you first."

"Probably. After eating with him and his mates Thursday and Friday it might look strange if we suddenly stopped."

The bell went and Sasha grinned. "Okay, I'll catch you then." Her grin widened even more. "There's these two hot guys I'm looking forward to watching while I eat my lunch."

Maddy smiled slightly as she watched her friend run off. One of them was crazy and she was beginning to wonder if it was her and not Sasha. Shaking her head, she headed to her class, unable to stop worrying about everything.

* * *

Maddy and Sasha joined Mitchell and his friends for lunch on Tuesday and Wednesday too. No messages were delivered on either of those days. Maddy didn't know whether to hope her friends had decided to behave or to wonder what they were planning. She didn't have long to wonder. Arriving at school Thursday morning she was the one to find the note shoved into her locker.

'Saturday ten a.m. to three p.m. Queensland Museum.' She groaned and was about to shove it back in her locker when Mitchell grabbed it from her hands. He glared at her after he'd read it, shoving it back at her.

"I didn't ask for it," Maddy grumbled.

Mitchell ignored her as he turned away to stride down the corridor. Maddy saw Logan follow him and wondered if that had been a set up. Sasha came towards her with a grin. Yep, it had to be. It was too convenient Mitchell had been about when she'd received the message.

"I thought I told you not to plan any more outings," Maddy said when Sasha reached her side.

"It wasn't me."

"But I bet he had your help."

"It's so sweet. Like a modern day Romeo and Juliet."

Maddy snorted. "Yeah, right. Not even close."

"Oh, not with the dying part. Just the romance and the parents trying to keep them apart."

Maddy shook her head. "You're mad. Did you know that?"

"Yep. And quite proud of it too." Sasha grinned and patted Maddy on the shoulder. "Don't worry. In time you'll be as crazy as me, I promise."

"That doesn't make me feel any better."

Sasha laughed. "Give it time. It will."

Maddy sighed when the bell rang. It felt like her life was constantly being interrupted by bells. She couldn't wait until the Christmas holidays started. Not just because she'd be at her mum's place, the school year was way too long. She headed for her class, wishing the day was already over. No, wishing the month was already over. By the end of the day, she was still thinking the same as she waited with Mitchell for Sinclair to pick them up.

He pulled up as soon as the road was less busy and they hurried to the car. Maddy sat in the back seat, buckling up as she waited for her father's usual greeting. There was none. He indicated and pulled out onto the road, not speaking a word. Dread pooled in her stomach and she worried he'd found out Logan and Sasha had joined them at the Botanical Gardens.

She couldn't think of anything else he might have found out about.

During the drive Mitchell turned to glance at her twice as if to ask her what was happening. She didn't know. How could she? She'd never been able to understand her father and she wasn't likely to start understanding him this afternoon. All she could do was give a slight shrug of her shoulders in answer to Mitchell's silent question.

Sinclair didn't speak until they arrived home. "I want both of you in the kitchen."

Maddy reluctantly followed her father and Mitchell. She froze when she entered the kitchen and saw the crumpled piece of paper on the bench. She'd forgotten to take the article back to school to get rid of it after bringing it home to read. It had probably been found when the house cleaner had changed the sheets that morning and given it to her father.

"Well, Madeline?"

"I didn't know how to ask you about it. It was horrifying. I even wondered if it was a sick joke, but there were several similar articles online," Maddy said.

"Mitchell?"

Even though her father's attention was no longer on her, Maddy didn't feel the slightest bit relieved. If Mitchell ended up in trouble there was no way he'd be able to find a way for them to go out Saturday. She dreaded to think what would happen if he found out it was Sasha pulling his strings. "As if he knew. He would have told you immediately. I couldn't tell you so there's no way I would have been able to tell him." Maddy clasped her hands behind her back to prevent herself from grabbing the article.

"Is that true, Mitchell?" Sinclair persisted.

"I'm not sure what's going on, Dad." Mitchell looked from the crumpled piece of paper to Maddy and then back to Sinclair. "Is it important?" He gestured towards the paper.

Sinclair didn't answer the question, not even with a shake of his head. "You may go to your room. This only concerns Madeline."

When Mitchell hesitated, Maddy felt like yelling at him. She'd given him an out, why wasn't he taking it? He glanced over at her and then at Sinclair. With a nod, he left the kitchen.

"I'm very disappointed in you, Madeline."

She managed not to point out that it seemed to be a constant state for him.

"Haven't you anything at all to say for yourself?"

"What happened to Eleanor?"

"Focus on the situation, Madeline. You are so easily distracted."

"That's the only reason I kept the article. I wanted to ask you if I have a sister."

"One should never dwell on the past. How many times must I tell you that? It only holds you back in life."

"Sometimes the past impacts on the future and you need to know about it to understand current events." Or so her year eight history teacher had informed the class years ago.

"I think you might be spending too much time at your mother's place. What does she let you do when you're there?"

She wanted to yell at him. There was no way she was about to stay here full time. Holding onto her temper was an effort. "I tell you every little thing I do there." Maddy gestured to the article. "Is this why you don't trust me? I'm not Elspeth. I'd never make her choices. I wouldn't climb into the car with a guy I barely knew." Thoughts of getting into Davey's car came to mind and she firmly pushed them away. That had been different.

"Where did you get the article from?"

Maddy shrugged. It was probably best to stick to her original excuse. "I don't know. Someone put it in my locker at school."

"How many people at your school know about this?"

Maddy could only shrug again. "I don't know. I haven't told anyone." Technically she hadn't. Sasha had been the one to tell her and Logan had read the article when Mitchell had.

"You can see why I don't let you have the internet. It's full of rubbish. Sensational garbage with very little relationship to the truth."

"There's educational stuff on the net too."

"Talking of your education, I'm not sure this school is the best place for you."

Once again she fought against the urge to argue with him, lowering her gaze to the floor. She tried to think of how to answer him. "I like knowing I have a brother at school that I can turn to if I have any problems. It makes me feel safe." She almost crossed her fingers as she waited to find out if her comment would appeal to his old fashioned beliefs.

"Go to your room, Madeline. And don't bother coming out again tonight. You need to think about what you've done. I don't want this subject brought up again. And you are not to discuss this with anyone else. It is extremely rude to sneak around behind someone's back and research them. I really don't think this school is a safe enough environment if people are leaving this sort of rubbish for you and you need to rely on Mitchell to feel safe there."

Her jaw tightened, her teeth aching at how firmly they were clamped together. Angry words wanted to pour from her. She couldn't let them escape. With the mood he was in, nothing would help. She wanted to say she'd refuse to go to any other school, but knew he wouldn't listen. Nodding, she headed to her room. She alternated between worrying she'd have to change schools and mentally calling herself an idiot for leaving the article in her room. But there'd been so many things going on lately. She hadn't thought about the actual article since the moment she'd hidden it.

Chapter Twenty-Four

Seeing Mitchell standing at her bedroom window, looking out it, Maddy paused in her doorway. He turned to face her.

She wasn't in the mood for him to gloat. "What do you want?"

"Why didn't you tell him I knew?"

Great. He would have to ask that question. Telling him it was because she needed him to get them out of the house probably wasn't the best plan. She didn't want to make him angry. It wasn't the only reason she'd taken the blame. Partly she didn't think he should be in trouble for her idiocy. But she wasn't about to mention that and encourage him to blame her for the problem. "I never thought about how our parents' marriage affected you. I only focused on how it annoyed me."

"I don't need your sympathy."

So much for the plan not to make him angry. "I wasn't giving you any. I was trying to tell you I'm sorry I acted like I was the only one who was affected by the marriage."

"And you think this is going to make up for all of that?"

"Of course not. Look, do we have to do this now? Dad is likely to come and check on me at some stage so I need to look productive. And maybe then he'll relent and let me out for dinner."

"I should have said something–"

Maddy interrupted him. "And have both of us miss out on dinner and be on his hit list? Don't be an idiot."

"I'm not an idiot," Mitchell growled.

"Than stop acting like one."

Mitchell stared at her for a moment before he strode from the room. Maddy sighed and pulled out her schoolwork. She didn't think she'd be able to concentrate on it, but at least she could look like she was busy if her father checked on her. Hopefully this was the only punishment. She didn't want him saying she couldn't go to her mum's house the following weekend. She wouldn't survive if he did that. Concentrating on her homework was almost impossible, but she forced herself to work on it, not wanting detention. Then she definitely wouldn't be allowed to go to her mum's place.

By the time her father checked on her, she'd finished most of her homework. She looked up, seeing him standing in her doorway. He said nothing and finally walked away again. She checked the time and realised dinner was over. She sighed heavily. It looked like she'd be going to bed hungry tonight. She guessed it wouldn't be the last time and it certainly wasn't the first.

A sound at the door made Maddy turn again. It was Mitchell. He placed a square object wrapped in a disposable serviette on her desk.

"Try not to leave the evidence lying around this time." He gestured towards the serviette before hurrying from the room.

She stared at the white object before she opened it, smiling when she saw the large slice of chocolate cake. Within minutes she'd eaten it and rushed to the bathroom to flush the serviette down the toilet. Leaning her head against the wall, she watched as the small crumpled ball disappeared. If only she could get rid of the rest of her problems as easily. Closing the lid, she headed back to her room and got ready for bed. It was probably going to be a long night. As big as the slice of cake had been, it wouldn't stop hunger from waking her during the night.

The next morning, Maddy forced herself to eat breakfast slowly. She didn't want to get in trouble for eating like an animal. But she was starving after only a single piece of chocolate cake for dinner. She hated it when he sent her to bed without food. It didn't seem fair. At least it didn't happen too often.

Marla breezed through the kitchen, dropped a kiss on Sinclair's head and ran her hand over Mitchell's hair. "I'll see you Monday night."

"What?" Maddy stared at Marla.

Sinclair frowned. "Manners, Madeline."

"Where are you going?" Maddy tried to sound polite.

"I have a conference to attend. There are meals prepared in the freezer. They're labelled for each day. Only call if it's an emergency."

Maddy stared as Marla left the kitchen. "No one ever tells me anything."

"If it concerns you, then you will be told."

Maddy forced herself not to answer her father back. But it was hard. How could Marla being away for several days not concern her? Well, maybe Marla didn't have much to do with her, but still, she should have been told. Maddy continued to steadily eat her breakfast. She wanted to shovel it in just in case she upset her father again and he took it away from her.

As soon as she'd eaten, she got ready for school then went looking for Mitchell. He was in the backyard kicking a ball around. She watched as the ball bounced off a tree and he caught it.

"What do you want?"

"Did you know your mum was going to be away for the weekend?"

"She's my mum. What do you think?"

"Nope."

"Whatever." Mitchell threw the ball against the tree and caught it on the first bounce.

"I hate it when they do that. Do you think it'll make it harder to go out tomorrow?"

Mitchell tucked the ball under his arm. "How would I know?" He stalked inside and Maddy was left standing there alone.

"And aren't you in the best of moods today," she muttered under her breath. She was about to go after him and say a lot of uncomplimentary things when it hit her. She might complain no one had told her Marla would be away for the weekend, but Marla wasn't her mother. No, she was Mitchell's mother and she hadn't bothered to tell him either.

She sighed. How could she be mad at him when

he was probably mad at the world for giving him such pathetic parents? Why hadn't Marla at least told her own son? Because she couldn't be bothered? Or didn't she think he was important enough to know. Or maybe she'd forgotten to tell him. Who knew? She couldn't comprehend half of what her father did. She wasn't about to try and figure out why Marla did things. Another heavy sigh and Maddy headed for her room to get her schoolbag. She didn't want to feel any sympathy for Mitchell. She wanted to continue to be annoyed with him. Maybe these outings with him weren't a good idea. It was harder to ignore how something would affect another person when you got to know them better. And she had enough of her own problems without worrying about someone else's. She needed to tell Sasha the letters had to stop. Becoming friends with Mitchell wasn't a good idea.

* * *

Saturday evening Maddy sat at the kitchen table as her father fired one question after another at her. Until this moment, she'd enjoyed spending the day at the museum. It wasn't somewhere she would have gone out of her way to visit, but the four of them had actually had fun. Even Mitchell had lightened up a little. When they'd returned home, Logan had turned up half an hour later to make it look like he hadn't been a part of their group. She would have liked it if Sasha had been able to visit too, but she knew her father wouldn't let her have a friend over while she was grounded. At least Sasha had been able to go to the museum with them by telling her parents she was going shopping in the city.

Leaning against the kitchen bench, Mitchell ate the sandwich he'd made while Logan stood near him, arms crossed on his chest. Neither of them looked at her, but she knew they were paying attention.

Maddy nearly cheered when her father's mobile phone rang and he had to take a break from his polite interrogation. Within minutes she realised he was talking to Marla.

"What does it have to do with me that one of your speakers have pulled out at the last minute?" Sinclair turned his back to Maddy as he talked. There was silence for a moment before he spoke again. "And who is meant to take care of things here… of course I realise how important this is to you… they are only children… I know they'll be seventeen before I know it, but right now they're only sixteen… that doesn't mean- of course I do…I don't like that idea one bit… you know I do…are you sure you couldn't find a single person to watch them… I didn't realise they would be there… if you are certain… yes, I guess he always has shown a great deal of maturity for his age… organise it then." Sinclair put his phone away as he turned to look at them. His gaze came to a stop on Logan. "I know you'd planned to stay the night, but is it possible for you to go home instead?"

Logan shook his head. "My parents aren't there. I guess they thought this would be a good opportunity to get away for the night since I'm staying here."

Sinclair's lips thinned. A sharp nod for answer and he turned to Mitchell. "You are in charge. Maddy needs to be in her room after dinner." He slid a key off the set he kept in his pocket. "You will make sure that is where she stays. Check on her once at bedtime in case she needs to use the bathroom. Can I trust you, Mitchell?"

Mitchell took the key. "Of course you can, Dad."

"You have proven yourself to me numerous times. That is the only reason I'm going to trust you to take care of things here. Are you sure you're capable of looking after yourself and your sister?"

Mitchell nodded.

Sinclair stared at him a moment longer. "I hope so. You break my trust once and you will never regain it. I don't like the idea of leaving you home alone, but Marla couldn't find anyone to stay with you. She rang everyone. She needs my help and believes you're mature enough to handle this responsibly. You both better behave and not cause me any problems. If a prominent philanthropist, who is also a highly respected member of the business community, hadn't bought tickets for the event I wouldn't think of leaving you alone. This is what Marla has been working towards for the past couple of years." He strode from the room before anyone could speak.

Chapter Twenty-Five

"What just happened?" Maddy stared after her father even though she could no longer see him.

"I think your father is leaving us home alone," Logan said.

Mitchell stared at the key he held. "He left me in charge." Mitchell sounded as dazed as Maddy felt.

Logan lowered his voice. "You're not going to actually lock her in her bedroom, are you?"

"Stay out of it." Mitchell strode from the kitchen.

Maddy rose to her feet, knowing she couldn't stay in a room with only Logan.

"Don't tell me you're going to run off and leave me too."

Maddy nodded. "I can't stay in here with only you. Apparently I need supervision." She couldn't keep the bitterness from her tone.

"Maddy–" he reached for her.

"No. Not here. And not yet. I'll talk to you later."

Logan dropped his arm and nodded. "I'll find Mitch."

Twenty minutes later the sound of a horn caught Maddy's attention. She went to one of the windows and saw Sinclair clasp Mitchell's hand before he got into a taxi. Anger bubbled up in her that he hadn't bothered to say goodbye. She knew he was still angry about the article, but to treat her like she didn't exist was going too far. He'd let Mitchell see him off while she sat in her room. That was it. She wasn't going to be locked in. First she had to find out when her father would return. Striding from her room, she went to find her stepbrother.

He was in the lounge room arguing with Logan. They fell silent the moment she entered. She briefly wondered if she'd been the topic. "When does he get back?"

"Monday night. They return together. I can't believe he did that. I mean, I know Mum regularly talks him into things, but he left us here. Alone. I never would have thought he'd do that."

"I bet that philanthropist is someone who can help him with his career. That's the only thing that makes sense," Maddy said.

Mitchell shrugged. "I don't know. But he left me in

charge so you're not going to do anything to get me in trouble."

Maddy's hands went to her hips, her eyes narrowing. "I'm not going to let you lock me in my room."

"You know the rule when someone stays over."

Maddy shrugged a shoulder. "I don't care. You aren't my father and we're the same age. It isn't right you should be left in charge because you're a boy."

"Do I have to ring him and tell him you're not cooperating?"

"Think of it as payment for not getting you into trouble."

"Come on, Mitch," Logan said. "Don't be an idiot. There's only the three of us here. How about I control my impulse to have non-stop sex with your sister all night, if she controls hers."

"Ha, ha, you're hilarious," Mitchell said dryly. He looked over to Maddy as he slid the key into his pocket. "If anything goes wrong I'm not accepting responsibility for it. I'll be telling Dad you refused to go to your room."

"He'll want to know why you didn't ring him immediately. Don't be a pain. I'm not going to do anything that will make him rethink leaving us here for a couple of nights. I'm hoping he'll do it again."

"I doubt anything like this will come up again," Mitchell said.

Maddy shrugged. "It doesn't have to be the same situation. Just him leaving us at home without any adults to annoy us."

"So what are we going to do since we've got the place to ourselves?" Logan asked.

"Watch a movie?" Mitchell suggested.

"No way." Logan shook his head. "I saw what movies you have. You don't have a single decent one. Who picked all of them?"

"Dad."

Maddy laughed. "I think he was hoping they might improve our manners and the way we behave.

Logan shuddered theatrically. "I like my manners exactly the way they are."

"Since you seem to think you have all the ideas, why don't you suggest something," Mitchell said.

Logan grinned, then looked at Maddy again. "I don't think you'd like any of my ideas."

She returned his grin. "Oh, I don't know. Try me."

Logan laughed. He paused a beat before he turned to Mitchell. "There's a party we could all go to."

"No way. Are you insane?"

"Probably. Anyway, how would he know? Leave the phone off the hook and say you mustn't have hung it up properly and that way if he does ring it'll eventually say it's busy," Logan said.

Mitchell didn't hesitate. "No."

"You're wasting your breath. Mitchell won't do anything to upset Dad." Maddy's tone dripped disgust. "He's the perfect son, didn't you know? Daddy's perfect little prince."

"Yeah, right." Mitchell glared at her. "You should hear how many times Mum points out how perfect you are to me." His tone changed to mimic his mother. "Why can't you be as organised as Madeline? Why aren't your grades better? Madeline gets straight A's. Your room is a mess, you never see Madeline's room looking like that."

Maddy stared at him, her mouth gaping. "Me?"

"And you do it deliberately. Last week Mum told me to clean my room at breakfast. When I hadn't done it by dinner she pointed out how you'd cleaned your room without being told and why couldn't I get mine done?"

"I tidy my room every day or Dad uses it as an excuse not to let me visit my mum. That's the only reason I behave. One thing wrong and I'm grounded. And half the time it's your fault I'm grounded."

"Only because you're impossible to live with. Why can't you be like any other person our age? Then

Mum wouldn't constantly tell me to act more like you."

Maddy slowly shook her head. "I didn't know she did that." She smiled wryly. "Dad often tells me how much better than me you are. I guess our parents are completely screwed up."

Logan laughed. "Aren't most parents?"

Maddy stared at him thoughtfully. "I've never heard you say much about your parents. What are they like?"

"Ahh, I guess the best way to describe them is… umm… artistic."

Maddy grinned at how uncomfortable he looked. "And? What do they do for a living? Where are they tonight?"

Logan shrugged. "I wouldn't have a clue where they are tonight. Mum runs an art gallery and is as strange as some of the modern art she sells and Dad is a lawyer and that word is about as normal as it gets when I talk about him. He takes on all the interesting cases as he puts it. If you ask me, he only represents the certifiably insane. And he doesn't think or look like a lawyer. I guess it might help a little if he didn't keep letting Mum buy his clothes for him."

"I'd love to meet them. They sound cool," Maddy said.

Mitchell shook his head. "They sound odd to me."

"They are odd," Logan said. "But I actually think that's the thing I like most about them."

"Anyway, why would he want you to meet his parents?" Mitchell asked.

Maddy fought the feeling of panic that washed over her. She'd forgotten for a minute that Mitchell couldn't know about her and Logan. "He didn't say he wanted me to meet them. I said I'd like to. I like meeting interesting people. Better than being locked in a bedroom."

"You're not going to start about that again, are you?" Mitchell shook his head. "I've got better things to do than stand around and listen to you whine."

"How about a board game?" Maddy asked.

"I'd rather have a doctor appointment," Mitchell said.

"I haven't played one in ages. What do you have?" Logan asked.

"I'm going over to Rob's. You coming?" Mitchell asked.

"What about Maddy?"

"She can stay and answer the phone in case Dad rings. Tell him I'm having a shower and then ring my mobile and leave a message. I'll screen my calls," Mitchell said.

"I'll stay and play a board game with Maddy."

Mitchell stared at Logan like he'd done something completely crazy. "You're going to stay here? With Maddy?"

Logan shrugged. "Well you said you don't like board games. I feel like playing one." He turned to Maddy. "You never said which ones you have."

"Monopoly, pictionary, scrabble, snakes and ladders, chess." She shrugged. "I don't know all of them. You'd have to look."

"Maybe I should stay." Mitchell looked from one to the other.

"Suit yourself." Logan turned back to Maddy. "Where are they kept?"

"I'll show you." Maddy started to move away, but was stopped when Mitchell grabbed hold of her arm. "What?"

"I'm not going to play a board game."

"Fine. Don't." She pulled away from him.

Mitchell glared at her. "I can't leave you here alone with Logan."

"I'm sure he can resist throwing himself at me. It's not like I have to beat the boys off." Maddy put as much sarcasm as possible into her words.

"You're welcome to join us." Logan grinned. "I always beat my grandparents at monopoly when I was a kid. Guess it's time to see if I really was good at playing or if they were letting me win."

Mitchell hesitated. He looked from one to the other. "You better not do anything to get me into trouble." He glared extra hard at Maddy. "I'm going to Rob's house."

"Do I look like I care?" Maddy turned away, glad Mitchell had reacted the way she'd hoped. Her father made them play scrabble once a month to help improve their vocabulary. Mitchell hated every minute of it since he never got a very high score. He'd probably be gone at least an hour. It was fifteen minutes to walk to Rob's house and he wouldn't turn around and come straight back. She grinned when the back door slammed.

"What's wrong with using the front door?" Logan followed her to the cupboard the games were kept in.

"Security camera." She opened the cupboard. "Does it matter which game? We aren't really going to play are we?" She grinned.

Logan laughed softly. "I certainly hope not." He looked into the cupboard. "Monopoly is easy to set up to look like we've been playing."

"Do you know that from experience?"

Logan laughed, his eyes bright with untold stories.

"As if I'd answer that question." He shook his head slightly. "So… Monopoly?"

Maddy nodded and pulled the game from the cupboard. They headed to her room.

Chapter Twenty-Six

Maddy was kneeling on the floor, setting the game up when she realised Logan wasn't helping her. He remained in the doorway. "What?"

"I guess I'm worried that somehow your father will find out I was in here and you'll be grounded longer."

"Come in and shut the door. There's only two cameras set up in this place. One is on the front door and the other is in the backyard aimed at my window." She put a random amount of money out in two piles, placed a car and ship on the board and handed out some of the properties.

"I like the dog." Logan pointed to the piece.

Maddy made a face at him and swapped the ship for the dog. "Happy?"

"Come here and I'll be able to say yes." He held his arms open.

Maddy rose to her feet and willingly went into

them. "This weekend isn't turning out to be as bad as I thought it'd be."

Logan grinned. "It's looking pretty good to me too." His lips met hers and Maddy's arms went around his neck.

By the time Mitchell returned, they were making out on Maddy's bed. When Mitchell called out to Madeline, looking for where she was, they scrambled to their feet and tried to straighten their clothes as they sat on the floor around the board game.

"In my room," Maddy called out as she picked up the dice and rolled them.

Mitchell opened her door as she moved her piece. "Why's your door closed?"

"Because I can."

"That doesn't make sense." Mitchell took a couple of steps into the room.

Maddy handed the dice to Logan. "You get to do what you want when you want. I don't. So I closed my door because Dad wasn't here to tell me not to." She grinned. "Or that I wasn't allowed to have a boy in my room."

Mitchell glanced at her bed. "Maybe he's right about that."

"Don't hint, just spit it out." Maddy stared at Mitchell. She refused to back down.

Mitchell opened his mouth, then closed it again with a shake of his head. "It's after ten, maybe you should pack up the game and go to bed."

Maddy laughed. "Nice try. I plan on seeing daylight and sleeping in till lunch."

"Madeline-"

"What will it matter?"

Mitchell started to speak again and then closed his mouth. He looked at her for a moment and then shrugged. "I guess it doesn't. Fine. Go to bed when you want, but you better sound awake if Dad rings and wants to talk to you in the morning."

Maddy smiled. "Not a problem." She turned back to the game.

"I brought some movies back from Rob's with me," Mitchell said.

"Which ones?" Logan asked.

"A handful of action movies. I'll grab them."

Logan turned to Maddy as soon as Mitchell had left the room. "I thought for a moment he was going to comment on your wrinkled bed. I didn't even think about straightening it."

Maddy giggled. "I don't think we would have had time anyway." They both fell silent when they heard Mitchell's returning footsteps.

"Here." He walked over to Logan, handing him the pile of DVDs.

Logan glanced through them and held one up for Maddy to see. "What do you think?"

Maddy shrugged. "Sure. At least no one can cheat when watching a movie."

"I only see one cheat around here." With his back to Mitchell, Logan winked at her.

Mitchell took the movies off Logan. "I'll go and put it on."

"Can you make some popcorn too?" Maddy started to gather up the paper money.

"If you're lucky." Mitchell strode from the room.

Logan scooped up the playing pieces and put them in the tray. "Think we'll be lucky?"

"It doesn't matter if we aren't. We can make it ourselves. It doesn't take too long. We've got a popcorn maker." She slid the lid onto the game and rose to her feet with it. "Dad believes in healthy junk food and apparently that falls into the correct category. Although when he's around, he doesn't let us put anything on it."

Logan stood and tugged her back to him. His lips brushed across hers. "I guess there's no chance I can distract you from watching this movie."

Maddy's lips slowly curved into a smile. "I wish.

But I think Mitchell might have something to say about that. Not quite as easy to ignore as a messy bed."

"I guess I'll have to hope and dream."

"Hopefully I'll be at Mum's next weekend. You can distract me through a dozen movies then if you want."

Logan grinned. "Sounds good to me. I've got a TV and DVD player in my room."

"Friday night?"

"It's a date."

Maddy's smile became a grin. "Good." She headed for the board game cupboard, finding it hard to maintain a normal pace. She wanted to dance down the hallway and sing. Maybe throw in a few energetic jumps. But Logan followed her and she didn't want to be that obviously happy about the plan.

When the game was away, they headed for the kitchen where Mitchell made popcorn. Maddy grabbed the icing sugar from the cupboard and grinned at her stepbrother. "Aren't you a sweetheart?"

"Keep it up and I won't make it again," Mitchell grumbled.

Maddy laughed and gave in to the urge to twirl around. "Isn't life wonderful?"

"Yeah, right." Mitchell looked at her like she was a lunatic.

That only made Maddy laugh again. She grabbed the bowl of popcorn Mitchell had made and put icing sugar in it. She shook it slightly to mix it through.

"I wanted salt," Mitchell said.

"Then make another lot. I'll even get the salt out for you." Maddy turned to Logan. "What about you? Any special requests?"

Logan grabbed a handful and popped some in his mouth. He shook his head. "These taste good to me."

"If you ask nicely I'll let you share them." Maddy put the salt on the kitchen bench next to Mitchell.

"How nicely?"

Maddy recognised the look in Logan's eyes and grinned. If only. "I don't know. How good are you at grovelling?"

Mitchell held a bowl under the popcorn maker. "I can make you your own bowl."

"Don't ruin my fun." Maddy made a face at Mitchell.

"I hate to see someone grovel."

It took Maddy a second to realise Mitchell had joined in the joking. She grinned. "I bet it's only because he's grovelling to me."

Mitchell tipped salt into his popcorn. "I should

leave him to suffer through the indignities of grovelling since he ditched me to play a board game earlier."

"Hang out with a couple of guys or stay with a pretty girl. What else was I to choose?" Logan asked.

"Huh! Not much of a compliment coming from you. Isn't your definition of a pretty girl one that has a heartbeat?" Maddy asked.

Mitchell headed towards the lounge room. "Have you heard the rumours too?" He glanced at Maddy.

"The ones where he thinks he's a modern day Don Juan?"

"Now that's not fair, two of you picking on me. If I look pitiful from this treatment will that mean I get to have some of your popcorn?" Logan aimed for a pitiful expression.

"I'd have to grade that look as a fail if you're aiming for pitiful. The only thing pitiful about it is the attempt." Maddy pulled two lounge chair cushions out and dropped them onto the floor.

Logan grabbed another two cushions and put them near hers. "I guess I'll have to resort to grovelling. Although a demonstration would be helpful since I've never done it before."

"That wouldn't surprise me." Maddy held the bowl

out to him. "Don't strain yourself. I don't think I could watch what would be a painful attempt."

Logan grabbed a handful of popcorn and leaned back against the lounge chair. "You want to get the lights, Mitchell?"

Mitchell turned out the lights before he sat in an armchair, the bowl in his lap, the remote on the arm of the chair. "Are you ready for me to start the movie?"

Maddy placed the bowl between her and Logan. "Yep." She reached for a handful of popcorn and found Logan's hand already there. She looked up at him, the flickering light from the television showing his smile. She returned his smile, helping herself to the popcorn.

Minutes later, Logan's fingers linked through hers. She used her opposite hand to grab some popcorn as she glanced at Mitchell. His gaze was trained on the television and he seemed oblivious to the fact she held hands with Logan.

Logan's fingers tightened on hers and she turned her attention to him. She saw the question on his face and supposed he was asking if it was okay to keep holding her hand. Annoyance filled her. Why should Mitchell be able to have a girlfriend, go to parties and do what he wanted when she couldn't even sit in her lounge room holding Logan's hand while she watched a movie? Too bad if Mitchell objected. She smiled to let Logan know it was fine and moved a little closer to him.

Chapter Twenty-Seven

Maddy drifted off to sleep some time during the second movie. She slowly woke to the sound of a whispered argument. She tried to open her eyes, but it seemed like far too much effort. Either that or someone had glued them together. Next she tried to move, but there seemed to be nowhere to move to. Instead, she snuggled back into the warmth at her side.

"I'm going to watch another movie, so it isn't a problem," Logan said.

"She can't sleep with you," Mitchell hissed.

"Let her sleep. Why wake her?"

"Madeline was the one who said she was staying up till dawn," Mitchell said.

"So? You don't do everything you say, do you?"

"She's my responsibility."

Logan sighed. "Do you honestly think I'm going to do anything to her while she's asleep?"

"You always have a lot of girls hanging around you at school," Mitchell said.

"Exactly. Why would I have to wait for one to be asleep when I have plenty of awake ones throw themselves at me all the time."

There was a pause before Mitchell answered. "Sinclair would kill me if anything happened to her."

"Sinclair? What happened to calling him dad?"

Mitchell snorted. "He's not my father, even though he insists I call him that. Half the time he's not much better than the bastard who provided the sperm that made me. I know how to stay on his good side so I can keep my freedom."

"Then why do you make it so hard for Maddy to keep hers?"

Mitchell was silent for a few seconds. "You like her, don't you?"

"Are you trying to avoid answering the question?"

"Are you?"

Logan laughed softly. "I guess it depends on what you're going to do with the answer."

"Probably nothing. What can I do without getting myself into trouble since Sinclair sees you as my friend? I'd be in trouble for introducing you."

Logan ran his hand across Maddy's forehead, brushing her hair back. "Yeah, I like her."

She could hear the smile in his voice and it took all her control not to open her eyes to look at him. She concentrated on keeping her breathing even. It wasn't every day she got to hear other people's confidences.

"What's going on between the two of you?" Mitchell asked.

"As if Sinclair would let anything happen between the two of us."

"I wouldn't have taken you as the kind who'd let that get in their way."

"Normally I wouldn't, but I don't think Sinclair is rational where Maddy is concerned."

"I don't think he's rational about a lot of things," Mitchell said.

"Are you going to stand there all night and make sure we behave or are you going to bed?"

Mitchell paused. "Can I trust you?"

"About this you can."

There was another pause before Mitchell answered. "She's a complete pain, but Sinclair made her my responsibility. And not just this weekend. But at school too. I get the blame if she does something wrong and I don't tell him before he finds out. So if you do anything…"

Maddy wondered if he'd made some kind of gesture to finish that sentence. Like run his finger across his throat.

"I wouldn't hurt her."

"I think your definition of hurt and Sinclair's are very different."

"Go to bed, Mitch. If you're worried I'm going to have sex on the lounge room floor with her, you can forget it. First, I wouldn't start something knowing you could walk in on us at any moment and second, there are better places than on a floor."

"I'll be keeping an eye on you."

"I've already told you I won't do anything tonight."

"I wasn't talking about tonight, Logan. I'll be watching you at school too."

"Whatever, but I think it's going to be a very boring chore."

"We'll see."

Maddy heard Mitchell's footsteps move away. Then Logan sighed and moved about a bit as if he tried to get more comfortable. She heard another movie start and considered talking to him and letting him know she'd heard part of the conversation. Instead, she drifted off to sleep again.

She didn't know how long she had slept, but it seemed like minutes before she was being woken by Logan gently shaking her shoulder. She blinked as she tried to focus on him. "What?" Her word came out as a croaky whisper.

"I'm going to bed. Do you want a hand getting to yours?"

Maddy struggled to sit up and was glad of Logan's help. She yawned, her hand covering her mouth. "Yeah."

Logan helped her to her feet, putting his arm around her waist. "I thought you wanted to see the sunrise."

"Plan changed."

"Do you still want to see it?"

"How far away is it?"

"About now."

Maddy nodded.

"Come on then." Logan led her to the back door and they slipped outside into the cool morning air, avoiding the area near Maddy's window.

She leaned against Logan as she looked around. "It's so peaceful."

"Yeah."

They stood together as the sky lightened and the sun rose above the clutter of houses that blocked the skyline. The longer they stood there, the more noise filled the neighbourhood as people rose and more cars could be heard driving through the suburb. Maddy yawned, swaying slightly.

"Let's get you to bed," Logan said.

She tried to answer, but only managed to yawn instead. She smiled as they went inside and locked the back door behind them. "I might not have made it to daybreak, but I bet I could sleep until lunch."

Logan chuckled. "I'll definitely be in on that." They reached Maddy's bedroom. "Do I say goodnight or good morning?"

"How about sweet dreams?"

Logan's lips brushed hers. "Sweet dreams."

She watched him walk away before she turned and climbed into her own bed. She was still smiling when she fell asleep.

* * *

Maddy was woken by Logan pushing his mobile phone into her hands, grunting as she tried to focus. "What's happening?"

"Sasha. Tell her she's dead next time I see her." Logan dropped onto Maddy's bed beside her, closing his eyes.

Maddy put the phone to her ear. "Sash?"

"What took you so long? Listen, I think I might have your sister's phone number."

Maddy sat up, struggling to wake up properly. When Logan groaned at her movement, she pressed a finger against his lips to quieten him. She pulled her finger away when he nibbled at it. "How did you get it?"

"Long story. But the basic one is I owe this guy big time, and you will owe me for life."

Maddy laughed. "You're the best. So what's her number?"

"Have you got pen and paper?"

Maddy glanced around. Only on her desk. She wanted to groan at how far away that looked. "Ahh…"

"I'll text it to you on Logan's phone. And while I think of it, what are you lot all doing still asleep? Doesn't your father drag you out of bed at dawn?"

"Nearly." Maddy ran a finger lightly across the side of Logan's face but he didn't move. His eyes were closed. "I actually got to see sunrise this morning before I went to bed. Well, maybe I kind of fell asleep for a little bit before then, but I still got to go back to bed after sunrise."

"How on earth did you manage that?"

"Both Marla and my father are away this weekend."

"What!"

Maddy held the phone away from her ear for a second. "Send me deaf why don't you?" She let her finger trail across Logan's chin and over to his cheek. Still he didn't move or open his eyes.

"Why didn't you ring me and let me know? I would have been over there in a second."

"And what would you have told your mum you were doing?"

Sasha groaned. "I hate that she can't keep a secret."

"Me too." Maddy trailed her finger across Logan's lips. He nipped her finger and she yelped.

He opened his eyes and looked up at her with a smile.

"What's going on there?" Sasha asked.

"Uhmm, yeah."

"Okay. I think I can guess. I'll let you get back to it and I'll text the number straight away."

"Thanks, Sash."

"What are best friends for?"

Maddy hung up and stared down at Logan, who watched her. "Morning."

"What's going on here?" Mitchell asked from the doorway.

Chapter Twenty-Eight

Maddy's heart leapt as she struggled to think of what to tell Mitchell.

"Bloody Sasha rang on my phone wanting to talk to Maddy." Logan lifted his head enough to slide his arm under it. "So much for sleeping until lunch."

"How did she know you were here? And what makes you think a phone call is a good excuse to climb into bed with Madeline?"

"I guess Maddy must have told her last night. And a phone call that drags me out of a good sleep involves collapsing on the nearest comfortable spot." Logan closed his eyes. "Hassle me later. I'm tired." He rolled over onto his side, his back to Mitchell.

"Madeline."

She ignored the warning in Mitchell's voice. "Oh, go do something else other than annoy me. I'm tired too."

"Not until he's out of your bed."

"I'm too tired to do anything other than sleep," Maddy moaned. "You can come back and police me in a couple of hours."

"I'm not moving until he's out of your bed."

"Fine." Maddy pushed at Logan. "Get on the floor so I can go back to sleep."

"You're cruel and heartless." Logan grabbed her pillow. "I'm taking this with me." He rolled over and awkwardly dropped onto the floor.

"Happy? Now let me get back to sleep." Maddy flopped onto her stomach. She closed her eyes only to open them when a message came through on Logan's phone. She was tempted to ring her sister immediately, but decided not to. She guessed it would be best to wait until she was properly awake.

"That wasn't what I meant," Mitchell said.

"Shut up," Maddy mumbled at the same time as Logan groaned, "Go away."

Mitchell hesitated in the doorway before his footsteps could be heard retreating.

Maddy opened one eye and lifted her head a fraction. "He's gone if you want to hop back up here."

"Too tired to care where I sleep."

"Hmmm." Maddy let her head drop and relaxed back into sleep.

Next time she woke it was to someone tugging on her fingers that hung over the edge of the bed. She lifted her head and peered over the edge to be greeted by Logan's smile.

She grinned. "I can't believe you slept on the floor. Aren't you sore?"

"I've slept in worse places." He sat up. "What did Sasha want earlier?"

"Ohh." Maddy reached for Logan's phone and checked the message that had come through. She smiled when she saw the landline phone number. "To give me my sister's number."

"Really?" He reached out and took his phone back. "Are you going to ring her? You can use my phone."

"Yeah. As soon as I figure out what to say. What if she doesn't want to talk to me? I mean, my father wants nothing to do with her so she might be mad about that. At least I guess he wants nothing to do with her since he says not to dwell on the past." Maddy frowned. "This is so confusing."

"What do you want to say to her? Or ask her?"

"I don't know. What can I say to her? She must be twenty-four now." She frowned. "Or maybe twenty-five. What if she doesn't believe in dwelling on the past either? And why did my father write her off? Maybe she did something. I mean, I know he's strict, but there's usually a reason why he does things. Apparently."

"That's something you could ask Eleanor."

"What if-"

"Ring her, Maddy." Logan used the bed to pull himself to his feet and sat beside her. "I'll stay with you while you talk to her if you want."

"Thank you," she said softly.

When Maddy continued to sit there, Logan grinned. "You want me to dial the number too?"

Maddy shook her head. She could do this. What was the worst that could happen? Eleanor could hang up on her. And since she'd only learned about Eleanor recently, it wasn't like she was used to having a sister in her life.

Her fingers trembled as she dialled the number. The phone rang in her ear. Should she hang up? Was she ready to talk to her sister? Someone picked up the phone on the other end and it was too late to hang up.

"Hello?"

"Ahh... hi. Could I speak to Eleanor Dowling, please?"

"Speaking. Who is this?"

"Ahh… I'm… that is… you don't actually know me, but… well, I'm Maddy Dowling. My father is S… Sinclair Dowling." Silence stretched out long enough that Maddy thought Eleanor had hung up the phone. "Are you still there?"

"How old are you?"

"I turned sixteen in September."

"Mum heard something about him marrying not long after he left us. Why did you ring me?"

"Because I just found out about… ahh… well, you and…"

"Elspeth? The hell child? The biggest slut imaginable? She wasn't as bad as they made her out to be."

Elspeth wasn't? She struggled to think of a reply. "I didn't think she was. Most articles are exaggerated to make people want to keep reading them."

"Don't misunderstand me… what was your name again?"

"Maddy."

"Well, Maddy, I'm not saying she was a saint, but she wasn't anywhere near as bad as the media painted her. Sensationalising it made the papers and magazines sell better. So, what do you want from me?"

"I didn't know I had a sister."

"You're lucky. I've known and been blamed for having one most of my life."

"I'm sorry."

Eleanor sighed heavily over the phone. "I guess it's not your fault. So, what do you want? Surely you had some reason for calling."

"Dad says not to dwell on the past, but I guess I like to know. I'm not as good at letting go of it."

Eleanor laughed abruptly. "I don't think anyone is as good at shutting out the past and making certain nothing else can disturb them regarding it. Dad is an expert."

"Yeah, I'm finding that out. Not through him either. Through other people."

"How did you find out about me then if he never talks about us?"

Maddy hesitated. But what else could she say? "A friend and I were googling Dad online and came across some of the articles about Elspeth."

"It's okay. You can talk about her. I know what happened usually makes people worry about how I'll react when her name is brought up, but I'd rather talk about her than completely forget she once existed. She was my sister." There was a pause. "What do you want, Maddy?"

"I don't really want anything. Well, I'd like to meet

you, but I guess that's not possible since you live so far away."

"Do you still live in Brisbane? I heard Dad moved there when he left us."

"Yeah."

"I'll be up there next weekend. If you're serious about meeting me, give me a call Saturday. Have you got a pen? I'll give you my mobile number."

"Hang on." Maddy hurried over to her desk. "Okay." She wrote down the number and read it back.

"Is this your phone number? The one you're on?"

"No. But you can leave a message for me at this number. I don't have a phone you can call me on."

"What about your home number?"

"I can't give it to you. Dad would kill me if you asked for me. He ahh…" Maddy's voice trailed off. Should she say he acted like Eleanor didn't exist? That seemed harsh.

"It doesn't matter. You call me if you want to see me. I'm not going to chase after you."

"Okay."

"Bye."

"Yeah, see-ya."

Maddy handed the phone back to Logan and then looked at the number she'd written down. "Can I store this number in your phone? And can you take the piece of paper with you? I don't want to be caught with it."

"Yeah, sure." Logan took the paper off her. "So what did she have to say?"

"She'll be in Brisbane next Saturday. I was thinking I might catch the train back and meet up with her."

"I bet Davey wouldn't mind giving you a lift. Do you want me to come with you?"

"Would you? I mean, it's not that I'm scared to meet her, but well…"

Logan smiled. "I'd get to spend the day with you. Why wouldn't I want to come?"

Maddy's worried expression became a smile. "Good."

Logan entered the number into his phone. "So I guess you wouldn't be able to keep my phone number since you can't even keep your sister's."

"Tell me and I'll try and remember it."

Logan handed her his phone. "It's on the screen since I don't always remember it."

Maddy read the number over several times before she handed the phone back to him. She watched him put it in his pocket.

"Don't tell me you know it already."

Maddy laughed. "Not hardly. I'll read it over a lot

more times before I do." Her gaze dropped to his lips when they curved into a smile.

"What are you thinking about?" Logan's voice was barely a whisper.

"I'd rather show you than tell you." Maddy leaned forward. He met her half way. She was so lost in the kiss and the feelings swirling through her that the first she knew Mitchell had entered her room was when he shouted.

"Madeline!"

She jerked away from Logan then glared at Mitchell. Anger rushed through her and she slid across the bed so she could lean against Logan. "What?"

"Dad would kill you."

"He's not here. Are you going to tell him?"

"I should." Mitchell glared back at her.

"Mitch–"

Mitchell glared at Logan. "I trusted you. Aren't there enough girls chasing after you? Did you need to add the ice princess to the list?"

Maddy jumped to her feet, striding forward. "He hasn't done anything wrong."

Logan followed Maddy. "Don't get her into trouble, Mitch."

"How would you like it if you weren't allowed to

do anything?" Maddy jabbed a finger at Mitchell's chest. "Would you like to be locked in your room? How about never going to a party? Or what about not being able to hang out with your mates? Tell me if you'd enjoy sitting in your room day after day doing schoolwork and making sure everything is spotless. You'd hate it!"

Mitchell took a step back. "Madeline-"

Maddy followed him, her finger still jabbing at him. "You think your life is so hard because occasionally your mum complains you aren't as well behaved as me? It's not. Try being the one who always has to behave. I swear if you dob me in for one more thing I'll make sure your life is as miserable as mine."

"And how do you think you'll manage that?" Mitchell's expression changed from startled to smug. "Dad doesn't believe a word you say about anything."

Maddy smiled. It was a smile that would have sat well on a shark that had seen the perfect prey. "Don't try me, Mitchell. I know I can do it, but I'd be a fool to tell you how so you can prevent it."

Logan dropped an arm around Maddy's shoulders. "And I'll help her with it."

"So that's the way it's going to be, huh? You're her friend, not mine."

"I shouldn't have to choose between you. But if you make me, I won't side with you if you're going to deliberately get Maddy into trouble for something she hasn't done. She has enough crap to deal with. Do you honestly think it's right that Sinclair locks her in her bedroom when you have friends over?"

Mitchell shrugged. "He's a little strange. It's not like he beats her."

"Words can leave a mark that will last longer than those left by a fist," Logan said.

"You're full of shit." Mitchell stalked away.

Logan raised his voice so Mitchell could hear him. "Only because you know I'm right." He turned to Maddy when Mitchell kept walking. "Are you okay?"

"Just angry."

"So what will you do if he dobs you in?"

Maddy shook her head. "I'm not about to tell you either. It's not nice and you probably won't like me very much afterwards."

"I might surprise you."

"I'm not about to risk it. How about breakfast?"

Logan grinned. "Fine, I'll let you change the topic. But only because I'm starving."

Chapter Twenty-Nine

Maddy met up with Sasha at lunch on Monday morning. They hadn't had enough time to talk before school, not when Sasha had shown Mitchell the new message. Maddy had thought he might explode when he read it. She'd nearly grinned when she'd taken the page from him. 'Sensible of you to listen to the puppet master. You'll never know when I'll give the next order. It could be tomorrow, it could be next week, it could be next year. You are under my control.'

Once Mitchell had stopped swearing and stormed off, the bell had rung. And since Maddy had spent morning tea with Logan, this was the first chance she'd had to catch up with her best friend. Sasha stared at her in amazement as she filled her in on all the details, including her conversation with her sister.

"I wish I could have come over Sunday. Stupid

family outing. I miss out on all the fun. I would have loved to have been there when you said that to Mitchell. I bet he went into shock. Especially since he's been able to lord it over you all this time."

"I know, but I suddenly lost the plot. Or maybe I found it. He made me so mad and then I had the best idea. Or maybe I should say the worst since it's so far from nice it's evil."

Sasha grinned. "Tell me all about it. I'm dying of curiosity here."

Maddy's grin matched Sasha's, even though the thought of ever going through with her threat made her feel uncomfortable. "I'll tell my father he tried to make out with me."

Sasha burst out laughing. "Sinclair would kill him. He wouldn't even give him a chance to deny it."

Maddy nodded. "I know. We'd be going to his funeral within days of me telling him. But don't you warn Mitchell. I don't want him to be able to warn Dad in case I have to use it. And I will use it if I have to. I'm sick of being so powerless all the time."

"At least you get to go to your Mum's this weekend and won't have to put up with Mitchell, Marla or Sinclair. Unless of course you end up grounded."

"Apparently they're going away this weekend so I

doubt it. Mitchell is sleeping over at Rob's. He isn't speaking to Logan anymore."

"What does Logan think about that?"

Maddy shrugged. "I wouldn't have a clue. He mentioned it this morning. But I guess he wouldn't have mentioned it if he wasn't bothered by it. I meant to ask him, but," she grinned, "we had other things on our minds."

Sasha laughed. "I can imagine."

"I bet you can. Especially the couple of times I've seen you with a boy." Her grin remained firmly in place.

"Talking of boys…"

"Yeah?"

"You know those two hot ones that hang out with Mitchell…"

"Yeah."

"I'm going to a party with the cutest one this weekend."

"Which one is that?"

"Seriously, no wonder I have to worry about you. The one with the dark curly hair of course. He's be-lud-ee purrrr-fect."

"That good, huh?"

Sasha hit her on the shoulder. "You're a horrible friend."

Maddy laughed. "Go on then. Tell me all about him."

"His name is Dale and he has the most gorgeous eyes. They make me squirm when he looks at me. I can't wait until Saturday. It's ages away."

Sasha spent the rest of lunch telling Maddy all about Dale and grumbled over how little time they had to talk when the bell went. Maddy headed for her next class, agreeing with Sasha. Saturday was ages away. She both looked forward to and dreaded it. What if her sister changed her mind and didn't come to Brisbane after all? Or what if she came to Brisbane, but decided she didn't want to meet her. She tried to push it from her mind, but thoughts of Eleanor kept intruding. Often at the worst possible time. Like when she had to answer her father's interrogation that night about the weekend. She was tempted to interrogate him about his weekend, but she didn't want to risk any future groundings. Just because he needed her to go to her mum's this weekend, that didn't mean he couldn't take away other weekends.

* * *

Friday afternoon, Maddy trailed after Mitchell as he walked out the gate. He looked like he wanted to hit something so she did the smart thing and didn't talk to him. An arm slipped around her waist and she turned to face Logan. "Can't you wait?"

Logan shook his head. "Nope." He gave her a quick kiss. "Later."

Maddy smiled as she watched him walk away. It wasn't often she was glad her father wasn't waiting for them the moment school ended, but today would have to be one of those days. And she hoped no one her father talked to had been about either. She probably should be more careful, but she was sick of watching every single thing she said and did.

"What would you have done if Dad had seen that?" Mitchell demanded.

"He's too predictable to turn up early."

"When I figure out what you've got to tell him, you will pay."

"Shut up, Mitchell."

Mitchell glared at her. "You think you're going to be able to keep hiding everything from him? You should be more careful what you do in public. Someone might take a photo that Dad would be very interested in."

"If I go down, you do too. Think about that, darling brother." She tilted her head to the side and looked him over. "What's got you so mad? Anyone would think your best friend has died."

"He's sick."

"What?" Maddy frowned, trying to figure out what he was going on about.

"Rob is sick. I've got nowhere to stay this weekend. And that bastard who can't keep his hands off you reckons he's going away this weekend."

"He is. To his grandad's place."

"He's really going away?"

Maddy nodded. "If he didn't want you to stay at his house, he'd just say, not make up stories."

"It wouldn't surprise me if he did. Not after he used me to get close to you."

Maddy was surprised at the bitterness in Mitchell's voice. "He didn't try and apologise Monday so he could continue to stay close to me. For some stupid reason he wants to remain your friend."

"Yeah, well, at least Rob has never tried to use me."

Maddy stared at him. Should she tell him Rob had once tried to hook up with her one weekend? No, definitely not. He hated her enough as it was.

"What? What did Rob do?"

Maddy shook her head. "Nothing. I was just wondering where you're going to spend the weekend since our parents won't be there."

Mitchell looked at her suspiciously before he shrugged. "Maybe they'll let me stay at home on my own. They did last weekend. There's no way in hell I'm going to Grandma's. I hate it there."

"Why?"

Mitchell opened his mouth then closed it. He shook his head and looked away. "It isn't important."

Maddy couldn't prevent a smile from forming. "Why do I think it's one of the reasons why I hate staying at Dad's house?"

Mitchell turned abruptly back to Maddy. "Because she hovers over me, asks me stupid questions and won't let me out of the house. Happy?"

Maddy stared at him. "No."

"Why not? I thought you'd be thrilled I got to put up with what you do, even if it's usually only once a year."

Before Maddy could answer, Sinclair pulled up. She walked quietly to the car and sat in the back. Mitchell followed and opened the front door.

"Rob is sick."

Sinclair glanced over his shoulder and indicated before he pulled out onto the road. "Then I guess you'll have to stay at your grandmother's place this weekend."

"Can't I stay home? I did last weekend when you weren't there."

"Madeline was there too. And no, you can't. There is no reason why you can't stay at your grandmother's. She wouldn't have been able to cope with two of you, but she always says she doesn't see enough of you."

Maddy nearly laughed. Yeah, right. The old bat hated her and wouldn't have had her there if someone had paid her a million dollars.

"But, Dad-"

"Mitchell, the subject is ended. When we get home you'll ring your grandmother and ask if you can stay the weekend. I'm sure she'll be delighted to have you."

Maddy opened her mouth before she could stop herself. "He could come to Mum's with me." She immediately started mentally arguing with herself. What are you saying? You idiot. He's going to ruin the weekend. But she couldn't let him go to his grandmother's. Not after he'd told her how much he hated it. Besides, they were almost friends now. Okay, so maybe that was an exaggeration, but she still couldn't leave him to suffer through the weekend at his grandmother's. She'd always known getting to know him was going to cause her problems. It looked like they were well and truly starting.

"That is very thoughtful of you Madeline, but I can't expect your mother to put up with an unexpected guest."

"I'll ring her. I'm sure she won't mind. It's not like we have anything planned for the weekend. He won't be interrupting anything. I think Mum said something about cooking a roast dinner Saturday night, but she always cooks extra so that wouldn't be a drama."

"Madeline, I don't think you understand the situation clearly," Sinclair said.

"I do. It won't bother her in the least that he's your stepson if I say I'd like to bring him with me this weekend. She always asks after everyone. When I told her how Mitchell looks out for me at school she said she'd love to meet him one day." Maddy felt like patting herself on the back for her last inspired comment. Instead she kept her expression neutral.

"I don't know, Madeline."

She could hear the hesitation in her father's voice. "Actually, I think Mum would appreciate having him there. He could walk with me to get the paper Sunday morning so Mum could have a bit of a sleep in rather than having to get up early to go and get it.

She doesn't like me to go out on my own. She always says that even though it's a quiet neighbourhood you just never know." You are so full of it, she told herself, struggling to maintain her neutral expression.

"Well… if Joscelin is fine with it, I can't see a problem. I'm glad to see the pair of you getting along so well. Marla had worried there might be problems between the two of you. I'm pleased to see they never eventuated."

Maddy stared at her father. How could he be so blind? Instead, she smiled. "It's nice having a brother to look out for me."

"Yeah. It's good not to be the only kid in the family." Mitchell glanced back at her, his expression blank.

She wondered what he was thinking, but it wasn't like she could ask him while her father was in the car. They fell silent and the moment they arrived home, Maddy made her way to the phone. Her mum was surprised by her request, but didn't mind. Marla was full of instructions about how Mitchell was to act and to make sure Joscelin didn't gain the wrong impression about how he'd been raised.

When they both finally boarded the train, Mitchell steered them to a seat surrounded by vacant seats and stared at her. "Why?"

Maddy played the innocent. "Why what?"

"You could have let me go to my grandmother's. Why didn't you?"

Maddy shrugged as she unplaited her hair to let it fall around her shoulders. She ran her fingers along her scalp, glad to have it down.

"Come on, Madeline. Tell me. What? Did you feel sorry for me? I don't need your pity."

"Get over yourself, Mitch."

Mitchell's mouth dropped open when he turned to see Logan standing in the aisle.

Chapter Thirty

Maddy smiled and shifted to the empty seat across the aisle. She leaned against Logan when he sat down beside her. "There's no flies to catch around here, Mitchell."

Mitchell closed his mouth and leaned across the aisle to talk to them. "What's going on? I thought you were going to your grandad's place."

"I am." Logan grinned. "His house isn't far from Maddy's mum's place."

Mitchell looked from one to the other. "How long have you known each other?"

"The last school holidays." Maddy paused. "I'm trusting you to keep this weekend to yourself." She grinned. "You're about to meet my alter ego."

Logan laughed. "Lighten up, Mitch." He turned to Maddy. "By the way, why is he here with you?"

"My stupid conscience kicked in and wouldn't let

him suffer the same treatment I endure." Maddy wrinkled her nose.

Logan dropped a kiss on the tip of her nose. "Pesky thing, a conscience." He grinned. "But that's okay. The more the merrier. You still up for a party tonight? And can I get a lift to your place? We can catch a taxi from there to my place."

"Ah, I guess so."

"What happened to your mum not letting you out of the house on your own. Not even to get the Sunday paper?" Mitchell was clearly confused.

Maddy laughed. "I know, I thought that was inspired." She sobered. "And if you dare take one pic this weekend of me doing something Dad would freak out about, or in clothes he'd find inappropriate, you will die a slow and painful death. Or you will wish you were dead before I'm through with you."

"Who are you?" Mitchell stared at her.

She smiled. "Maddy. Madeline is a stuck up snob who I really can't stand."

Logan wrapped his arm around her. "I don't know about that. I've found her to be rather friendly on occasions."

Maddy laughed. "You sure that was Madeline?"

"Hmm, I don't know. It certainly looked like her.

Neat and tidy school uniform, hair tied back in a plait."

"I knew you two were meeting somewhere at school," Mitchell exclaimed.

Maddy rolled her eyes. "Of course we are."

"Where?"

"As if I'm about to tell you that if you haven't figured it out." She shook her head. "One idiotic action allowed per day. I think I blew my quota for today."

"Are you saying you regret inviting me?" Mitchell demanded.

Maddy shook her head again. "Not yet. Don't do something to make me regret it. There's a lot happening this weekend that I don't want Dad to know about."

"Like what?"

"I'm going back to Brisbane tomorrow to meet up with my sister."

Mitchell was left gaping at her again. Twice he tried to speak. Twice he failed to say anything. He slowly shook his head. "Eleanor?"

Maddy nodded. "Yeah. Did you want to come too? Logan and his cousin are coming with me."

"Are you insane? Dad would kill you if he found out," Mitchell exclaimed.

"I know. Are you going to tell him?"

"How can I?" Mitchell swore. "You did this deliberately, didn't you?"

Maddy frowned. "What?"

"Make sure I'd owe you."

"No. I'm sick of us being enemies. You're angry with the wrong person. I'm not the one who has you jumping through hoops. That's your mum. It's not my fault she uses me as an example. That's exactly what Dad does to me. It's almost like they don't want us to be friends. Have you ever considered that? If we aren't friends then we'd be less likely to keep each other's secrets."

"Are you sure your father would think like that, Maddy? It sounds awfully devious," Logan said.

Maddy nodded. "Yeah. It's exactly the way he'd think."

Mitchell nodded too. "Yeah. And Mum is as bad as Dad. They both love to manipulate other people. Including each other."

Maddy recalled the secrets she'd heard the night Mitchell had stayed. "You don't have to call him Dad when you're not around him. I'm not about to go running to him and tell."

Mitchell stared at her for a moment then smiled wryly. "I guess we've got so many secrets to keep for each other it'd be stupid to run to him with something so minor."

"Does that mean we have a truce?" Maddy asked.

Mitchell hesitated. "I guess."

"What about us?" Logan asked. "Are you going to stop treating me like I don't exist?"

"I guess."

Logan held out his hand and Mitchell shook it. Logan grinned. "Are you going to complain if I make out with your sister?"

"Logan!" Maddy elbowed him.

Mitchell laughed. "I'll go back to pretending you don't exist for a while so I don't have to watch the revolting display." He sat back in his seat and pulled out his phone.

"That phone better not take a single pic tonight," Maddy warned.

Mitchell glanced over at her and grinned. He faced the phone at her. "Smile."

"You better be joking."

Logan placed a hand on her cheek and turned her to face him. "Ignore him." His lips met hers and Maddy easily forgot Mitchell sat nearby.

When they pulled in at their station, Maddy led the way off the train. She threw herself at her mum and hugged her before turning to Mitchell with a grin.

"This is my brother, Mitchell."

Mitchell sent her a look of annoyance before he turned to Joscelin and held out his hand. "Thank you for having me this weekend, Mrs Dowling."

"Oh please, not so formal. Joscelin will do."

"Mum, do you mind if Logan comes home with us?" Maddy slid her arm around Logan's waist as she spoke.

"Does he want a lift to his place?" Joscelin strode towards the car, all of them keeping pace with her.

Maddy shook her head. "Nah. We're going to a party tonight. I wanted to grab something to eat and get changed into real clothes first."

Joscelin glanced towards Mitchell. "Do you think that's wise?"

Maddy laughed. She knew she'd have to find time to explain about Mitchell's change of heart. She'd complained often enough about him getting her into trouble over the years. "He's cool Mum. Honest. He won't say anything. We can have a normal weekend."

"Okay. I guess you'd know best." Joscelin didn't look convinced.

Maddy hopped into the car and gestured towards the front seat for Mitchell. She dragged Logan into the back with her. Once they were all buckled and headed for home she said, "Mitchell knows he'd never be able to sleep again for fear I'd retaliate if he said anything to Dad."

"Ahh…" Mitchell looked uncomfortably between Maddy and Joscelin.

"Don't look so worried, Mitchell. Maddy has a terrible sense of humour. She's pulling your leg." Joscelin glanced in the rear view mirror. "What are your plans for this weekend,?"

"Party tonight, Brisbane tomorrow to meet my sister Eleanor and Sunday with Grandma."

"You know that's not the sort of news you should be telling me when I'm driving," Joscelin said dryly. "Did you actually say Eleanor will be in Brisbane tomorrow?"

"Yep."

"Maddy, have you really thought about this?"

"Mum." She drew the word out.

"I don't want to see you make more trouble for yourself."

"It's fine, Mum. I've got it all under control." Or as much as possible.

Joscelin pulled up at her house. "I really hope so." She turned off the ignition. "Show Mitchell to the spare room, Maddy. I've got to dash out and do a few things. If you're gone before I'm back, have a good night."

Maddy nodded. "I'll scribble Logan's number down and put it on the fridge in case you need to get in touch with me. I won't be with Melissa and Carrie tonight." Her mum usually rang her on one of their phones if she needed her when she was out. She'd have to try and find time to catch up with them soon or they'd think she hated them.

"Thanks. I had planned to ask you about that." Joscelin smiled. "I hope you've put me down for some of your time in your busy schedule."

Maddy's eyes widened. "You mean to say picking me up and dropping me off isn't enough?"

Joscelin laughed. "Go have some fun."

Maddy grinned. "You always get Sunday night, Mum."

"Before I forget, Maddy, your cousins will be expecting you to email them during the holidays. Their mums said they were excited they'd be hearing from you."

"Thanks, Mum." She got out of the car and stood between Logan and Mitchell as she waved her Mum off. "Come on. I need to get changed before someone around here sees me in these revolting clothes."

She let them into the house, showed Mitchell to the

guest room and raided her wardrobe. As soon as she'd showered and dressed, she applied makeup and added some gold highlights to her hair. Luckily they'd wash out easily. She slid on a couple of bracelets and went to look for the boys. She found them in the kitchen.

Chapter Thirty-One

"Aren't you the domestic one?" Maddy grinned at Logan, who was making toast to go with the boiled eggs sitting in eggcups on the table.

Logan turned to face her and whistled. "You clean up all right, Maddy."

"All the compliments are going to go to my head." She moved closer to him.

"Maybe I shouldn't give you so many then."

Maddy laughed and lightly kissed him. When he tried to hold onto her, she pulled away. "You'll wreck my lipstick."

"Then you better bring it with you if you hope to have any on you at all tonight."

Still grinning, she sat at the table. "Waiter. I'm hungry."

Logan put the buttered toast on the table in front

of her and leaned close. "I'm going to make you pay for that comment."

Maddy glanced up at him. "I'm sure we can think of something you'll be happy with." A strangled noise made her look over at Mitchell who was seated across the table from her. "What?"

He shook his head.

"Come on, spit it out."

Mitchell shook his head again. "I'm speechless."

Logan laughed. "Leave him alone. It takes a bit of getting used to seeing how you can be two completely different people." He glanced at his watch. "Now eat up. The taxi will be here in fifteen minutes."

"Yes, sir," Maddy said disrespectfully.

"I'm keeping tally," Logan warned.

"You want interest too?" Maddy cut open her boiled egg and sprinkled salt on it.

"Absolutely." Logan sat at the table beside her.

She grinned before cutting up her toast and having a bite of it with egg. Her grin faltered as her gaze was drawn to Mitchell. He better not say anything to her father. Pushing her worries aside, she focused on eating and bantering with Logan.

When they arrived at Cliff's house, the party was well and truly going. Logan shouldered his bag and wrapped an arm around Maddy. "I need to ditch my bag in my room."

"We'll go and lose ourselves in the crowd." Maddy grinned, pulling away from him. "I'm sure I can find someone to dance with while you desert me."

Logan grabbed her around the waist and drew her back to him. "I'll find you." He kissed her thoroughly before he let go of her and headed into the house.

Maddy turned to Mitchell and grabbed his hand. "Come on."

Mitchell allowed himself to be dragged inside, still speechless. He looked around at all the people, shaking his head when someone with a handful of cold beers offered him one.

"Come and meet Davey." Maddy dragged Mitchell through the crowd. "Hey, Davey."

"Maddy!" Davey threw his arms around her and gave her a noisy kiss on the cheek. "You ready to ditch that cousin of mine and go out with me instead?"

"Very tempting." Maddy grinned at him before turning to Mitchell. "Mitchell, this is Davey, Logan's step cousin. Davey, this is my stepbrother, Mitchell."

Davey kept an arm around Maddy's shoulder as he held out a hand to Mitchell. "Nice to meet you. Want me to grab you a drink?"

Mitchell shook his head. "I'm fine. Thanks."

"Mind if I steal your sister for a dance?" He turned slightly and raised his hand in the air. "Hey, Lindy." He waved the blond girl over who turned at his shout. He turned back to Mitchell. "Lindy will keep you entertained." He grinned at Lindy as she reached them. "This is Mitchell. Logan's mate from Brissie."

"Cool. Brisbane is awesome." Lindy grabbed his hand. "Come and dance." She dragged him into the crowd.

Mitchell sent a pleading look in her direction but Maddy grinned at him and waved. She turned to Davey. "Aren't I important enough to offer a drink to?"

Davey laughed. "Dance first?"

Maddy willingly followed him to where everyone seemed to be dancing. She didn't get the drink since Logan soon found her and stole her away from Davey. Several hours later, Davey found them on the back verandah snuggled on one of the cane lounge chairs. He handed over a glass that had droplets of condensation on it.

"What is it?" Maddy took the glass.

Davey grinned. "Have a drink and find out."

Maddy sniffed it.

"Here." Logan took the drink and had a mouthful.

"Rum and lemonade." He held the glass out to Maddy.

She took a tentative sip. Swallowing it, she breathed in sharply. "Is there any lemonade in it?"

Davey laughed. "All I get are complaints. First I didn't offer you a drink, now it's not the right mix."

Maddy took another sip.

Logan brushed his lips across her cheek, stopping near her ear. "You don't have to drink it."

"I know." She took another sip. After hassling Davey to get her the drink it didn't seem right to immediately ditch it.

Davey leaned against the verandah rail. "A handful of us are going for a swim. You pair want to join us?"

"I haven't got anything to wear." Maddy put the glass on the floor beside the leg of the chair.

"No one will mind."

Maddy made a face at Davey. "I will."

"I've got some old board shorts I grew out of ages ago. They might fit you. And you can help yourself to one of my shirts," Logan offered.

"Well…" Maddy hesitated. She was tempted. She hadn't been swimming at night in ages.

"Your brother is joining us."

"How is Mitch doing? I haven't seen him all night," Logan said.

"Lindy is looking after him." Davey grinned. "She's got a thing about Brissie. Don't know why myself. Who'd want to live in the city when you can step out your door and be on the beach." He waved his hand towards the straggly grass that eventually gave way to sand. "So? Swim?"

"Maddy?" Logan turned to her, waiting for an answer.

"Sure. Why not?"

"Great. I'll see you pair down there." Davey pushed away from the rail. "Don't get distracted now." With a grin, he was gone.

"Where are the board shorts?" Maddy asked.

Logan held up a set of keys by a single key. "I'll get them and meet you in my room. Pick out a shirt while you wait for me." He rose to his feet. "There are some white ones in there."

"Very funny."

"I can hope."

Maddy rose to her feet. "Go get the boardies." She walked away from Logan, ignoring his laughter. Once inside, she had to thread her way through the crowd, which seemed to be bigger than before. She unlocked Logan's door when she reached it and slipped into the cool room. A lamp cast a soft glow across the room from beside the bed and she made her way to the drawers to look for a shirt.

"A white one," she muttered. "Not likely." Spotting a black shirt with the image of a band printed on it, she threw it on the bed and closed the drawer. She was picking up a book that sat beside the lamp when the door opened. Expecting Logan, she dropped the book back into place and turned, ready to speak. It was Mitchell.

He closed the door behind him. "Is this what you normally get up to at your mum's place?"

Maddy grinned. "Basically."

He shook his head. "No wonder you never want to come home to Brisbane."

"It's not Brisbane I object to, it's staying with Dad. He's too unrealistic. I mean, I get where he's coming from with Elspeth and everything, but he shouldn't punish me for what happened to her."

Mitchell was silent a moment. "Are you going swimming?"

Maddy nodded. "Yeah. I'm borrowing some clothes from Logan. I actually thought it was him when you came in here."

"It's not dangerous, is it?"

Maddy shrugged. "It's not like there's no moon. It's fairly bright outside. And not everyone has been drinking heavily so there should be enough people to rescue anyone that might risk drowning."

"I always thought you were this boring, perfect…" he waved his hand, trying to find the right word. "Robot."

Maddy laughed. "Nope. Not me. I've learned to act a part when I'm around Dad. The perfect little princess he expects me to be."

"Have you thought of acting as a career? I never would have known." Mitchell slowly shook his head.

The door opened again. Logan entered and turned to Mitchell, carrying a pair of board shorts. "Did you find the boardies?"

Mitchell shook his head.

Logan strode across the room and opened a drawer. He grabbed a blue pair out and threw them to Mitchell. "Catch." He gestured towards the door. "Bathroom is towards the right."

"Thanks." Mitchell closed the door softly behind him.

Logan handed the pair of board shorts, he'd brought into the room, to Maddy. "Need a hand?"

"Nice try." She grinned and gave him a shove towards the door.

He grabbed another pair of board shorts and left her in the room alone, locking the door behind him.

Maddy stripped off and pulled on the board shorts and shirt. They were both a little large on her, the shirt more so than the shorts, but they would do. She folded up her clothes and left them on the desk. Then she went looking for Logan. Anticipation curled through her. She loved swimming at night. As Sasha said, it was be-lud-ee purrrr-fect.

Chapter Thirty-Two

Saturday morning Maddy reluctantly dragged herself out of bed at eight. She took the piece of paper she'd written Eleanor's number on last night, before she'd left the party, and went to the lounge room to ring her sister.

The house was quiet and she wondered if she was the only one awake. She picked up the phone and stared at it. Her stomach did some acrobatic feats as she sat down, wondering if she was doing the right thing. Maybe she should forget about her sister. If her father found out-

She cut that thought off immediately. She would not go down that road. If she worried about her father's antiquated views, she'd never do a single thing. She dialled the number before she could change her mind.

"Hello."

"Eleanor?"

"Yes. Is this Maddy?"

"Yeah." She didn't know what else to say then began to feel uncomfortable as the silence dragged on. Finally she blurted out, "Are you still in Brisbane today?"

"Have you got a pen and paper? I'll give you the address of where I'm staying."

Maddy grabbed a pen and scribbled the address on the piece of paper with the phone number. "What time will you be there?"

"From one onwards. What time do you think you'll get there?"

"One?"

"Fine. I'll see you then."

"Okay." Maddy barely managed to speak before Eleanor hung up. She put the phone down and sat staring at it. One o'clock. Her stomach did another flip.

"Hey."

She turned to see Mitchell in the doorway and was glad to have something to take her mind off her plans for the day. "Hey." She grinned. "How did you like the party?"

"Do you mind if I don't go with you today? Lindy invited me around to her place."

Maddy laughed. "That's okay. I wouldn't want to get in the way of your love life."

Mitchell looked troubled. "She's actually a year older than me."

"And?"

"I don't know. It's kind of odd, I guess."

Maddy grinned. "Who cares about ages? Go for it."

"She wants to move to Brisbane when she finishes school this year. She's applied to a few unis there."

"Neat."

"Yeah. It is." Mitchell glanced at the phone. "Do you mind if I give her a call? Sinclair always checks the phone bill to see who I ring. I don't think I could explain this call. Not since we're meant to be spending the entire weekend sitting around your mum's house. There's no way I'd have a chance to meet a girl doing that."

Maddy handed the phone over. "Help yourself." She rose to her feet. "I've got to get ready. I have to be in Brissie by one."

"Good luck with meeting your sister."

"Thanks." Maddy left Mitchell to his phone call, almost relieved to be able to leave the room. It was odd to have such a conversation with him. She guessed it would take time for them to get used to not being enemies.

Maddy had a shower and washed her hair, which smelt of seawater. She grinned as she remembered their late night swim. She loved late spring and summer evenings. They were warm enough for swimming. She hoped she'd get the chance to have a night swim when there was a full moon. Not too much longer and it'd be the Christmas break. There should be time for one then. She frowned as she tried to figure out how long until school ended for the year and finally decided it must be about a month. She grinned at the thought of all those weeks without putting up with her father's rules. And she'd be able to get her learner's license that her father didn't think she was capable of holding. The first party Melissa and Carrie threw in the school holidays was going to be a celebration of her return to freedom. Which reminded her, she still had to find time to catch up with them. But right now, she needed to get ready to go to Brisbane.

After her shower, Maddy had breakfast with Mitchell. They were barely finished eating when first Lindy arrived to pick up Mitchell followed by Logan and Davey. Maddy scribbled a note to her mum to let her know she could reach her on Logan's mobile phone if she needed her. She put it on the fridge under a magnet.

Not feeling very sociable, Maddy refused the offer of the front seat and hopped in the back. About a quarter of the way to Brisbane, Logan gave up trying to get her to join in the conversation.

"That's it, I'm getting in the back with you." Logan glanced around at the traffic before undoing his seat belt.

"No! If we end up in an accident you might die," Maddy exclaimed.

"Davey wouldn't dare have an accident. He knows I'd have to come back and haunt him if he did." Logan slid between the two front seats and dropped onto the back seat.

"Having my own personal ghost might be cool," Davey said.

"Buckle up," Maddy ordered and then glanced at Davey. "And you, don't have any accidents."

"I don't know. I even get bossed around in my own car," Davey grumbled good-naturedly. "And not only do I get treated like a chauffeur, now it's plain to see I am one since all my passengers are in the back."

Logan snorted. "If a chauffeur was anything like you, they'd be bankrupt within a week."

"I get no thanks. I'm completely unappreciated."

"Yeah, yeah, better go eat some worms," Logan said with a distinct lack of sympathy. He put his arm around Maddy. "If your sister doesn't like you we promise to hate her too."

Maddy smiled weakly and leaned against Logan. "Thanks."

They fell silent again, but this time Maddy didn't feel removed from the situation. The warmth of Logan at her side and his fingers linked with hers reminded her she wasn't alone. Although none of that helped when Davey pulled up in front of an old Queenslander that had been recently painted. Her stomach went back to doing acrobatics and she began to regret the lunch she'd eaten when they'd stopped at a service station along the way.

Davey turned in his seat. "We're here." He paused to have a look at Maddy. "If you're going to be sick, think you can do it out of the car?"

Maddy unbuckled her seat belt. "Well, I know who to go to when I'm looking for sympathy."

"Not me." Davey grinned. "If you're looking for fun, I'm your guy. Sympathy," he shook his head. "Not my thing."

Maddy slid out of the car, closely followed by Logan. Davey joined them before they reached the steps. She paused at the bottom of them. Logan's fingers tightened on hers and she looked at him.

When he smiled, she tried to return it, but didn't have much luck.

"You don't have to do this," Logan whispered.

Maddy nodded and forced herself to use the stairs. She did have to do this. Her worst fear was that her father would somehow find out. Well, she wasn't going to let that stop her. She knocked hard on the door.

A man with dark hair and a small beard opened it. "Yeah?"

"Is Eleanor here?"

"Are you Maddy?"

She could only nod in answer. Why couldn't Eleanor have answered the door?

The man looked behind Maddy. "Who's with you?"

"My friends Logan and Davey." She pointed to each of them in turn.

He gave a short nod and stepped back. "I'm Matt." He gestured them inside. Maddy looked around. The house looked like it was still being renovated and there was mismatched furniture and furnishings.

"El," the man bellowed as he led them down a dark hallway.

Eleanor appeared in the doorway ahead of them. Her gaze brushed over the boys then remained on

Maddy. She was a bit shorter than Maddy, was slight of build and fair-haired with her father's blue eyes.

"Come in and sit down. Does anyone want anything to drink? Tea, coffee, soft drink, fruit juice?" Eleanor hovered in the doorway as she gestured towards the table.

"Water would be nice." Logan sat at the table and tugged on Maddy's hand to get her to sit beside him.

"I'll have water too," Maddy said. Decisions, even minor ones were currently beyond her.

"Coffee," Davey said.

Eleanor started towards the fridge when Matt put a hand on her shoulder. "You sit down. I'll get the drinks."

"Was there much traffic on the road?" Eleanor asked.

"Not too bad," Maddy said.

"I'm surprised there's not more. You'd think everyone would want to head to the beach. It looks like it's going to be a perfect day for hitting the beach," Eleanor said.

Traffic and now the weather? Maybe Eleanor was as nervous as she was. Maddy eyed her sister carefully. It was hard to tell. Maybe she was awkward with all new people. "Thank you," she said when Matt put a glass of water in front of her. She searched around for something to say. "Do you come to Brisbane very much?"

Eleanor shook her head. "Matt was transferred up here a couple of months ago. I came up to see him then. It was my first time here."

"Oh." Maddy couldn't think what to say next.

"What work do you do?" Davey took a sip of his coffee and looked over to Matt.

"Financial consultant." Matt grinned. "Don't worry, I won't hassle you to look at portfolios."

Davey gestured towards the house. "Who's doing the renovating?"

"I am. My weekend project." Matt remained standing, resting his hand on Eleanor's shoulder.

"Do you mind showing Logan and me around?" Davey asked.

Matt shrugged. He looked down at Eleanor who smiled weakly. He turned to Davey and nodded. "Sure. Most of the stuff I've done is in the backyard."

Maddy watched them leave the room before turning to Eleanor with a slight smile. "I'm afraid Davey isn't very subtle."

Eleanor's smile came more readily this time. "I guess they got sick of sitting around listening to the silence."

"I don't know what to say. I mean, I do, but it's

just a tonne of questions. I don't want to sit here and interrogate you like Dad does to me whenever I go anywhere."

"At least he'll let you go places. In the end, I wasn't allowed out of my room."

"Barely. I'm allowed to go to my mum's and school. Oh, and the occasional supervised educational excursion."

"I guess he hasn't changed." Silence stretched out again before Eleanor spoke. "Ask your questions. It's got to be better than sitting here staring at each other, trying to figure out what to say."

Chapter Thirty-Three

Maddy giggled nervously as all the questions tumbled through her mind. It took her a few seconds to decide which one to ask first. "Why did he stop having anything to do with you?"

"He found out I'd covered for Elspeth a few of the times she went out when she wasn't supposed to. And sometimes I said she was with me when she was actually with friends. The first he heard about some of the things Elspeth used to get up to he lost his temper. It's the only time I can ever remember that happening."

"I've never seen him lose his temper."

"I think I prefer that to the day he stared me in the eyes and said it was just as much my fault she was dead. I believed him for a long time."

"Weren't you only six when it happened?"

Eleanor nodded. "That didn't matter. I was

responsible for my sister's death." A wry smile formed. "It took me a lot of years to realise I wasn't."

"How did you cover for her?"

"I'd stay in our cubbyhouse and pretend I was in there playing with her. Sometimes she'd take me to the park and leave me there and I'd have to tell our parents she'd stayed with me the whole time. That was scary. I hated when she did that. I'd hide until she came back. It wasn't often. Most of the time they weren't at home and didn't realise she was out."

"You were only little. How could she leave you in the park like that?"

Eleanor shrugged. "She never thought of the consequences. She was like a butterfly. Nothing held her attention for long and she never thought about what her actions might cause to happen. It was like she wasn't capable of living past the moment she was in. I loved her. Everyone did. You couldn't help loving her." Eleanor's voice trailed off and her gaze lost focus. "She was so clever. She was good at learning stuff off by heart, sometimes after only reading it once. She had a hard time at school to start with. She started school really young and struggled to fit in for years. In the end she learned that if you don't want to be bullied, you have to be the bully."

"How did she manage that?"

"Her best weapon was words. And she was so good at manipulating people. Sometimes she reminded me of Dad, especially when she was focused on something. She'd be completely ruthless. Whatever it took, it didn't matter as long as she got what she wanted. At times like that she wasn't being deliberately nasty to people. It was that she was so focused on her goal she couldn't think of anything else, including how it would affect others. Or even herself." Eleanor paused. "Especially herself."

"Is that why she died?"

Eleanor shrugged. "Who knows why she got in the car with him. He was a fair bit older than her. She never slept with any of them. The papers all said she slept around. It was like they were trying to find a way to blame her for getting killed. It wasn't her fault. No matter what she did, she didn't deserve that. Everyone believed what they read, even Dad. And he never forgave her for it, even though it wasn't true. Elspeth loved having boys worship her, being the centre of attention. Something she never got at home. She told me one day it made her feel like she was someone. Like she existed. That sometimes she felt like she'd fade away to nothing because no one knew she existed. I knew she was talking about our parents."

"So Dad never kept you at home all the time?"

Eleanor shook her head. "No. He was barely there himself. He was trying to establish himself. And Mum was a neurotic mess. Dad kept telling her she needed different cosmetic surgery to improve herself. It got to the stage where she couldn't even sleep without tablets. And because of the sleeping tablets they labelled her a drug addict. It wasn't until Elspeth died that Dad changed. He was always strict, but after that, he paid attention and made sure we did as he said. Even Mum. He ordered her around too, blaming her and me for everything that had happened. It became unbearable."

Maddy took a sip of her water, trying to find the right words. Unable to think of what to say, she was relieved when Eleanor continued to speak.

"We were hounded by the press. It was awful. It didn't help that the neighbours hated us and told a lot of lies. Elspeth had upset them a few too many times. So had Dad. He'd called their teenage daughter a whore because her boyfriends never lasted longer than a month. I guess they were happy to have the opportunity to pay us back."

"What did they do?"

"They spoke to the reporters. Told them all sorts of lies with just enough truth to make it seem correct.

They told them Elspeth often came home drunk. Which was a lie. She never drank."

"Didn't the articles say she had alcohol in her system when they found her?"

"Yes, but she wouldn't have drunk it. He must've made her. She hated not being in control of a situation so she never drank." Eleanor paused. "But everyone believed the worst. No matter what I said they still believed it." She fell silent again.

Maddy struggled to think of something to say. Words seemed inadequate for what Eleanor had endured.

"One day a reporter came into our backyard and tried to interview me while I was playing on my swings. All I remember was his big white teeth and the microphone he kept shoving in my face. The cameraman was perched on the top of the fence, recording it all. Dad came outside and, without a word, grabbed me off the swing and carried me inside. I was terrified. Not only of the reporter, but of Dad. He'd looked so angry as he locked me in my room. After that, he barely let me out again."

"I know how that feels. I'm sick of my room." So many things now made sense. She wanted to ring her father and tell him she wasn't Elspeth. Demand that he let her have a life. But she'd never be able to speak those words to him. She didn't dare.

"How did you manage to come over here if Dad doesn't let you out?"

"This is the weekend I'm at Mum's. She's more laid back."

"They're not together anymore?"

Maddy shook her head. "Dad married again. Marla. She has a son my age. Well, he's a few months older."

"His third marriage. Wow. How long?"

"A few years."

"What's our brother like?"

Maddy stared at her for a moment. She hadn't thought about the fact Mitchell would be stepbrother to both of them. "His name is Mitchell and I guess he's okay. He used to dob me in for everything I did wrong, but he's getting better. He didn't like me because his mum kept using me as a positive example of the way he should behave."

Once the questions had started, they managed to keep them going. They compared childhoods and in particular their experiences with their father. They talked about friends and other family members and Maddy learned Eleanor would move to Brisbane in the New Year.

When the boys rejoined them, they were talking

easily and soon included them in the conversation. Late afternoon arrived before Maddy was ready for it and she was saying goodbye to her sister.

Logan hopped in the back of the car with her and grinned at the look his cousin gave him. He slipped an arm around her shoulders and pulled her against him. "How do you feel?"

"Relieved. She's nice."

"How long is she here for?"

"She flies home tomorrow and won't be back until early next year. She has a lot of stuff to finish sorting out before she moves here. She only flew here this morning because she had a job interview." Maddy yawned. "I can't believe how tired I am."

Logan bent his head closer to her ear. "And here I'd planned to watch DVDs in my room with you."

Maddy turned her head and met his gaze. A shiver went through her as she remembered talking about him distracting her through a dozen movies. That plan had changed when Davey had rung Logan and suggested a party Friday night. Her gaze was drawn to Logan's lips as a smile formed.

"I take it you like that idea?"

Maddy's lips parted to speak, but her mouth had gone dry at the look in his eyes. She nodded. The drive back to Logan's house was going to take forever. The sound of the car stereo being turned up startled her. She glanced towards Davey who appeared to be focused on the road.

Logan laughed softly. "Guess he's worried about what he might hear."

"There won't-" Maddy started to argue the statement, but Logan's lips met hers and she forgot what she wanted to say as she pressed herself as close as the seat belt would allow.

Chapter Thirty-Four

Sunday morning Maddy stumbled out of her room at nearly nine. She yawned and stretched. Still yawning, she headed for the kitchen to get a drink. She stubbed her toe on a chair, that wasn't pushed under the table properly, and swore. A knock at the back door startled her. Swinging it open, she was surprised to find Mitchell there.

Maddy frowned. "What are you doing out here?"

"Lindy dropped me home an hour ago. I knocked but no one answered."

"You must have barely missed Mum. She said she'd be going out at eight this morning." Maddy stepped back to let him in. "Davey and Logan are picking me up in an hour and we're headed to the beach for a couple of hours. You want to come?" She couldn't stop another yawn.

Mitchell shook his head. "Nah. Lindy will be back for me at lunch. I need a few hours sleep."

Maddy grabbed the water bottle from the fridge and eyed the distance she'd have to walk to get a glass. "Make sure you're back by four. We need to catch the train this arve. Dad would be so unimpressed if we missed it." She took a mouthful out of the water bottle.

"Pig."

Maddy grinned and wiped her mouth on her sleeve. "I'm so tired that every centimetre looks like it'd take an hour to walk it." She returned the bottle to the fridge.

"When did you get home?"

Maddy shrugged. "About three I think. I wasn't exactly watching a clock."

"What were you doing then?"

Maddy turned away when she felt her cheeks warm. "Watching movies."

"You didn't…"

Maddy turned and caught the uncomfortable expression on Mitchell's face. "None of your business."

"You did!"

"So?"

"Madeline! Are you crazy? If you get pregnant Sinclair won't just kill you, he'll kill me too."

"We used condoms."

"Condoms! As in more than one!"

"Oh, leave me alone, Mitchell." Maddy started to leave the kitchen.

Mitchell grabbed her by the arm. "You've not long turned sixteen. I can't believe-"

Maddy pulled away from him. "It wasn't like we planned to. Anyway, what did you and Lindy get up to last night?"

"That's different."

"Why?" Her hands went to her hips and she glared at him.

"Because…" Mitchell couldn't meet her gaze.

"Because you're a boy?"

"Madeline-"

"No! I have just as much right to do whatever you do."

Mitchell started to speak again, but sighed heavily instead. "Be careful."

Maddy's anger evaporated at the concerned expression she saw on his face. "Of course."

Mitchell grinned wryly. "I can't believe we're having this conversation."

Maddy laughed. "Not one I would have ever

expected to have with you." She became serious. "We cool?"

"Yeah." Mitchell nodded. "Thanks for inviting me this weekend."

"Make sure you warn Lindy that if she ever meets our parents she isn't to mention how she met you. Get her to say you met in Brisbane or something."

"How do you keep it all straight?"

"Easily. Nothing happened." She smiled. "At least not as far as Dad is concerned.

"What do we tell him happened this weekend?"

"That's why you need to be here at four. We'll go over the official story of the weekend."

"Okay." Mitchell yawned. "I better get some sleep. Otherwise I'll need to come up with a reason why I'm so tired. It's not like I can tell Sinclair I was out all night."

Maddy grinned. "Or what you were doing." She laughed at the hint of colour that filled Mitchell's cheeks. "I tell him there was a cat fight that woke me up and I had trouble getting back to sleep after it. Or one of the neighbours was away for the weekend and their dog barked all night because they weren't there."

"You have an answer for everything."

"Not quite, but I've had a lot of practice at it." She

glanced at the clock, swearing. "I've got to get ready or I'll still be in my nightie when Davey and Logan get here."

"Somehow I don't really think Logan would complain."

Maddy made a face at him before she fled to the bathroom. She was still throwing her swimming gear in her backpack when they arrived.

"Did you sleep in?" Logan snagged her around the waist and drew her close for a kiss.

"Considering I hardly got any sleep, is it any wonder?"

Logan lowered his voice. "Are you complaining?"

Maddy glanced away. "No," she said softly.

"Good." He kissed her again.

Maddy reluctantly pulled away. "Give me a couple of minutes then we can go."

"We don't have to. If there's something else you'd rather do…"

Maddy recognised the look in his eyes and grinned. She lightly pushed him away from her. "Behave. We're going to the beach. And then to visit our grandparents after lunch." The weekend was never long enough.

* * *

Maddy sat in the back of her mum's car, her fingers entwined with Logan's as they talked over the official story for the weekend again. Mitchell sat in the front, on an angle so he could talk to them.

The last thing she wanted to do was return to her father's house. She had to keep reminding herself the Christmas holidays would start next month. Then she'd be able to be herself and hopefully spend more time with Logan instead of stolen minutes in the storerooms at school.

When they pulled up at the train station, Maddy threw her arms around her mum. "I'll miss you."

"Love you, Maddy."

"Love ya." She started to pull away but her mum held her a moment longer.

"Be careful."

Maddy looked confused and Joscelin glanced towards Logan. Maddy smiled. "Everything is fine."

"I hope so. You're only young. There's time enough to get serious later on."

"Don't worry, Mum." She hugged her again before pulling away, glad Logan and Mitchell had moved closer to the train station to give them some privacy. "I'll see you in a fortnight."

Joscelin nodded and waved as they headed into the train station without her. They didn't have long to wait before the trained pulled in. It was more crowded than the one had been on Friday night. They ended up squished on a seat that was meant for two, Maddy between the boys.

"Is it often like this?" Mitchell glanced around the crowded carriage.

"Sometimes." Maddy shifted in her seat trying to get more comfortable.

Logan's arms went around her. "Here." He pulled her onto his lap.

Maddy laughed. "Trust you to turn a crowded train to your benefit."

Logan's mouth brushed her ear. "Aren't you more comfortable?"

Maddy turned her head to look at him, her smile an answer.

"Cut it out you pair. I'm sitting here too you know," Mitchell grumbled.

"You're only annoyed you won't see Lindy for ages." Logan pulled Maddy back against him and rested his cheek against hers.

"She's going to drive to Brisbane next weekend. If she can find somewhere to stay I'll see her Saturday and Sunday. Otherwise she'll only come for Saturday," Mitchell said.

"She can stay at my place," Logan said.

"Won't your parents mind?" Mitchell asked.

Logan shook his head. "Nah. If they're about next weekend they probably won't even notice her. But you've got to do me a favour too."

"I knew there'd have to be a catch." Mitchell looked disgusted.

"It's only a little one. I want you to break Maddy free."

"That might not be possible," Mitchell complained.

"If it's possible, will you do it?" Logan asked.

Maddy slowly grinned. "I think I can come up with an excuse."

Logan laughed softly. "We should always ask the expert of duplicity."

Maddy wrinkled her nose. "Stop showing off with big words."

"The downside of having a lawyer for a father. He sometimes forgets he's not in the courtroom." Logan grinned. "So what's the plan?"

"Lindy's Mum won't let her go out for the day with Mitchell unless he can provide a chaperone. And she thinks a sister would be the perfect person."

Mitchell gaped at her. "You've got to be kidding."

"It fits Dad's thought pattern perfectly. Tell him we're going on a picnic at Southbank. A nice family orientated day out. Then we'll go over to the art gallery and have a wander through. The bonus of an educational excursion thrown in too. It's not like we have to go there. We can drive by Southbank, dash through the art gallery and still gain enough info to spin him a great story. Then we can do what we want."

"The way your mind works is scary." Mitchell stared at her. "It really makes me wonder what plan you have for me if I step out of line."

"You never know, I might even tell you one day."

"And me?" Logan asked.

Maddy turned enough so that her lips brushed his. "No."

"That's not fair."

"If I tell Mitchell and he wants to tell you, then fine."

Logan kissed her briefly before he turned to Mitchell. "You'd tell me, wouldn't you Mitch?"

"Not if you're going to sit there making out the whole trip."

Maddy laughed at the look on Mitchell's face. "You wouldn't be complaining if Lindy was here."

Mitchell opened his mouth to argue when his

phone rang. He pulled it out and looked at the display. A grin instantly formed. "Hey, Lindy."

Logan whispered in Maddy's ear. "Does this mean I can kiss you now he's distracted?"

Maddy laughed. "Do you ever think of anything else?"

"Yep."

Maddy's smile faded when she saw his expression. Her heart sped up and speech was momentarily impossible. She finally managed to speak. "Typical." Her lips met his and her hand rested against his heartbeat. It was as fast as hers. How was she going to survive with only stolen moments for the next two weeks?

Chapter Thirty-Five

The next week dragged for Maddy. Monday she told Sasha about her weekend and had to shush her when she squealed. They weren't sitting very far from Mitchell, Logan and their friends and she didn't want them to wonder what she was talking about.

Wednesday Maddy ended up with detention because Logan distracted her in Mr Gallo's class and Mitchell surprised her by covering for her. He rang Sinclair and asked if he could pick them up later because he wanted to practice with his teammates after school and Maddy had agreed to sit in the stands at the oval.

Maddy and Logan were nearly sprung in the storerooms on Thursday and decided it might be best to stay out of them since more props for the end of year play were being completed every day. That made Friday go even slower when Maddy couldn't spend time alone with him.

Then it was Saturday and Maddy was glad her father expected them to rise early as she didn't think she would have been able to sleep in. Sinclair gave them the third degree over breakfast and Maddy put together a picnic basket as soon as she had eaten. She draped the picnic blanket over the basket and frowned as she mentally ticked off what she'd packed. Props were always important. She only wished she didn't need to wear the revolting dress her father thought was the appropriate garment for someone her age. Yeah well, not in this century it wasn't. Or the last one either for that matter.

A knock on the door signalled the arrival of Lindy and Maddy had to suppress a smile when she saw the conservative dress she wore. She could see her father was extremely impressed by the quiet, well-spoken girl who arrived. With a lot of smiles and last minute orders, Sinclair said goodbye to them.

Maddy got in the back seat of Lindy's small, pale blue sedan while Mitchell put their gear in the boot. Lindy started the car the moment they were all in it and headed down the street.

"I'm desperate to get out of this dress." Lindy

glanced at Maddy in the rear view mirror. "Doesn't it annoy you wearing such outdated clothes?"

"It could be worse," Maddy said.

"Impossible," Lindy muttered.

Maddy laughed. "He might expect me to wear a veil and be covered from head to toe. At least I can show my ankles."

"What a bonus." Lindy pulled over onto the side of the road.

Before Maddy could ask what was happening, Logan opened the back door and got in the car. Maddy grinned. "I was wondering when we'd pick you up."

Logan slid close to her and buckled up. "It wasn't like I could turn up at your place. I don't think that would have impressed your father."

"No, I think it might have actually had the opposite effect." Maddy linked her fingers through Logan's.

He bent his head near her ear. "Not much of a greeting."

"Really? And what exactly were you hoping for?" Maddy tried to hold back her smile, but she was unsuccessful.

Logan grinned. "I might follow your example and show you instead of tell you." His lips met hers, only breaking away to laugh when the comments from Mitchell got too much.

Maddy tried to glare at Mitchell, but her smile ruined it. "You're lucky I don't have anything to throw at you. Besides, I bet if Lindy wasn't driving you'd be doing the same."

"Where are we going to first?" Lindy asked.

"Southbank. Then over to the art gallery. After that, do you want to go to my place?" Logan asked.

Everyone agreed and they headed for Southbank. When they arrived, Maddy took note of everything that was happening so she could realistically describe the day to her father and then they rushed through the exhibitions at the art gallery. She memorised the names of a couple of artists that produced traditional work so she could mention them later.

They arrived at Logan's house around ten o'clock and he unlocked the front door and waved them in. "Welcome to my humble home."

Mitchell snorted, walking inside with the picnic gear. "Yeah, if you compare it to a palace."

Logan grinned. "I know, terrible, isn't it? I swear my parents should have provided me with a castle to live in. I'll probably never recover from the emotional scarring."

Mitchell put the basket on the floor and dropped

the blanket on top of it. "I think your problem is more mental."

"Do we get a tour?" Maddy glanced around.

"And where do I crash?" Lindy carried an overnight bag.

"Come on. I'll show you to one of the guest rooms." He took them upstairs and showed Lindy and Mitchell the room. He pointed to a closed door further down the hall. "That's my room. Knock when you're ready for the grand tour."

Lindy nodded. "I've got to change into my usual clothes first."

Logan tugged on Maddy's hand, and with a grin, led her to his room. She looked around and found it fairly similar to what he had at his grandad's house, even to the colour scheme. She smiled when she noticed his built-in-wardrobe was partially open and there was a tangle of clothes on the floor and DVDs scattered all over the shelf the television sat on. Yep, nearly identical to his other room.

Seeing where Maddy looked, Logan slid the doors closed and leaned against them with a smile. "Leave my mess alone."

"What if I wanted to watch a movie?"

"Then I'd open the door again. But I don't think you do, you're just being a pain."

"Really?" Maddy took a step towards him. "Are you sure about that? Maybe I actually want to see an entire movie when I'm with you. And not just the beginning and the menu."

Logan took the last step that separated them and wrapped his arms around her waist. "Really?"

"Possibly."

The conversation ended when Logan's lips met hers. And nothing else was said until Mitchell knocked on the door and called out to them. Logan swore while Maddy half laughed and half groaned.

"He has terrible timing." Maddy pulled away from Logan.

"Can't argue that." Logan unlocked his door, swinging it open.

Mitchell grinned at them. "I'm not interrupting anything, am I?"

Logan started to swing the door shut again. Maddy stopped him. "We can't stay in your room all day."

"Want to bet?" Logan asked.

"No. Come on. You offered us a tour of the house. I'm sure that will take a while." Maddy linked her arm through Logan's and he reluctantly stepped out of his room.

The tour finished at an in-ground pool and outdoor entertainment area. It was all under a roof and the landscaping consisted of tropical trees and shrubs. Maddy stared at the pool longingly. It was certainly a hot enough day for a swim, but she had no swimmers with her. Even though they could easily have stayed in the air-conditioning, it wasn't the same as having a swim.

She sighed and turned her back on the pool. "It's nice out here."

"I might be tempted to move in." Lindy ran her fingers along the edge of a large pool table. "Anyone for a game?"

"Count me in," Mitchell said immediately.

Logan shook his head. "Maddy and I are going for a swim."

"But–" Maddy started to protest.

"Check out the dressing room." Logan gestured towards the closed door of the garden shed sized building.

Maddy glanced between Logan and the building before she decided to see what was in there. She closed the door behind her and smiled when she saw his board shorts she'd worn last weekend. Beside them was a white shirt and the black one she'd borrowed. She couldn't stop the burst of laughter that escaped as she moved the white shirt to one side.

Changing her clothes, she headed back to the pool.

She shook her head with an expression of mock disappointment at Logan.

He grinned. "It was worth a try. It might have been my lucky day."

Maddy rolled her eyes. "Dream on."

"Oh, I will." He ran towards the pool and tucked up his legs as he jumped in.

Maddy turned her head away when water splashed everywhere. The moment she saw him surface, she joined him in the pool, trying for an equally large splash.

The day passed quickly. Once she'd finished swimming, Maddy showered, washed her hair and dried it. No one would know she'd been swimming by looking at her. For lunch, they spread the picnic blanket out under a shady tree and then retreated to the air-conditioned media room to watch a movie. Maddy didn't see much of the movie and she had a suspicion that no one else did either. When it was time to return home, Lindy changed her clothes before they headed out to the car.

Maddy's feet dragged as she got in the car. The last thing she wanted to do was go back to her father's home. They were nearly there when Logan's phone rang. He handed it over to her. "Your mum."

Chapter Thirty-Six

Lindy pulled over to the side of the road near where she'd picked Logan up earlier. She waited for Maddy to finish her call so Logan could take his phone and get out of the car to wait for her to drop them home.

"Hey, Mum. How did you know to call me on this number?"

"It was the only other one I had. Maddy-" Joscelin fell silent.

"Mum? What's wrong?"

"I rang your father but he said he wasn't going to tell you. He wouldn't even let me talk to you, but I finally got it out of him that you were out with your brother. I'm glad he lets you out sometimes."

"Mum? You're rambling."

"I'm sorry."

"Are you crying?" Maddy reached out and grabbed hold of Logan's hand. She had a really bad feeling.

"He won't let you come and see her. She got sick early this week and I thought she was going to get better. Like last time. But she took a turn for the worse."

"Grandma?"

"He won't let you see her."

Maddy could clearly hear her mum was crying now. "Where is she?"

"In the public hospital. They said she won't make it through the night. That there's no chance she'll see the morning."

Maddy didn't know what to say. There was no way her father was going to stop her from seeing her grandma for what would be the last time. "Don't worry, Mum. I'll get there somehow."

"Don't go doing anything silly, Maddy. I don't want anything to happen to you too. I feel guilty enough I didn't fight for you. Don't-"

"It'll be fine. I'll be there as soon as I can." Maddy hung up the phone and handed it back to Logan.

"Can we go now?" Lindy asked.

Maddy shook her head. "I'm thinking." She frowned. "Mitchell, ring Dad and tell him Logan rang you. Actually, Logan ring Mitchell first since Dad checks his phone sometimes." Maddy rubbed at her forehead.

"What do I tell him Logan said?" Mitchell answered his phone with a grin. "Hey, Logan. What's happening?"

Maddy rolled her eyes as they both hung up. "Tell him Logan invited you to stay the night and Lindy offered to drop you off." She turned to Logan. "Can you get out so we can go?"

"You'll let me know what happens, won't you?"

Maddy kissed him. "I'll see you again very soon." She grinned at his expression. "Go on. I'll explain everything when I see you."

They drove off the moment Logan was out of the car and Mitchell rang Sinclair. The conversation was short and Mitchell had a grin when he hung up. "Now what?"

"You pack an overnight bag and Lindy keeps Dad busy in the lounge room. His favourite topic is himself and his work."

"What will you be doing, Madeline?"

"Running away from home."

Mitchell stared at her, opened mouthed. "What?"

"Stay calm. Act like everything is normal. As long as Lindy keeps Dad in the lounge room he won't see me sneak out the back way. And Marla won't be home until tonight so we won't have to worry about her. I need you to not be there tonight, Mitchell. You don't want to be a part of this," Maddy said.

"He'll kill you when you come back," Mitchell warned.

"I've got a feeling I won't be back." Not now there was no one to protect. She glanced out the window and saw the house. "We don't have time to go into details. Stick to the plan. Oh, and don't take off with Logan until I get there." She grinned fleetingly before she got out of the car. Before she reached the door, her hand was pressed against her stomach and a pained expression was on her face. She knocked on the door and waited for her father to answer. It was nothing like her mum's place. There she was allowed a key.

Sinclair stared down at her when he opened the door. "What's wrong with you?"

"Can I have some Panadol? I think I need to lie down for awhile. Menstrual cramps." She grimaced.

Sinclair nodded and stepped back to let her inside. "You know where they're kept. It can't be too bad if you were willing to stay out all day."

Maddy didn't stick around to see if Lindy did her part. She headed straight for her room, stopping in her doorway. There wasn't much she needed to take. All her personal stuff was at her mum's house. People in prison probably had more of their own things around them then she did in this house.

She grabbed the photo frame that contained a picture of her and Joscelin from several years ago, a bracelet she'd had since she was a kid and her school uniforms, shoving them in her schoolbag. Next she slipped her laptop into its carry bag that she'd rarely had the opportunity to use. That was all she wanted from this room. The rest of the stuff, including the clothes and books, had all been bought by her father. Bought for a person who had never existed outside his mind. It looked like she'd no longer be living her life like that. Her grandmother wouldn't make it through the night. No one needed to protect her anymore. She closed the door and turned her back on it, surprised at the sadness that washed over her. A sadness that wasn't only for her grandmother. She wouldn't miss the house or her father or Marla. But she'd miss her brother.

Maddy headed for the back door without a single glance behind her. She never wanted to return to this house. Ever. Although, if it meant her grandma could have lived she would have willingly endured years in her father's house. She slipped outside, running towards the back fence. She peered over the wooden palings and saw the yard was deserted. Within minutes she was over the fence and headed for the road. Before she'd walked a block, her schoolbag began to feel like it weighed a tonne and she started to wonder if she really needed her laptop. She was relieved to see Logan run towards her when she turned into the next street.

Logan took her schoolbag. "Do you think you can tell me what you're up to now?"

"I'm leaving home."

"What about your grandma?"

Maddy shook her head, her throat going tight. She couldn't think about that right now. "She's dying. I have to see her. Do you have some money I can borrow to catch the train?"

Before Logan could answer, Lindy pulled up beside them. Mitchell started before Maddy was even buckled up.

"What do you think you're doing? Sinclair will kill you. He'll probably kill me."

"No he won't. Why do you think I wanted you out of there tonight? He'll have no one to blame it on except me."

"I can't believe I went along with everything you said. You sounded so much like him. You were barking orders like you expected us all to obey without question. And we did. I can't believe we went along with you," Mitchell grumbled.

"Sorry. There wasn't time to explain. When he rings you later to interrogate you about me, tell him the only time I wasn't with you today was when I went to the ladies. Okay? Once just after lunch and once before we came home. You have to make sure he can't blame you for any of this."

Mitchell shook his head. "You're insane."

"Probably. But my grandma is dying and I need to see her. Can you drop me at the train station, Lindy? I have to get back to the coast tonight. Before it's too late."

"I could drive you back if you wanted. But I wouldn't be able to afford the fuel to return tomorrow." Lindy sent an apologetic glance to Mitchell.

"Why don't we all go to the coast?" Logan asked. "We can run back to my place, pick up Lindy's gear and leave a message for my parents in case they come home before me. And I don't mind paying for fuel." He grinned fleetingly. "My parents never seem to complain about what I put on the credit card they gave me."

"I don't want to drag all of you into this. It might

get messy." Maddy reached out and caressed his cheek.

"You don't have to do this alone. Unless of course you want to." Logan placed his hand over hers and turned his head so he could place a kiss on her palm.

Maddy's eyes filled with tears, but she managed to hold them back. "He might come to the hospital."

"I'm in. As long as I can lay low," Mitchell said.

"Me too," Lindy said.

"Okay." Maddy couldn't have said another word. She leaned against Logan and closed her eyes as she tried to gain control of her emotions. All she could think of was the frail woman she'd played cards with on three occasions. That was it. They'd met only three times. And she'd never known her as a grandmother. Her grandmother had been the little sister who'd pestered her to spend time with her. It didn't seem right.

Chapter Thirty-Seven

Mitchell and Maddy waited in the car when they reached Logan's house. As soon as they were alone, Mitchell turned in his seat so he could face her.

"Does this mean I won't get to see you again?"

Maddy shrugged. "I don't know, but I hope not." She smiled wryly. "You're not such a bad brother anymore."

"You aren't so unbearably perfect these days."

Maddy smiled. "Maybe you'll be able to visit in the school holidays. Even if you can't stay with me, maybe they'll let you stay with Logan."

"I hope so. I want to see Lindy in the holidays. Next year she'll be living in Brissie so I'll be able to see her heaps then, but that's ages away." Mitchell fell silent for a moment. "I'm sorry your grandma's dying. I didn't even know you had one until last weekend."

"Yeah, I only learned about her recently too."

"Sinclair must be the strangest person in Australia."

Maddy couldn't help grinning at that comment. "If he isn't, he must be in the top ten." She looked over as Logan opened the car door.

He dropped an overnight bag on the floor and slid across the seat. "What top ten are you talking about."

"Of strange people. Dad probably makes the list."

Logan grinned. "You know, if your mum needs a good lawyer I bet my dad would find the case interesting enough to take it on. Actually, he'd take it on just because I asked him to. You should have seen him when he was making sure I didn't get expelled from my last school. I never would have thought of the things he said, not in a million years."

"Thanks."

"I'm serious, Maddy. He'd use your lack of freedom, being locked in your room, constant interrogations and not being able to have friends as reasons for you to never return."

Maddy nodded. "I don't want to think about it right now, but I do have a few ideas floating around."

"Fair enough." He grinned. "Should I pity him?"

She managed a weak smile at his teasing.

They fell silent, only the stereo breaking the quiet and even it was down low. When they were about halfway, Sinclair rang Mitchell and demanded to know if he knew where Maddy was. She smiled at him when he finally hung up.

"I'm so proud of you. An award winning performance," she teased.

Mitchell held out his hands, which trembled slightly. "I'm a mess. I was terrified he'd tell me to come home. I don't know how you do it. Aren't you always worried you'll be caught?"

"That's part of why I do it. I don't like to give into fear. Dad controls enough of my life without giving away any more control of it to something else."

"What about school? You've nearly finished this year. You can't exactly go somewhere else. You'll fail your year eleven exams," Mitchell said.

"I'll see if I can stay with Sasha during the week and go home to Mum on the weekend," Maddy said.

"Sounds like you've got it all figured out. Am I in your plans somewhere?" Logan asked.

Even though his tone was light, she could see the worry in his eyes. "Of course you are. I'm hoping that now I won't have to pretend I don't know you that you won't lose interest." Maddy grinned. "You know, the thrill of the forbidden and all that."

Logan grinned. "I didn't know you were forbidden when I first met you." He lowered his head close to her ear. "And I wanted you from the moment I saw you."

Maddy felt a rush of heat at his words and wished they were alone. Instead she contented herself with a quick kiss. "If I move to the coast full time next year will you visit every weekend?"

"And ring, text and message you. All those things I haven't been able to do. I'm hoping your mum gets you a mobile phone so I can ring you whenever I want to talk to you instead of having to wait until I see you," Logan said.

"Don't you know patience is a virtue," Maddy said primly.

"I'll leave it to your father to focus on virtues. I've never been all that worried about them," Logan said.

Maddy laughed. "I guess he does have a bit of a fixation on them." Her expression became serious. "Can I use your phone to call Sasha? I need to let her know what's happening."

Logan handed his phone over and Maddy explained the situation to her friend. Sasha complained they could have picked her up too, but told her to ring any time she needed someone to talk to. She didn't even care if it was in the early hours of the morning.

When they reached the hospital, Maddy asked

them not to come in with her in case her father turned up. She was glad she hadn't let them stay when, after sitting beside her grandmother's bedside for a couple of hours, she nearly ran into her father when she went to get a soft drink from a vending machine.

"Time to go, Madeline. This will be the last stunt like this you ever pull."

Maddy backed away from him. She didn't dare take her gaze off him for a minute. She tried to remember how far back the nurses' station was. "It isn't a stunt. I've decided I'm going to live with Mum from now on." She'd managed to talk to her mum about it and she'd agreed it was time for Maddy to move in with her. There'd be no miracle for Sara.

"Don't try my patience, Madeline."

"Then stop acting like you own me." She kept retreating.

Sinclair followed. "I'm not going to tolerate this behaviour. You can expect a lot of time in your room over the next few weeks."

"No, I can't. I won't be there."

"Is everything okay?" a nurse asked.

Maddy felt a surge of relief. "No."

At the same time, Sinclair said, "We are fine, thank you."

"We are not fine because I am not going home with you."

"Do I need to call security?" the nurse demanded.

"That won't be necessary," Sinclair said in his most soothing voice. "We were leaving. It was only a slight difference of opinion regarding living arrangements." He turned to Maddy. "Come on now. No more inappropriate behaviour. It's time to go home."

"I'm sixteen, surely that means I can choose who I live with," Maddy turned to the nurse in the hope she'd agree with her, while keeping an eye on her father.

"Choosing to live with your mother because she lets you run wild is not an acceptable reason for leaving my care." Sinclair sounded reasonable and concerned. "Come on, Madeline. You've seen your grandmother. This is not a healthy environment for a child."

She hated how reasonable he always sounded. Reasonable and concerned. "I want to stay until the end. You never let me get to know her. This is my last chance to spend time with her."

"Madeline, this is ridiculous. The woman isn't even aware you're here." There was a touch of annoyance in his voice.

"But I'll know." Maddy tried to remain calm. She

knew she had to do something drastic soon or he'd have all the staff on his side. He was good at that. Half the time people didn't even realise they'd been manipulated into seeing his side of an argument. She turned to the nurse again. "Please, can't you have security take him outside? I can't go back to his house."

"Madeline, the staff here don't want to see one of your temper tantrums. Now please say goodbye to your mother and be sensible. It's time to go home. The courts wouldn't have awarded custody to me if they didn't think it was in your best interests."

"They only gave it to you because you blackmailed Mum so she'd stop fighting for me."

"I've told you before not to listen to wild accusations from your mother. I have surgeries to perform tomorrow. We need to leave now."

It was now or never. Maddy took a deep breath, slowly letting it out. She turned to the nurse, making sure she could see her father. The words caught in her throat, but she forced herself to speak them, knowing they were the only ones that would make him lose his temper he always controlled so well. And not only that, she hoped they'd be the ones that would cause him to cut her from his life. "You can't let him take me. I'm terrified about what he'll do when he finds out I'm not a virgin anymore." She would have spoken the words even if they hadn't been true.

Sinclair roared, launching himself at Maddy. "You whore!"

Maddy ducked behind the nurse who screamed when Sinclair collided with her. Within seconds the corridor was filled with people and security guards dragged Sinclair away as he yelled at Maddy.

The nurse sat shakily on a seat someone brought into the corridor and Maddy slid down the wall to sit on the floor. She covered her face with her hands, not able to talk to anyone. She'd done it now. There'd be absolutely no going back. He'd never forgive her. In his mind she'd be as bad as Elspeth and Eleanor. A hand stroked her hair and she looked up at her mum.

Maddy burst into tears as Joscelin wrapped her arms around her. "Shh. It'll be all right, Maddy. Everything will be fine. You and I will be fine together."

She clung to her mum, wanting to believe the words, but worried about what the future would bring.

Chapter Thirty-Eight

Sara Leason passed away at four twenty-seven in the morning. Both Joscelin and Maddy were there. When they walked out the front doors of the hospital, Maddy almost shrieked when someone ran across the road towards them. Realising it was Logan, she threw herself into his arms.

"Have you been out here all night?" Maddy walked with one arm around his waist while he draped an arm across her shoulders.

"It wasn't too bad. You meet some interesting people at this hour." Logan stared at her for a moment. "How are you?"

"Dad came in and made a scene."

Logan laughed softly. "I'd say that was an understatement from what I saw when they threw him out."

"He didn't see you, did he?"

Logan shook his head. "Nah. He was too busy abusing the security guards who threatened to call the police."

"He'll never forgive you, Maddy," Joscelin said. "He's never been able to forgive. No matter the reason. He doesn't even hold a grudge. It's like he wipes you from his life."

"I know. But it's better this way. He would have written me off when I left at the end of school next year anyway. Once he's over his initial anger I know he won't want me back. I want it that way." Maddy turned to Logan. "Where's Lindy and Mitchell?"

"I gave them the keys to my place. They didn't need to sit around here all night. Especially not Mitchell. So I guess I should ask if I can crash at your place since I don't have my keys." Logan turned to Joscelin.

"Only if you promise not to wander when I put you in separate rooms," Joscelin said.

Logan grinned. "I'll be on my best behaviour tonight." He glanced up at the sky. "Ahh, today."

"I hope so. Just because the pair of you are having sex doesn't mean I'll let you have it in my house. Nor do I think either of you are old enough," Joscelin said.

Logan gaped at her. "You… what…" he looked

at Maddy. "You didn't…" his voice trailed off as he glanced away.

"No." Maddy laughed, surprised she was still capable of not only smiling, but laughing. "I told Dad, which is why he went psycho and tried to kill me."

Logan paled. "You told him you and I–" he gulped.

"Relax. You're safe from castration. I didn't give him any names."

"Don't joke about it." Logan shook his head. "I nearly had a heart attack."

They reached the car and Joscelin unlocked it. She faced Logan. "Do I have your promise?"

Logan looked extremely uncomfortable. He cleared his throat. "Yes."

Joscelin nodded before getting in the car.

Maddy didn't recall the drive home or how she managed to get to bed. But when she woke after lunch, her stomach rumbling, she was in her own bed. She used the bathroom and staggered out to the kitchen where she found Joscelin and Logan, at the table, eating bacon and eggs.

Joscelin gestured towards the frypan that sat on the stove, a lid on it. "Yours is in the pan. It should be warm."

"Thanks." Maddy served herself before sitting at

the table. She let the conversation wash around her, too tired to join in. She listened as Logan told Joscelin about his family. Some of it she hadn't heard before, but some she had. The one thing she did notice was he clearly liked his family no matter how strange some of them were or what they did. And it wasn't only him that could accept people as they were, but it seemed like his entire family could, if his stories were anything to go by. She only wished her father could have accepted her as she was and not wanted to change her. Wished that he could have understood she was a person with her own thoughts and feelings, not a piece of clay in need of moulding.

When Maddy started to rise, Joscelin put a hand on her wrist. "Wait a moment, Maddy."

She sat down, her stomach lurching at the serious tone her mum used.

"I want to hold the funeral next Saturday. That way you can be there without missing school and having to go back and forth to Brisbane in the one day."

Maddy nodded, relieved it hadn't been more problems. "Okay. Can I invite some people?"

"Whoever you want. She was part of your family too. We also have to figure out where you'll stay for the rest of the school year and organise for you to start the next year at a local high school." Joscelin smiled slightly. "But that can wait a bit. We need to focus on this year for now."

"I was thinking of asking Sasha if I could stay with her."

"She's always welcome at my place." Logan grinned. "In separate rooms of course."

Joscelin nodded. "I'm sure you'll understand if I leave that as a last resort."

Logan looked like he was trying not to grin. "Yeah."

Joscelin turned back to Maddy. "Can you ring Sasha and see if it's fine to stay with her?"

Maddy nodded and this time when she rose from the table, her mum didn't stop her. She rang Sasha and winced at the squeal her friend gave at the thought of Maddy staying with her over the next few weeks. Within minutes she'd talked to her mum and was back.

"Yes. Yes. Yes."

"It sounds like it's going to be a real chore to have me there."

Sasha laughed. "Absolutely." She sobered. "I'm going to miss not seeing you nearly every day next year though."

"You'll have to come out on the weekend sometimes. Catch the train with Logan."

"Only until I get my license in February," Sasha said. "I can't wait till I turn seventeen. Mum and Dad said they'll get me a car for my birthday."

"Bitch."

Sasha laughed again. "Yep. I'll think of you stuck with public transport while I'm enjoying my car."

"Next year is going to be so different."

"What are you worried about? You've survived living in hell for years. Next year will be a breeze."

"Yeah. I guess so."

"I know so."

"Sash?"

"Yeah?"

"My grandma's funeral is next Saturday. Will you come to it with me?"

"Of course I will. I'll stay the entire weekend."

"Thanks, Sash."

"You're my best friend. You don't even have to ask. Just tell me when and where."

"Okay. I'll see you tonight."

"You want Mum to pick you up from the train station?"

Maddy shook her head even though Sasha couldn't see her. "Nah. I'll organise something."

"Okay. I'll set the camp bed up in my room for you."

"See-ya."

"Yep. Bye."

Maddy stared at the phone for a moment after she'd hung up. She always felt good after talking to Sasha. Like no matter what she did there was someone who wouldn't look down on her for doing it. Someone who'd cheer her on or even join her. She looked up when Logan kissed the top of her head.

He perched on the arm of the chair she sat in and leaned against her. "All sorted?"

"Yeah. I can stay there for the rest of the school term."

"How disappointing."

Maddy grinned and lightly hit his arm. Her grin faded. "It'll be strange not being met at the train station by my father."

"My aunt is picking me up. She can give you and Mitch a lift to wherever you want to go."

"Oh." Maddy covered her mouth with her hand. "I completely forgot he was on the coast too."

"He's fine. He rang me earlier." Logan grimaced. "He woke me up or I'd probably still be asleep."

"How thoughtless of him."

Logan grinned. "I know. Anyway, Lindy will drop him over here around three so he can catch the train back to Brissie with us."

Maddy nodded. "Okay." She glanced at the clock on the wall. "But that still leaves us with a few hours to kill."

"I've got a few ideas about what we can do."

"I'll bet you do," Maddy said dryly. "But I believe Mum said something about you behaving yourself. And you made a promise."

"I believe she was talking about not wandering into your room." Logan glanced around. "This doesn't look anything like your room."

"Logan!"

He looked completely innocent. "What did you think I was talking about? You haven't kissed me yet today. That's all I was looking for."

"Sure." Maddy's voice was heavily laced with sarcasm.

Logan grinned, completely unrepentant.

Her lips slowly curved into a smile. "Good morning, Logan." She wrapped her arms around him, giving him the kiss he was waiting for.

Chapter Thirty-Nine

Monday morning, Maddy nervously walked beside Sasha. She tried to ignore all the stares she was getting, but it was hard. Logan greeted her the moment they stepped in the gate, an arm going around her waist as he drew her close.

"You look good. Your hair suits you like that." He ran his fingers through her layered hair that now only fell to a little past her shoulders. "Ah, and earrings too." His lips met hers. They pulled apart when someone cleared their throat behind them.

Mr Gallo frowned at them. "You know school policy, Mr Ridley."

"Sorry, Mr Gallo. I forgot where I was for a minute."

"And you, Miss Dowling? What is your excuse?"

"Ah… the same?"

"Don't let it go to your head that the seniors have

graduated and your grade is at the top of the ladder now."

"No, Mr Gallo," they said together.

"And I expect you to remember where you are in my class too. I'll be keeping an eye on both of you." Mr Gallo abruptly walked away.

Sasha giggled. "Looks like you'll have the rumours flying today."

Maddy put an arm around Sasha's waist and one around Logan's. "Let them talk. Who cares what they say. Has anyone seen Mitchell?"

"I don't think he's here yet," Logan said.

"Oh. I wanted to see if he'd come with us next Saturday." She'd already asked Logan to come to the funeral with her.

"He can stay at my place," Logan offered.

"Thanks," Maddy said. The bell rang. "I guess we better head to class." She reluctantly let go of Logan who needed to go in a different direction.

Maddy didn't catch up with Mitchell until lunch. He grabbed her hands when he saw her and pulled her out of earshot of his mates. "You're never going to believe what happened when I got home last night."

"You didn't get into trouble did you?" Maddy was worried, but he didn't look upset.

Mitchell shook his head. "Nah. Mum is pregnant."

"What!"

Mitchell laughed. "You should see your expression."

"It better not be a girl. The poor thing wouldn't survive his style of parenting."

"You don't have to worry. Mum had a scan and found out it's a boy."

"How far along is she?"

"Four months."

"So good of them to share the news with us immediately," Maddy said dryly.

Mitchell shrugged. "They're always like that. Anyway, Dad was going on about you and how ungrateful you are and blaming everything on your mother. I was getting so sick of listening to him. I was just about to leave the room when Mum told him not to worry, he'd have a son in five months. I nearly fell off my seat."

"I can imagine. That pair are demented."

"Yeah well, we're going to have a brother." He grinned. "It'll be a nice change from all these sisters I seem to have."

Maddy laughed before she became serious. "You make sure they don't completely ruin him."

"I'm not a miracle worker."

"Make sure he doesn't learn that females are a lower class citizen. He'll have major dramas in life if he learns that lesson from Dad."

Mitchell nodded. "I'll try, but I'm not sticking around any longer than I have to. As soon as I finish school I want to get a job and get out of there."

"What about uni?"

"I don't know if I can put up with them that long."

Maddy placed her hand on his shoulder. "Don't go making any rash decisions." Then she grinned. "I'm sure I can come up with a reason why you'll need your own place when you've been at uni for a few months."

"Like what?"

"Cross your fingers that our brother is noisy and then you'll have the perfect excuse."

Mitchell laughed. "I can't believe I ever thought you were a perfect little princess." He sobered. "Are you ever going to tell me what you would have told Sinclair?"

Maddy hesitated. She guessed he deserved to know, although she wasn't sure she'd ever be able to tell him who'd been leaving the messages in her locker. "That you tried to hook up with me."

Mitchell paled. "That I-" he broke off with a

shudder. "He would have killed me. He wouldn't have even given me a chance to deny it."

Maddy nodded. She was relieved she'd never needed to follow through with the threat. "Aren't you glad we're no longer on opposite sides?"

"That would have been a really nasty thing to do."

"Nasty? I was thinking more along the lines of evil."

Mitchell stared at her for a moment. "Next time I get in a fight with someone I'm coming to you for payback ideas."

"Cool. I've never done that before."

Mitchell slowly shook his head, putting an arm around her shoulders. "Come on, sis. Let's join the gang. They're annoying me with their constant looks in this direction to find out what we're up to."

"Are you going to tell Logan?"

"About what?"

"My threat."

"Only if you don't mind."

"Only if you think he won't be completely shocked by it."

Mitchell laughed. "I doubt it. I'll have to tell you a few stories Davey told me about Logan."

She hoped they were more interesting than what

Davey had told her the first time she'd met him. "Deal."

Chapter Forty

Maddy looked around the cemetery. Her sister had flown up to be there for her and stood beside Matt. Sasha was on one side of her, Logan on the other and Mitchell near him. There was a handful of her other friends she hung out with when she was at her mum's, including Melissa and Carrie who were both thrilled she'd be at their school next year. Davey stood with Cliff and a handful of other residents and staff from the nursing home. And best of all, her great aunt Sally was there with her two daughters, Marie and Carol. She looked forward to catching up with them and seeing all the pictures, they'd brought with them, of her cousins.

There were other people she didn't recognise. Some her mum had introduced to her as workmates. Her attention was brought back to the grave as people started to drop handfuls of dirt on the coffin.

Maddy shuddered. There was no way she could do that. She felt Logan's arm tighten around her and she turned to give him a watery smile.

"I am so not going to be buried," Sasha whispered. "Make sure they cremate me."

Maddy reached out and took hold of her friend's hand. "Me too." She noticed she wasn't the only one with damp eyes, or the only one who stayed back from the grave.

Once the ceremony at the graveside was ended they returned to the church hall for morning tea. Maddy listened to people tell stories of Sara, especially when Sally talked of her childhood. Maddy grinned when Carol exclaimed over her looks.

Carol shook her head in amazement. "I swear you could pass for Mum's twin when she was younger. She always teased that she didn't know if she'd brought the correct kids home from the hospital since we all looked so little like her. But you," she shook her head again and turned away. "Marie, come and check out Joscelin's girl."

"The spitting image of Mum, isn't she?" Marie said when she reached their side.

"Oh look, you're making the child uncomfortable," Carol said.

Maddy couldn't help laughing at this comment

since Carol had been the one to start it. "It's okay. Grandma thought I was Aunt Sally at the end." She had so many questions she wanted to ask them, but they could wait until later.

The morning tea ended up turning into a lunch until people began to drift away in ones and twos. Maddy stood out the front with Joscelin and waved off Sally, Marie and Carol when they headed back to the hotel they were staying in. Most of her friends had already left and Mitchell had taken off with Lindy earlier. Only Logan, Davey and Sasha were still with her.

Joscelin dropped an arm across Maddy's shoulders. "How are you doing?"

"Probably better than you. I keep feeling I should be sadder than this, but I guess I didn't know her very well. I feel more sad I'll never have the chance to get to know her."

Joscelin's arm tightened. "I'm sorry about that."

"I know." She didn't blame her mum. "Dad is the one who should be saying sorry, not you."

"That will never happen." Joscelin smiled wryly. "What are you planning to do this afternoon?"

"I don't know," Maddy said.

"We can head back to our place," Davey suggested.

"It's too hot to do much. We can turn the aircon up to freeze and laze about watching movies."

"Sounds good to me," Sasha said.

Maddy nodded.

"Make sure you're back in time to go to dinner with your aunts." Joscelin turned to Davey. "You're welcome to join us." She'd already invited Logan and Sasha was expected to join them since she was staying with them. Eleanor had already headed back to Brisbane.

"Thanks," Davey said. "I will if you don't mind eating with the hired help." He grinned. "I mean, after all, I'm only the chauffeur."

There was a ripple of laughter before they headed to Davey's car.

Maddy and Logan got in the back seat of the car and Sasha in the front. Maddy turned to wave to her mum, who stood alone. She felt a twinge of guilt at that. At least she'd be able to spend more time with her next year. They'd even talked about going to visit the family in England for a white Christmas. She hoped they ended up doing that. She'd never been on a plane before. Or seen snow.

When they reached Cliff's house, Davey turned up the air-conditioner in the lounge room and started suggesting movies. Once one was chosen, he put it on.

"What about popcorn?" Sasha asked. "How can we have a movie without popcorn?"

"You'll have to survive," Davey said. "But I can provide chocolate."

"Yes." Sasha grinned. "One of the major food groups." When Davey had left the room to get it, she turned to Logan, her expression completely innocent. "I forgot to ask him to bring drinks. Think you could get some? I'm not fussy."

Logan laughed. "How convenient. You forgetting wouldn't have anything to do with wanting to talk to Maddy alone, would it?"

Sasha made a face at him and then grinned when he left the room. "He's too smart sometimes."

"You better hurry up and tell me what you want to say. They won't be gone long."

"Has Davey got a girlfriend?"

"Not that I know of."

"I don't suppose you could find some time for me and Davey to be alone, could you?"

"What happened to…" Maddy frowned as she tried to recall the name of the boy Sasha had been chasing.

"Oh him." Sasha airily waved her hand. "Yeah, he's

not worth remembering. I ditched him earlier this week."

"You never told me."

"It was such a forgettable occasion I completely forgot. I mean, I told him I thought we shouldn't see each other again and he said okay. That was it. I think he might have been tackled hard one too many times."

Maddy laughed.

"What's so funny?" Davey came back into the lounge room followed by Logan.

Maddy shared a look with Sasha before she turned back to Davey. "It's one of those 'you had to be there' kind of jokes."

Logan handed a can of soft drink to Sasha and then came to stand beside Maddy, offering her one. She took it and pressed it against the back of her neck, momentarily closing her eyes.

"Some days are too hot." She opened the can and had a mouthful.

"It won't take long and you'll cool down. Especially with how high Davey has the aircon," Logan said.

Maddy noticed Davey and Sasha had settled in front of the television and slowly smiled. "Really?

And here I was thinking things were likely to get hotter."

It took Logan only a second to catch her meaning. He grinned and grabbed her hand, heading for his room. "Watch the movie without us," he threw over his shoulder.

Maddy glared at Logan as he shut his bedroom door on Davey's laughter. "What's with the caveman tactics?"

"Sorry. I didn't want to give you a chance to change your mind. It's been ages since we've had any time alone." He took the can from her and placed it on his desk. "How about I try again?" He wrapped his arms around her waist.

"Possibly." Maddy tried to hold onto her offended expression, but it was rapidly melting.

His lips met hers and her arms automatically slid around his neck. He pulled away slightly. "How was that?"

"Uhmm…"

Logan grinned. "I'll take that as a yes."

Maddy gathered her scattered thoughts. "You can take that as, I'm still deciding. How about you try again?"

Logan laughed. "Willingly." His lips met hers.

After a moment, she murmured, "Much better."

"Does that mean you've decided?"

She met his gaze. There were a lot of things she'd decided lately, including who she really was. And it wasn't Madeline, the girl who'd kept her head down and gaze lowered. She was Maddy and she no longer needed to hide that fact. "Yeah. I have. Now shut up and kiss me." She barely managed to grin before he did. She had a few seconds to be amazed at how much her life had changed in only a couple of months before thoughts became impossible.

Free Ebook

Subscribe to Avril's newsletter to receive a free ebook. This ebook is exclusive to those on her mailing list. To find out more about this offer visit: http://www.avrilsabine.com/free-ebook/

*

We value your privacy and will not sell, rent, exchange or loan your email address to third parties. Your information is confidential and you are under no obligation to remain on the mailing list and can unsubscribe at any time.

Acknowledgements

Thank you to all those involved in creating this book. As always, I appreciate everything you've done.

To The Reader

If you enjoyed this book, why not consider leaving a review to help other readers discover it too? Reader engagement is one of the few ways that lets an author know readers want more books in a particular series or genre. So leave a review and tell friends, not only about this book but also about other ones you've enjoyed, so you can continue to enjoy books by your favourite authors for years to come.

Dreams are meant to be lived,

Avril.

About The Author

Avril is an Australian author who lives with her family on acreage in South East Queensland. She writes mostly young adult speculative fiction, but has been known to dabble in other genres. You can find more information about her at her website www.avrilsabine.com where you can also subscribe for her newsletter to be kept informed about new releases, current projects, blog posts and exclusive news.

Titles By Avril Sabine

Stories about strong characters and characters who discover their strengths.

SERIES

Assassins Of The Dead- Young Adult Fantasy/ Paranormal

Book 1: Dark Blade

Book 2: Dragon Touched

Book 3: Society Against Vampires

Book 4: King's Request

Dragon Blood- Young Adult Urban Fantasy (with elements of romance)

(5 book series)

Book 1: Pliethin

Book 2: Wyvern

Book 3: Surety

Book 4: Knight

Book 5: Mage

Dragon Mage- Young Adult Urban Fantasy (with elements of romance)

(Series two of Dragon Blood series)

Book 1: Promise

Dragon Blood Chronicles- Young Adult Urban Fantasy (with elements of romance)

(Companion series to Dragon Blood)

Book 1: Oath

Book 2: Betrayed

Guardians Of The Round Table- Young Adult Fantasy LitRPG

(Co-written with Storm and Rhys Petersen)

Book 1: Dexterity Fail

Book 2: Goblin Boots

Book 3: Singed Feathers

Book 4: Frog Mage

Book 5: Crystal Mine

Book 6: Cursed Harp

Rosie's Rangers- Young Adult Western Steampunk

(6 book series)

Book 1: Justice

Book 2: Vengeance

Book 3: Treachery

Book 4: Accused

Book 5: Wanted

Book 6: Corruption

Mark Of Kings- Children's Fantasy

(Upper middle grade/preteen)

Book 1: The Arena

Book 2: The Island

Book 3: The Assassin

Book 4: The King

STAND ALONE SERIES

Demon Hunters- Young Adult Urban Fantasy/ Horror (with elements of romance)

Book 1: Blood Sacrifice

Book 2: Retribution

Book 3: Tainted

Book 4: Premonition

Book 5: Cursed

Book 6: Feud

Book 7: Extrication

Plea Of The Damned- Young Adult Urban Fantasy/Paranormal

(6 book series)

Book 1: Forgive Me Lucy

Book 2: Forgive Me Aiden

Book 3: Forgive Me Jena

Book 4: Forgive Me Kobe

Book 5: Forgive Me Marti

Book 6: Forgive Me Dawson

Realms Of The Fae- Young Adult Urban Fantasy (with elements of romance)

The Sword (short story)

Heart Of Stone

Book 1: A Debt Owed

Book 2: Marked By The Hunt

Book 3: The Magic Collector

Book 4: An Unexpected Betrayal

Book 5: Imprisoned By Iron

Fairytales Retold (Short Stories)

Snow-White And Rose-Red

The Twelve Brothers

The Light Princess

Beauty And The Beast

Sleeping Beauty

Aschenputtel

The Golden Bird

The Frog Prince

The Death Of Koshchei The Deathless

Myths And Legends Retold (Short Stories)

Ion, Son Of Apollo

Sir Gawain And The Maid With The Narrow Sleeves

Princess Ilse, The Giant's Daughter

YOUNG ADULT NOVELS

Young Adult Fantasy (with elements of romance)

Elf Sight

Earth Bound

Young Adult Urban Fantasy

Stone Warrior (with elements of romance)

The Jungle Inside

Young Adult Contemporary (with elements of romance)

Through Your Eyes

The Ugly Stepsister

Perfect Little Princess

Young Adult Contemporary/Paranormal

Whispers In The Dark (with elements of romance and same sex relationships)

Over Too Soon (with elements of romance)

Young Adult Sci-Fi

Experiment X-One-Six (Urban Sci-Fi/Superheroes)

An Endless Dawn (Post Apocalyptic Sci-Fi)

CHILDREN'S BOOKS

Dragon Lord (Preteen/early teens) (Fantasy)

The Irish Wizard (Upper middle grade) (Urban Fantasy)

SHORT STORIES

Urban Fantasy

Eternally Late

Dealings With Joe

Glimpses (short story in That Moment When Anthology)

Contemporary

The Brat Next Door

Fantasy LitRPG

(Set in the same world as Guardians Of The Round Table Series)

Tales Of Inadon 1: The Disc (Co-written with Storm and Rhys Petersen) (short story in Game On! Anthology)

Post Apocalyptic Sci-Fi

Compulsive Directive

NONFICTION

A Year Of Weekly Writing Exercises (Creative Writing)

Cooking For Families With Allergies (Cooking) (Co-written with Storm Petersen)

Tell Me A Story, Grandma (Memoir)

For the most up to date details on available titles visit:

http://www.avrilsabine.com/books/bibliography

Disclaimer

This is a work of fiction. Names, characters, businesses, places, events and incidents are either the products of the author's imagination or used in a fictitious manner. Any resemblance to actual persons, living or dead, or actual events is purely coincidental.

www.ingramcontent.com/pod-product-compliance
Lightning Source LLC
Chambersburg PA
CBHW031001190726
48285CB00004BB/1416